Also by Kieran Scott

The He's So/She's So Trilogy
She's So Dead to Us
He's So Not Worth It
This Is So Not Happening

True Love
Only Everything

Complete Nothing

A TRUE LOVE NOVEL
BY KIERAN SCOTT

SIMON & SCHUSTER BFYR

NEW YORK   LONDON   TORONTO   SYDNEY   NEW DELHI

SIMON & SCHUSTER BFYR

An imprint of Simon & Schuster Children's Publishing Division
1230 Avenue of the Americas, New York, New York 10020

Text copyright © 2014 by Kieran Viola
Jacket photograph copyright © 2014 by Michael Frost
Jacket hand lettering and illustration by Bobby Haiqalsyah

SIMON & SCHUSTER BFYR is a trademark of Simon & Schuster, Inc.
For information about special discounts for bulk purchases,
please contact Simon & Schuster Special Sales at 1-866-506-1949
or business@simonandschuster.com.
The Simon & Schuster Speakers Bureau can bring authors to your live event.
For more information or to book an event, contact the Simon & Schuster Speakers Bureau
at 1-866-248-3049 or visit our website at www.simonspeakers.com.
Also available in a SIMON & SCHUSTER BFYR paperback edition
Jacket design by Chloë Foglia
Interior design by Hilary Zarycky
The text for this book is set in Granjon.
Manufactured in the United States of America
2 4 6 8 10 9 7 5 3 1
Library of Congress Cataloging-in-Publication Data
Scott, Kieran, 1974–
Complete nothing / Kieran Scott. — 1st edition.
pages cm. — (A true love novel ; 2)
Summary: True, also known as Eros, the Goddess of Love,
tries to bring together a second pair of soul mates in her quest to return to Olympus
and be reunited with her own true love, Orion.
ISBN 978-1-4424-7721-6 (hardcover) — ISBN 978-1-4424-7720-9 (paperback) —
ISBN 978-1-4424-7722-3 (eBook)
1. Eros (Greek deity)—Juvenile fiction. [1. Eros (Greek deity)—Fiction. 2. Goddesses,
Greek—Fiction. 3. Mythology, Greek—Fiction. 4. Dating (Social customs)—Fiction.
5. Love—Fiction. 6. High schools—Fiction. 7. Schools—Fiction.] I. Title.
PZ7.S42643Com 2014
[Fic]—dc23
2013032403

FIRST
EDITION

For my true love, Matt Viola,

who has never stopped believing in me

ACKNOWLEDGMENTS

I would never be able to do this job at all, let alone have so much fun doing it, without my incredible support team. Thank you so much to Sarah Burnes, Zareen Jaffery, Justin Chanda, Logan Garrison, Julia Maguire, Paul Crichton, Siena Koncsol, and Valerie Shea. Special thanks also go out to the amazing designers Chloë Foglia, Hilary Zarycky, and Bobby Haiqalsyah, for their incredible style and vision.

Humble thanks to all the fans, bloggers, librarians, and bookstore owners and employees who have been so supportive of my work.

Thank you to my ever-supportive friends (and family) Erin Scott, Wendy Stewart, Shira Citron, Kristy Gillio, Sharren Bates, Jessica Freundel, Meredith Rothouse, Courtney Elefante, Jen Calonita, Aimee Friedman, Katie Sise, Lanie Davis, Danielle Garretson, Rachel Hirsch, and Maura Deleo, for their unshakeable faith in me.

As always, thank you to my family, Matt, Brady, and Will, who make every day worth living.

PROLOGUE

After a time, I could feel nothing save the weight of his feet on my back, one heel pressing sharply between two lower ribs, and the other into the muscle of my shoulder. When he'd first told me to kneel before his throne and proceeded to thrust out his legs to use me as a footstool, I had thought it would be the humiliation that would kill me. But after half an hour, any pride had long since flown through the palace windows. Then it was only the cold, hard marble pressing into my palms and my bare kneecaps. The quivering of my muscles. The pain darting through my joints. I was forced to forget my pride as my brain focused merely on survival, on not collapsing, on refusing to beg for mercy.

It had been five hours, and my resolve was quickly crumbling.

"Orion!" the mighty King Zeus crowed, adjusting his feet, making sure to grind the hard soles of his sandals into my bones. "I know not how you do as a man, but you make for sturdy furniture."

The guards and lower gods assembled laughed, and Zeus gulped his thirtieth goblet of wine. Another rivulet of sweat snaked its way across my forehead and down my nose until the drop slipped to the tip and clung there, trembling inches above the pool of perspiration I'd been staring at these last few hours.

When it fell, so would I. There was no more surviving this.

And then, a commotion. Guards shouting. A woman's voice. A slam, a screech, an explosion. The mighty Zeus rose to his feet, and I collapsed in a heap on my side. My arms and legs curled in on themselves, jerking and seizing of their own accord. Several vile guards laughed over my plight, but I didn't care. I was free. For the moment, I was free.

"What's the meaning of this?" Zeus demanded of his nearest protector.

Before the guard could answer, a voice rang out through the lofty chamber, echoing against its vaulted ceiling and surrounding us, as clear as day.

"If Orion is alive, I demand to see him! I demand an explanation!"

"Artemis," I groaned. And in my weakened state I prayed that she would come save me. Even though she had once killed me. Even though she was the reason I'd spent the last two thousand years hanging among the stars, watching life on Earth go on as if I'd never existed. I prayed to her, the goddess protector of women, of all things. I begged.

"Artemis, please. Rescue me."

Zeus glared down at my coiled form, alarmed. There was a cacophonous crash as Artemis attempted to break through the wall of armored sentries. Then Zeus flicked his wrist, and I experienced a sensation like nothing I'd ever felt before. It was as if a tremendous cricket bat had hit me square in the face, chest, and knees. I flew backward, through the open doorway at the back of the throne room and that of my cell. I slammed against the back wall of the tiny chamber I'd spent the last week or month or ten years inside—I had no way of knowing—and hit the floor so hard I was sure no bone in my body had been left intact. I rolled onto my back and moaned.

"Eros," I whispered, my voice a mere croak. "Where are you, my love? Where are you?"

I imagined her hovering above me, the sun in the sky casting a beatific halo around the long black mane of her hair as I lay back in the soft grass outside our humble cabin. The smile on her lips brought peace to my heart, and as she gently wiped my brow with her fingertips, the relief was total. If only she were here. If only we had never been found, if only we had devised a way to escape together so that she'd never had to make that hideous bargain with the king. If only, if only, if only . . .

Tears stung my eyes, and I bit down on my bottom lip. I hated the broken, shivering slab of flesh that I'd become, begging goddesses to help me, praying, sometimes, for death. I had thought that I was stronger than this. That I could survive anything. But Zeus was an expert in torture. He had seen, quite literally, everything, and he was very fond of reminding me of this fact. Every creative means of delivering pain and psychological damage that had ever been devised by god or Gorgon or human—he had witnessed everything—and for however long I'd been his prisoner, he'd been perfecting every last technique on me.

"Is it true? Does Orion live?"

I lifted my head. Artemis had somehow made it into the throne room. When I turned my head, I was able to see the smallest sliver of the bright-white chamber, past the golden bars of my cell, across the stone-walled room outside it, and through an open archway. I opened my mouth to scream her name.

Nothing came out. And suddenly I was choking. My throat

collapsed in on itself as if an invisible rope was being twisted tighter and tighter and tighter around my neck. Then, just as suddenly, the rope was released, and I was left sputtering and choking and gasping on the floor.

"If you are keeping him here, King, I demand to see him," Artemis was saying when my coughing subsided and I was able to hear again.

"On what grounds do you make these demands of your king?" Zeus asked, amused.

"He belongs to me!" Artemis cried. "He was my love! I have spent these last two millennia attempting to return him to life, to return him to my side—"

"And you have failed," Zeus pointed out. "So perhaps, my dear Artemis, he does not belong to you, in the end."

"Where is he?" Artemis growled.

I saw a flash, and a mighty clatter rang through the palace. The guard at my door fell sideways across the threshold, his eyes rolling back in his head, and my heart began to pound in earnest. Artemis had felled Zeus's guards. I was both terrified and infused with pure, hot hope. This offense would not sit lightly with Zeus, but it also meant I had a chance. I somehow pushed myself to my knees.

"Artemis!" I rasped, grasping for the golden bars of my cage. "Artemis! Here!"

Again my throat constricted, and I fell back against the rear wall. I sensed the air inside the palace go still. She had heard me. She would come.

But I couldn't breathe. I couldn't breathe. I couldn't breathe.

"Orion!" Artemis cried.

My legs kicked out as I struggled in vain for air. I slammed my heels against the bars, rattling them as hard as I could, even as my vision prickled, even as my life began to drain from me.

"Orion? My love! Are you here?"

I heard her footsteps. Heard the cries of the remaining guards as they were flung aside, tossed through windows, slammed against the walls. My fingers clawed at the dirt floor in sheer desperation, trying to pull me closer to the bars, closer to my savior.

Zeus let out a mighty, furious roar. There was another explosion, so close this time the bars and walls shook, raining rocks and silt throughout my cell. She was dead. I was sure of it. And if she was, then so was I. My last hope. Gone. In an instant.

Until, like a vision, Artemis appeared in the doorway, as statuesque as ever in white robes, a gold-and-leather vest adorned with an intricate pattern of roses and stars, and a shimmering bronze crown. She was as beautiful as the day we'd fallen in love, her chestnut hair tumbling in ringlets around her perfect, sharp chin. Her skin was a creamy white, with the merest blush across her cheeks. Her emerald-green eyes widened at the sight of me, and suddenly I could breathe again.

I gasped in air—gasped in life—and reached for the goddess who would save me. I no longer loved her—hadn't in centuries—but that could be explained later. After she got me out of here.

"Artemis," I rasped.

"Orion," she whimpered.

She extended her trembling hand and I felt, for the briefest second, the slip of her fingertips across mine.

And then everything went black.

CHAPTER ONE

True

"I'm . . . fine," the love of my life mumbled, searching my face. "But who the hell are you?"

I gazed into his deep blue eyes and stopped breathing. I knew every green and brown fleck within them. I knew every dream and fear and hope they disguised. And yet they were a complete blank as they stared back at me. Slowly, achingly, a cold terror settled into my veins even as my lips tingled from our kiss. He wasn't joking.

"Orion, do—do you truly not know me?" I stammered.

He chuckled in an embarrassed way and smoothed the back of his dark wavy hair as he looked around, waiting for the punch line. I took a startled step back, catching my shoe on the curb. Automatically, instinctively, Orion reached out and grabbed my arm to steady me. His touch stopped my heart, and I stared at his tanned fingers, then into his eyes.

It's me, Orion. Please. Please, remember me. I'm the one who saved you. I brought you back to life after eons of hanging among the stars. I nursed you back to health and we fell in love. We spent hours, days, weeks together, telling our secrets, whispering our hopes, learning everything there is to know about each other. Please, you must remember me. Please, please, please.

He released me. "Sorry, no. How do you know my name?"

I felt Hephaestus's presence at my side, the left wheel on his chair coming to a stop right next to my leg. I stared mutely down at him, my dark-skinned, dark-eyed, leather-and-metal-and-denim-sporting friend, wishing he could snap his fingers and wake me from this nightmare. Like me, Hephaestus was a former god, and as such, was almost mind-bendingly handsome with his square jaw, flawless complexion, and perfect muscle definition, but while he had been human for generations, I had only been in this mortal body for two weeks. I was still getting used to its quirks. Like the psychotic, panicked pounding of the pulse that I was currently experiencing. I had thought that I was familiar with every working of the human heart. As Eros, the Goddess of Love, it was supposed to be my specialty. But this was something new.

Hephaestus nudged my leg with the rubber coating on the wheel of his chair, but my brain couldn't form words. My brain could form nothing other than a silent, anguished scream.

"Lucky guess?" Hephaestus offered.

Orion laughed again. "That'd be a first. Everyone's always surprised when I introduce myself. I think my mom was high when she named me. She never heard of Michael or David or James?"

"You have a mom?" I blurted.

His handsome brow knit. "Doesn't everyone?"

Hephaestus laughed loudly, forcibly. "Good one." He looked at me with wide eyes, urging me to get it together. But at the moment I didn't even know what "it" was, let alone how I could get it together. From the corner of my eye, I saw Darla Shayne and Veronica Vine in their matching outfits—Darla's a blue minidress, Veronica's a pink one in the same style—checking Orion out as they sauntered by on their way into school.

Back off, I thought, angry adrenaline surging through me. *Back the eff off.*

Darla turned to walk backward, slipping her sunglasses to the tip of her nose for a better look. Some skateboarder guy was performing tricks nearby, and without a thought I glared at his board, sending it flying out from under him and rolling into Darla's path. She tripped and fell right on her ass on the sidewalk with a screech.

That was what you got for coveting a goddess's man. But as I watched the boy retrieve his board and Veronica help Darla brush off her backside, I knew I was out of line. My power of telekinesis had only just returned to me, and I still had no idea why. The deal with Zeus was that I had to form three couples without my powers. To that end, he'd stripped me of every last one before depositing me here on Earth. So why had this one returned? What did it mean?

And most importantly, would I get in trouble for using it?

I decided not to think about that right now. It was too much to wrap my brain around. Especially now, with Orion standing two feet away from me. I'd deal with the power issue later.

"Yeah, well, Dad says it was her idea." Orion gestured toward the white SUV that had dropped him off, which was now idling at a stoplight near the corner. "He put his foot down when it came to my sister, so she lucked out and got Amy. Boring, normal Amy."

I swallowed a sharp lump in my throat. He had a mother? A father? A sister? What was happening? How was this possible?

"I'm Heath," Hephaestus introduced himself, extending one mesh-gloved hand. Orion shook it, then looked at me. "And this is True," Hephaestus added.

"Nice to meet you guys." He crossed his arms over his chest. "So, you greet all the new guys in school with a kiss like that?"

"No," I said.

They both looked at me, waiting for more. Expecting more. An explanation, a joke, an excuse. But I had nothing. Orion was right there. *Right. There.* So close I could smell the piney shampoo he'd used this morning and see the tiny cut on his neck from shaving. I could have reached out and brushed the lobe of his ear and knew exactly how it would feel beneath the pad of my thumb. I knew every last inch of him—each variation of his laughter, every lilt of his voice, and the nose-prickling scent of his skin. I knew the particular way he stretched upon awakening, how he smacked his lips when he tasted something sour, that his gaze would dart to the horizon whenever he was startled.

But to him, I was a stranger.

"Anyway . . . I'm supposed to go to the main office?" Orion said, raising his eyebrows. He directed this comment at Hephaestus, probably discerning that I was a lost cause.

"We'll show you, right, True?" Hephaestus said, turning his wheels toward the ramp outside the school's side door.

"Yes," I replied, finding my voice. "Yes. Of course."

Orion walked next to Heath up the ramp. When I turned to follow them, my knees went weak and I had to grab on to a NO PARKING sign to keep from going down. I clung to it and tried to breathe.

What is happening? What is happening? Why is he here? Why does he not remember me?

"True?" Heath prompted as the door automatically opened in front of them.

"Coming!"

I summoned every ounce of strength within me, called on every triumph of my endless, immortal existence to buoy me, and forced myself to stand. Then I cleared my throat and followed the love of my life and the former god who was my best friend into Lake

Carmody High. If ever there had been a sight more surreal than the two of them moving together under the huge HOMECOMING! banner, I wasn't aware of it.

"So where're you from?" Hephaestus asked Orion, glancing over his shoulder at me as we made our way down the front hallway. A few students milled around at their lockers, checked their phones for messages, and reviewed their homework. I was aware of them, but I didn't really see them. Orion was the only person I could see. I had never felt a longing like this in my life. It was as if he was pulling me along by a leash clasped around my heart.

"We just moved here from Boston," Orion said. "My dad got a new job in Manhattan and my aunt lives in Lake Carmody, so she found us a house."

This had to be Zeus's doing. There was no other god powerful enough for machinations like these. Creating an entire family? A history? A house and a move and a job? But why? Why had he sent Orion here? The deal was, he'd keep Orion with him while I completed my three love matches here on Earth, and I would be returned to Orion's side once I succeeded. No one had said anything about sending Orion back to Earth, or about him losing his memory—his entire personality. Why would Zeus do this?

Could this mean that our deal was off? It was possible that Zeus was somehow displeased with my last match, and his punishment was to condemn us to live in this random American town for good. But there was no reason for him to disapprove of Charlie and Katrina. The sand timer he'd sent to track me had turned when they'd sealed their love with a kiss. I had thought I was on my way to victory. And now, this.

Hephaestus opened the door of the front office, and Orion stepped inside. I moved to follow.

"Thanks, guys," he said, adjusting one backpack strap on his shoulder. "You don't have to come with me. I got it from here."

My arms went limp at my sides at the very thought of leaving him. I'd just gotten him back. Sort of. "But I can't—"

"Right. Well, good luck!" Hephaestus said, and he let the door swing closed.

"We can't just leave him!" I hissed.

"We have to!" Hephaestus replied, wheeling toward the wall. "He thinks he's just a regular human kid. He thinks *we're* regular human kids. Normal people wouldn't follow him around like puppy dogs."

I could see a tiny sliver of the side of Orion's head through the door's window—the wave of his thick dark hair—as he spoke with the administrative assistant, Mrs. Leifer. His muffled laughter sent my pitter-pattering heart into my stomach.

"What is he doing here, Hephaestus?" I whispered urgently. "What does this mean?"

"I don't know," Hephaestus said. "Perhaps Zeus sent him here to goad you on? Remind you of why you're doing this?"

I liked his theory better than mine. At least that would mean that there was still a potential end to this trial. That I could still complete my mission, form my three couples, and return home to Mount Olympus with Orion at my side, his memory perfectly restored. But I didn't quite believe it. Zeus had seemed so pleased at the idea of keeping Orion as his slave, at the prospect of torturing him while I did my work on Earth. Now, on a whim, he sends Orion here to torture *me*? It didn't add up. Something was off. I needed to know why Orion was here. I needed answers.

"We must contact Harmonia," I said breathlessly. "Find out what she knows."

It was my sister Harmonia who had dispatched Hephaestus to me after I'd sent up a desperate plea to her in the town square, begging for help. Now that I was human, he was my only direct line to Mount Olympus. Aside from praying and offering up sacrifices—two notoriously dodgy forms of communication and bargaining—I had no other way to contact home.

"That's not really how it works," Hephaestus told me.

"What do you mean?"

Orion disappeared, moving out of view inside the office. I leaned over Hephaestus, trying to catch a glimpse.

"Excuse me. Your breasts are kind of in my face," Hephaestus groused, gently shoving me away.

I groaned and stood up straight. "What do you mean that's not how it works?" I repeated.

"I mean, I don't contact her. She contacts me."

I heard Orion laugh again, and I couldn't take it anymore. I sidestepped Hephaestus and walked into the office at the exact moment Orion was shaking hands with a guy I'd seen around school. He was tall and muscular with shaggy brown hair, and his pretty blond girlfriend was at his side. He wore one of those blue-and-white varsity jackets that every other person at this school seemed to own. It looked like Orion had just met his peer guide.

"Peter Marrott," the guy said. "And this is my girlfriend, Claudia Catalfo."

"Welcome to Lake Carmody," Claudia said with a smile.

"Thanks." Orion nodded at Peter's jacket. "You play ball?"

"He's the starting quarterback," Claudia replied, looking up at Peter proudly. She sipped hot tea from a paper cup and entwined the fingers of her free hand with his. She was petite, the top of her head barely reaching Peter's shoulder. Her auburn hair was tied into a French braid, and she wore skinny pink jeans, a white button-down, and a flowered headband. Her face was familiar, but I couldn't place why. "He's going to play in college next year, right, Peter?"

"Maybe," Peter said, a blotchy blush popping up on his cheeks. He tossed his light-brown bangs off his head, and they fell right back into place. "You play?"

"I was starting running back at my old school," Orion replied, rounding his sexy shoulders. "I had twenty-one touchdowns and almost a thousand yards last season."

My brain went fuzzy and I felt faint. He had an athletic history too? What else had he left behind in Boston? A part-time job? A slew of clubs? A girlfriend?

"Really? That's awesome. We're a little weak at running back this year," Peter replied excitedly. "Our starter graduated, and the backup guy is kind of a bust."

"Think they'll let me try out?" Orion asked hopefully. The eager tone in his voice nearly broke my heart. I loved him so much. It killed me not to be able to reach out and touch him, hold him, tell him I was going to make everything okay.

"Definitely! Come on. I'll introduce you to Coach Morschauser right now."

They turned toward the door as one and paused, catching me standing there with what I was sure was pure desperation in my eyes.

"Um . . . excuse us?" Peter said.

I glanced behind me and realized I was blocking the door. "Oh. Sorry. Right. I'm . . . sorry."

I shoved the door open and stumbled out ahead of them, almost mowing over Hephaestus, who was still, loyally, waiting for me.

"Thanks again, you guys. I'll see you around," Orion said dismissively.

"You're . . . problem," I blurted. "I mean, no welcome. I mean—"

"True, stop," Hephaestus whispered, grasping my wrist.

But it didn't matter. They were already halfway down the hall. Claudia leaned toward Peter and loud-whispered, "That's that girl. The one who stole my scarf on the first day, remember?"

Right! That was why I knew her. I'd used her scarf to tie my hair back on my first day of school, before I started to get a handle on how covetous people were of their things. They glanced back at me, even Orion, with that look in their eyes. That look that I had, unfortunately, grown accustomed to. Orion's, at least, had a smidgen of sympathy in it, a touch of curiosity. But the fact remained:

Every last one of them thought I was a freak. Including the love of my life.

CHAPTER TWO

Peter

"Welcome to the team, man."

I walked up behind Orion and slapped him on the shoulder, so hard half the water in his cup sloshed over the rim. My best friend, Gavin Dunnellon, laughed, but Orion took it well. He turned to shake hands with us, then dumped the rest of his water over his sweaty head. Thank God this kid had transferred here. Without a solid running game, the offense was going to be totally focused on me, and I wasn't sure I could carry the whole team this season. Impressing the scouts meant running a well-rounded game plan. Now I at least had a shot at going to college. If any good schools actually came out to see me.

I was supposed to meet with my guidance counselor, Mr. Garvey, and the coach tomorrow to talk about it, a thought that kind of made me want to hurl.

"Thanks, guys," Orion said.

"We were just gonna walk the track," Gavin told him, his voice a low rumble. "Come on."

"Walk the track?" Orion asked, squinting one eye against the sun. The other members of the team were busy shoving their stuff into their duffel bags, rehashing the better plays of the session and shuffling back toward the locker room.

"Gavin needs to loosen up after practice," I explained, cocking a thumb at my massive linebacker friend. "It's his thing."

"Don't mock it, man."

Gavin cracked his knuckles, then his neck. His short brown hair stuck to his forehead like a second skin, and his freckles looked darker on his red cheeks. We used to call him freckle-fart-face in grade school. Until he got bigger than the rest of us. Now the guy was like a tank—thick neck, shoulders like boulders, fists like bowling balls. I even knew some adults who were intimidated by him. No one messed with him anymore.

Orion shrugged. "Cool."

He launched his cup into the garbage can and we started walking. At the top of the hill next to the bleachers, the JV cheerleading squad practiced their chants. Farther down the slope, Claudia and the other members of the Boosters Club were working on spirit signs for this week's pep rally and the game on Saturday while Greg Howell, one of the guys from yearbook, snapped pictures. I saw Claude bent over a long white roll of paper with a glitter gun, her lips pressed together as she concentrated.

"That your girlfriend over there?" Orion asked, shading his eyes.

I felt myself blush and was glad I was already red from exertion. "Yep."

"What's she up to?"

"That's the boosters," Gavin replied, rolling his shoulders forward and back, then stretching out his triceps. "Basically the hottest chicks in school who aren't cheerleaders are boosters."

"Oh." Orion looked them over as if he was shopping for arm candy. "Are any of them cool?"

"Who cares? They're hot," Gavin joked.

I laughed. "I can't really say. If Claudia hears I been talking, I'll get in trouble."

They both chuckled. "How long've you guys been together?" Orion asked.

"Almost a year and a half." I stooped to pick up a crushed cup someone had tossed on the blue running track. "She's awesome. She's not into this shallow crap like a lot of girls. Like, it's not only about her hair and her clothes and stuff like that. She cares about stuff that matters."

"Plus, she's obviously into football if she's on the boosters," Orion said. "That's gotta be good."

"Yeah, she likes to support her man," I replied with a grin, tossing the cup back and forth between my hands. "She's actually into ballet, so she knows what it's like to be on a regimen like I am. She just gets it."

"Plus, they're sickening together, so that's fun," Gavin joked, holding one arm across his chest to stretch his shoulder out. "They're, like, never *not* touching each other."

"Nice," Orion said with a grin.

"Shut up, dude!" I said, shoving Gavin as hard as I could.

He barely moved. Just took a tiny sidestep.

"I had a girlfriend back in Boston, but she dumped me as soon as I told her I was moving." Orion stared out across the trees as the wind rustled through them.

"That sucks." I said it lightly, but inside my heart did this awful spin-around-and-die maneuver. Me and Claudia were both seniors. In exactly nine months we'd be graduating, and in eleven months she'd be going to college and who knew where the hell I'd be. Sometimes I lay up nights just thinking about her off at Princeton—her number one choice—or Harvard or some other smart place like that next year, flirting with a brainiac in a corduroy jacket or some shit, forgetting I ever existed. I tried to tell myself it would never happen, that we would never break up, but who was I kidding? At least here I was good enough for her. I wasn't in the honors classes with her, but I was the star of the football team, the most popular guy in the senior class, and everyone at our church loved me because of the time I spent volunteering. I had other things to make up for the fact that I was never going Ivy League. But once she was out of this lame-ass town and meeting guys who were as smart as her? Guys with dreams and ambitions and the possibility of actually achieving them? Forget about it.

"What's up, man? You just went quiet," Gavin said.

"Nothing, it just . . . it sucks." I looked back over my shoulder at the boosters and couldn't see Claudia anymore. "There's, like, a ticking time bomb on this whole thing."

"What whole thing?" Orion asked.

I threw my arms wide. "This. Football. High School. Friends. Girlfriends . . ."

"Dude. Claudia's never gonna break up with you," Gavin said, giving me one of his don't-mess-with-me stares. "She lives for the Marrott love."

Orion snorted a laugh.

"What? She totally does," Gavin said. He cracked his knuckles again. Orion stopped laughing.

"Please. Everyone knows long distance doesn't work."

I started to jog. Just because. My blood was pumping suddenly, and I needed to do something to work it out. The two of them started to jog too. Within a minute we were rounding the turn and

I spotted Claudia again, holding up one end of a sign while her best friend, Lauren Codry, held the other. It read GO MARROTT! #11 in huge blue letters. I smiled, but my heart felt sick.

"You don't know, man. Maybe you guys'll end up at the same school," Orion said, pacing me.

I laughed him off. "Yeah, right. Claude's crazy smart. She's applying to Princeton early admission. My best hope is some triple-A school gives me a football scholarship, and who knows where the hell that'll be."

"Whatever, man. You think too much," Gavin said, shoving me. "We've got the whole year. Just chill."

I paused near the opening in the fence, with the boosters and cheerleaders right up the hill from us. The cup, which I was still holding, had been squeezed into a sweaty, twisted stick of cardboard. I threw it in the nearest trash bin.

"I'm chill," I said, raising my palms and forcing a smile. "Do I not look chill?"

"G! A! V! I! N! What's? That? Spell?"

We froze. The JV cheerleaders had just started up this loud chant. I looked at Gavin. He pushed his wet hair back from his face and shrugged.

"G! A! V! I! N! What's? That? Spell?" they repeated.

Six girls in front were holding up big placards spelling out his name in red, the sixth one holding a heart. Then this girl, a sophomore named Tara Schwartz, popped up from behind the line of them. Two girls held her up by her feet as she raised her arms in the air. Gavin had been tutoring her in Spanish since last spring, and I knew they'd hooked up a couple of times.

"Gavin!" she shouted solo.

Gavin was the color of a lobster and looked confused. Greg

Howell stepped up alongside us to take a few pictures of both the cheerleaders and Gavin's stunned face.

"Gavin Dunnellon! Will you go to homecoming with me?"

"Awwwwwww!" someone on the Boosters moaned.

It was official—homecoming season was here. Every year my school had this tradition where we asked each other to homecoming with these big, stupid displays. As soon as one person started it, there'd be, like, twenty crazy stunts a day, like dudes coming to class in gorilla outfits, girls having pizzas delivered to the caf for a guy and his friends. Last year someone even hired a skywriter.

Everyone looked at Gavin. The girls holding Tara up started to shake.

"Um, sure?" Gavin said.

The hill erupted with cheers. Tara popped up into the air and her friends caught her. Then Gavin climbed the whole hill in, like, five long strides to talk to her, and he was smiling for real, so I knew he hadn't just said yes to keep from embarrassing her in front of everyone.

"Dude. What was that?" Orion asked.

"Welcome to Lake Carmody High," I said with a grin. "Where nothing you do is too cheesy."

"Hey, guys! Come check out what we're doing!" Claudia shouted down to us.

Orion and I jogged up the slope next to the bleachers, and I kissed Claudia hello. She reached up and hugged me, full-body, not caring that I was covered in sweat. Then she gestured down at the signage.

"We're making one for each starter," she said. "We figure we'll hang them over your lockers tomorrow and then bring them out here the day of the game."

There were a couple dozen girls and, randomly, one guy on the boosters. They looked up at me, waiting for my reaction.

"Cool," I said with a nod. "They look awesome. And hey, you're gonna have to make one more. We got a new starting running back," I added, slapping Orion's chest with the back of my hand.

"Congratulations! That's so great!" Claudia said, her eyes lighting up. "But all the boosters are taken. We're gonna need someone to double up."

Every starter on the team is assigned their own booster. Basically the girl (or guy) decorates your locker for you, makes you a big basket of food the day before the game, and does other random cool stuff throughout the season.

"Does anyone want to be Orion's booster?" Claudia called out.

"I'll do it!"

The girl from that morning—the one who had stolen Claudia's scarf out of her bag at lunch on the first day of school—stood up from a seat on the bleachers. I hadn't even seen her sitting there until now.

"You're not even on the boosters," Claudia said, her face falling.

The girl clomped down the stairs and then walked up the hill and over to us. Her long dark hair streamed out behind her in the wind, and she had the most unbelievable blue eyes I'd ever seen. She was gorgeous, not that I'd ever admit that out loud. When it came to boosters, Orion could do worse. Maybe he'd even just landed himself the new girlfriend he was obviously looking for. At least he had two more years of high school to be with her. Lucky bastard.

"So? Sign me up," the girl said, looking directly at Orion. "I'm in."

Claudia sighed and turned to Orion. "Are you okay with . . . what's your name again?" she asked the girl.

"True," she and Orion said at the same time.

Claudia and I locked eyes, both surprised he already knew her name.

"True Olympia," True said with deep meaning, as if that was supposed to be significant to Orion somehow.

"With True?" Claudia finished.

"Sure." Orion shrugged.

"Okay. Go see Wallace over there," Claudia gestured toward the one dude in the group, who scrambled to his feet with his iPad. He was wearing a black T-shirt and checkerboard shorts with a chain connected to the wallet in his pocket and had dark floppy bangs like mine. He lifted one scrawny arm and waved. There was ink up and down his forearm, but it looked like a doodle, not a tattoo. "He keeps the booster lists and attendance and everything."

"Got it." True made her way over to Wallace, tripping over a paint can and half crumbling a sign. It seemed like she couldn't take her eyes off Orion, and she was plowing everything over to do it.

"You ready to go grab dinner?" I asked Claudia. "Me and a couple of the guys are going to Pizza City."

She checked her watch. "Crap. How'd it get so late?" Dropping to the grass, she shoved her phone and a notebook into her bag, then stood. "Lauren, can you hang out for a while and make sure everything gets put away?"

"No problem, Skipper," Lauren said, saluting.

Claudia rolled her eyes, but laughed.

"I'll see you at the Studio."

"Hey, guys, before you go, can I get a shot of the senior class couple?" Greg asked, wielding his camera.

Claudia and I grinned, both of us loving being called the class couple. Like I said, nothing was too cheesy. "Sure," I told him.

We turned toward each other and hugged, smiling for the camera. Greg reeled off about half a dozen shots, then gave us a thumbs-up.

"Thanks." He checked something on the screen and then moved off to photograph the cheerleaders.

"No problem!" I shouted. "Hey, Orion! You coming for pizza?"

His eyebrows rose. "Yeah? Cool."

"Gavin! Let's go!" I shouted, raising an arm to wave him down.

He said good-bye to Tara and jogged over to join us. I slipped my arm around Claudia as we made our way down the hill, Orion and Gavin in front of us. There was still an annoying pinch in my chest from my conversation with the guys, but I tried to ignore it.

"I'm so nervous!" Claudia said, raising her tiny shoulders as we walked.

"About what?"

"Tonight's the night!" She skipped once. So frickin' cute. "I'm gonna find out if I got the audition!"

She slipped through the opening in the fence ahead of me, and I paused for a second, my heart dropping. The audition. Right. Claudia had sent in an application to this prestigious dance program right outside Princeton for next year. The hope was, she'd get into her dream school and her dream dance program and they'd be within walking distance of each other. Suddenly my chest was heavy with dread. If she got this audition, it would be a sign. Because if she got the audition, she'd get into the dance program. And if she got into the dance program, there was no way she wasn't going to get into Princeton. After tonight, she could be one step closer to getting everything she wanted. And everything she wanted would take her away from me.

CHAPTER THREE

Claudia

"Can I get you guys anything else?"

The waitress at Pizza City stood at the end of our table, smiling at Peter. She was a girl from school, a junior I was pretty sure, and she was always here. I think her family owned the place, but I wasn't sure what her name was. What I did know was that she wanted my boyfriend. Of course she did. Everyone wanted my boyfriend. He was Peter "QB-1" Marrott. But this girl was making it totally obvious, with her sly half smile and by the way she was leaning one hand into the faux-wood table, pushing up her boobs by angling her triceps against one of them. Why didn't she flirt with Gavin? Or Orion? Or Peter's annoying friend Lester? One of the guys at the table whose girlfriend wasn't sitting right next to him.

"You can get *me* something else," Lester said, leering at her.

Well, okay. I understood why she didn't flirt with Lester.

She stood up straight and sighed, looking down her nose at him. "Oh yeah? What's that?"

Lester Chen's skinny face turned purple. "Oh, um, nothing. I was just kidding."

The girl looked hopefully over at Peter again. I leaned in closer to his side and looked her in the eye. "Thanks. We're fine."

Emphasis on the "we're." She gave me this look, like she couldn't believe I was sitting there with him even though we came in here together twice a week, every week. Then she finally, *finally* walked away, flipping her weirdly orange hair over her shoulder.

I tugged Peter's large class ring out from under the collar of my shirt, where it hung on a gold chain, and toyed with it. It wasn't as if I could blame the girl for her confusion. Honestly. It had been fifteen months, three weeks, and two days since Peter had first asked me out, and even I sometimes found myself wondering how and why it had happened in the first place. We're talking about Peter Marrott here, people. He was the hottest, most popular, most athletic guy in the senior class. Girls had started crushing on him in kindergarten. He'd been voted best-looking in eighth grade by a landslide (I was in charge of counting the votes, so I knew). Before me he'd gone out with Aura Sen, who was a year older than us and the hottest of Lake Carmody's legendary Hot Sen Sisters. (There were five of them, and the youngest had already won some pageant that put her on the cover of the local paper last year.) But they'd broken up after the junior prom scandal two springs ago. (Rumor was there was vomit involved. Lots of vomit.) Three weeks later he'd come to his sister's dance recital, which had just happened to also be my dance recital, and afterward he'd waited for me—yes, me—to come out of the dressing room and now here we were, sitting at Pizza City together for the hundredth time with his superhot and popular friends.

Lester excepted, of course. From the hot part, anyway.

So yes, I'd been surprised when he'd first asked me out. While I do have good hair and a tight body, I'm not Aura Sen–level beautiful. But now that I knew Peter so well, I wasn't surprised we'd been together as long as we had. We didn't have any classes together and we hung out with different crowds at school, but opposites attract, right? And besides, when it came down to it, we had more in common than anyone could imagine. We were both family-oriented athletes with responsible natures, and we supported each other. Would little miss cleavage-shover understand any of that? My guess was no.

"What do you want to do this weekend?" Peter asked me as I leaned into his side. Gavin launched a grape tomato at Lester, and Lester caught it in his mouth. Orion, meanwhile, texted on his phone with a crease between his eyes, like whatever he was doing was super serious.

"I don't know," I said, smiling up at him. "The usual?"

"You mean sit around and be boring?" Lester said with a cackle. A grape tomato hit him in the temple and bounced along the floor.

"Dude. Back off," Peter said, reaching behind me to shove Lester's head.

"Don't bother. I'm used to it," I told Peter, rolling my eyes with a smile. Nothing was going to bring me down today. Not even Lester's relentless mocking of me and my boring life and straight As. After almost a year and a half of being Peter's girlfriend, I *was* used to it. And besides, today was the big day. I was going to find out if I'd gotten the audition at the Lafayette School of Dance. I was so excited I'd had to use the bathroom between every single class. If I got that audition, my future was practically set. Then we'd just have to figure out Peter's.

"Are you ready for your meeting with Mr. Garvey tomorrow?" I asked him.

His leg started bouncing under the table, just like it always did whenever the subject of college came up.

"Um, yeah. I think so." He fiddled with the straw in his soda cup.

"Did you fill out the general application?" I asked. "Because if you want, I can come over after ballet and help you with it."

"What're you, his mom?" Lester asked.

Gavin kicked him under the table. We heard the pop, and then Lester bent over, rubbing his shin.

"It's cool. I got it," Peter said.

"Are you sure?" I asked. "Because he said he wanted you to have it done before you met. It's no problem if you want me to—"

"I said, I've got it," Peter snapped.

I looked down at my salad, feeling as if I'd been slapped. Every time I offered to help Peter with his applications or his school search, he got tense with me. I just didn't get it. Didn't he understand that I was trying to help? That I wanted to be part of his decision and his future? I loved him and I wanted him to have the life he deserved, but it seemed like he didn't want me involved. At all.

Maybe he didn't feel the same way about me as I felt about him.

"So, what does a booster do, exactly?" Orion asked me, putting his phone away. I could have kissed him for breaking the awkward silence. Except then Peter would have pounded him. Except, then again, maybe he wouldn't. Either way, I decided it was safer to spear a cucumber slice with my fork. Peter, meanwhile, wolfed down another slice of sausage pizza as if nothing had happened.

"We basically make you feel like a superstar," I explained, and Orion grinned. "I'm sorry you got stuck with that klepto, though. What was she even doing in the bleachers during practice? Stalking you?"

Orion shrugged and glanced out the window at the packed parking lot. "I don't know, I kinda like her. Did you know that she randomly kissed me this morning? Out of nowhere?"

My jaw dropped. "See? Freak!"

Orion laughed and blushed, reaching for a pizza slice. I wished him luck with that one. What kind of person just takes something out of your bag when you don't even know them? And then she didn't apologize when I confronted her about it. Weird.

I finished off my water and checked my watch. After our awkward moment, I was longing for some fresh air. And besides, the sooner I got to the Studio, the sooner I'd find out my fate.

"Do you mind if we head out?" I asked Peter. "I'm dying to get over there." A shadow crossed his face, and my heart stopped once more. "What's wrong?"

"Nothing. Yeah, no problem," he said. "Let's go."

I turned to Lester, who was, as always, oblivious to what was going on around him.

"Excuse me?" I said politely, lifting my bag off the floor.

"What?" he asked.

"Dude! Move!" Peter ordered.

Lester instantly shot up. "You guys're leaving already? What's up?"

"Claudia has to get to class, and I gotta pick up Michelle," Peter said, dropping a few dollars on the table.

"You are such an old married couple, picking up the kid and running errands," Lester groaned. "What's next, grocery shopping? Are you guys gonna watch HGTV tonight, then not have sex and go to bed?"

"We're not *your* parents," I joked.

"Oh!" Peter and Gavin shouted, high-fiving. Then Peter raised his hand for me to slap as well. Just like that, the tension lifted. The moments when I felt like I belonged among Peter's friends were few and far between, but when they happened, I reveled in them. I think Peter kind of did too.

"Burn!" Peter shouted in Lester's face.

We turned and headed out the door, and I suddenly couldn't stop smiling. Whatever had gone wrong between us back there, I'd set it right. Now I just had to survive the drive to the Studio without peeing in my pants.

"Will you come in with me?" I asked Peter when he pulled his old secondhand Buick up in front of the Studio. It was a large storefront on Maple Street, just off Main, and it was the place where I'd spent most of my life for the past thirteen years. Usually walking through that door was like walking into my own home, but today, I was crazy with jitters.

"Why?" Peter asked.

"Because! I'm nervous! What if I don't get in?"

Peter huffed a sigh and looked through the windshield. For a second his hands worked the steering wheel, his knuckles red, then white, then red, then white. What was going on with him today? Was he angry at me about something?

I was about to ask, but then, suddenly, he turned to me and squeezed my hand. "You'll get in."

I grinned. "You think?"

"Let's go find out."

He got out of the car, then jogged around and opened my door for me. Together we walked into the brightly lit studio. The reception area was empty, but a dozen dancers worked out on the wide wood floor of the rehearsal space, stretching out and laughing and chatting at the barres. I waved to Lauren, whose heel rested on the barre near the corner. Her black curls were up in a high bun, and she wore a light-pink leotard and skirt that perfectly complemented her latte-hued skin. She widened her eyes toward Madame Helene's office.

"Lance is in there!" she mouthed.

The butterflies in my stomach were straining to bust out. Peter put his hand on the small of my back, and we walked over to the open office door together. Madame Helene, a short, robust woman with gray hair in curls around her pretty face, stood at the center of the room in front of her desk, talking in hushed tones with my friend and frequent dance partner, Lance Turska. Lance had applied to the Lafayette School as well, and we were both finding out about our auditions today. He stood tall and straight, as always, his shoulders back in his tight white leotard and black tights. I couldn't see his face. Was he happy? Sad? What?

"Madame?" I said tentatively. I could feel Peter's heat behind me, and it made me feel brave. Both Madame and Lance turned to face me. Lance's whole face broke into a smile.

"We did it! We got the auditions!" he announced.

"We did?" I cried.

Lance crossed the room in one long stride and took me up in his arms, spinning me around. I felt as light as air, and I laughed into his shoulder.

"Both of us?" I asked Madame Helene as he replaced me on the floor.

She smiled as if she'd known this would happen. "My star pupils."

I turned to Peter and moved to hug him, but his face had turned to stone. I stopped and even took a step back at the sight of it. He looked so untouchable. I glanced over my shoulder at Lance, whose smile faltered. Peter had always been a little bit jealous of him, because we spent so much time together at rehearsal, but there was nothing going on between us. There never had been. Lance was like the big brother I never had.

"Peter?" I said, confused.

"Congratulations." He stoically looked Lance in the eye. "Both of you."

Then he turned around and walked out of the office.

"Peter!" I called after him.

But he didn't stop. He shoved open the door with the flat of his hand and was gone.

CHAPTER FOUR

Peter

"And then Kendall was all like, you can't make me head the ball, and Coach Tarkisian was all, if you don't want to learn the game, then why are you here? And Kendall was like, what do you know about soccer? You run a dry cleaner! And Talia completely freaked out and went all *TMZ* on her butt."

I pulled the car into the driveway and hit the brakes. "What does that even mean?"

It came out nasty, as if I was mad at her or something, and suddenly I felt worse than I already had, which I didn't think was possible. I took a deep breath and tried to blow out my anger, but I couldn't stop seeing the way Claudia had thrown herself at Lance back at the studio. I knew she wasn't interested in him. I did. But he was basically the perfect guy for her, and I'd spent the last year and a half waiting for her to see it. Now they were going to go to that audition together, get into the dance program together, and spend the next four years hanging out. While I was . . . where? Here? Taking classes at the community college and going to LCH football games on the weekends, trying to relive my glory days?

God. I was such a loser.

Michelle, meanwhile, didn't seem to notice my tone. She looked at me like I was the dumbest person alive. "You know, like on *TMZ* how they're always showing celebs kicking the paparazzi's ass?" She unhooked her seat belt and pushed open her door. "Talia was *not* cool with Kendall insulting her dad. She totally ripped the back off Kendall's practice jersey."

I smirked, trying to focus on my fairly awesome sister instead of my own lameness.

"Seriously?" I said as I got out of the car. "Sounds more violent than *my* practice."

"Eighth-grade girls' soccer is not a cakewalk, bro," she said, widening her blue eyes as she shook her head.

I laughed and ruffled her hair. "I might have to come be your bodyguard next time."

"Are you kidding? Talia takes Krav Maga!" Michelle joked, nudging my side. "She could take you with one hand tied behind her back."

"Ha ha." I got her in a choke hold and gave her a noogie. Not a hard one, though. More like a love-noogie. At least if I stayed home next year I'd get to hang out with my mom and Michelle. That was a bright side.

"Get off! Get off me! Foul! I call foul! You've got a hundred pounds on me!" I let her go and she straightened her hair and huffed. "You are *so* immature."

"My apologies, princess." I raised my hands in surrender. "What do you think Mom's making for dinner tonight?"

"I hope fried chicken," Michelle replied with a jump, forgetting how fed up she was with me. "We haven't had fried chicken in forever, and she said she was going to try some new seasoning or something."

She pushed open the door and we both paused. The house was

full of the scent of frying food. Even though I'd just eaten half a pizza, my stomach grumbled. My mom, who was a paralegal by day and a food blogger by night, was rushing around the kitchen, her semi-wet blond hair pulled up into a high ponytail, an apron strapped on over her sweats. Every day she came home, showered, and got right to work on some random recipe she'd try out on us. Then she'd write about our reactions for her blog, "Kid Tested."

Which was why I'd been my sister's chauffeur ever since I'd gotten my license. But I didn't mind. I liked the extra alone time with Michelle. And at least my dad had left behind his old car when he'd bailed on us eight years ago. My mom had kept it in good condition, so that I'd be able to use it as my own one day. She called it my dad's "parting gift."

"Hi, guys!" she called out happily. "How was your day?"

"Good," I lied, considering the way it had ended.

"Better now!" Michelle added, hopping over to the stove.

I put my bag down and was about to go grab one of the onion rings off the paper towel where they were draining on the counter, when something in the dining room caught my eye. Great. Just when I thought it couldn't get any worse. On the table were stacks of college brochures—dozens of them. My mother must have raided my room, and from the looks of it, she hadn't left a drawer unsearched, a pillow unturned, or a garbage can unemptied.

"What's that about?" I asked, trying to sound casual as I plucked an onion ring.

"You and I are going through those tonight, together," she said, and gave me a serious stare. She checked the temperature on her oil, which popped and sizzled. "If you're meeting with your guidance counselor to narrow down your choices tomorrow, I want my two cents in."

"But Mom—"

"No buts, Peter."

Michelle giggled.

"But I have volunteering tonight," I improvised. I wasn't scheduled to work, but they could always use help. It wasn't like Marcy Fiore, my church's middle-aged soup kitchen ministry adviser, was going to turn me away if I showed up at the door. "I can't miss that."

"Then we'll do it after," Mom said. "This is your future we're talking about, Peter. You have to start taking this seriously."

I felt that pressure—the pressure I always felt when Claudia brought up college—like someone was grinding a rock into my chest. The onion ring found its way into my mouth, even though my stomach didn't really want it anymore.

"Are there any schools near Princeton?" I asked, trying to lean back against the counter casually. "I mean, like, schools I could get into?"

My mom and Michelle exchanged a knowing glance.

"Well, there's Rowan," my mom said, carefully placing a chicken leg into the oil, then wiping her fingers on her apron. "And Rutgers is about an hour from there. But Rutgers might be . . ."

"A long shot. I know." I swallowed hard, feeling like a tool. What kind of moron couldn't even get into his own state school?

"Peter, listen, I understand what you're trying to do, but you can't decide your future based on where Claudia's going," my mother said, adding a wing and then a thigh to the oil. "We love Claudia as much as you do, but it's a high school relationship."

The onion ring turned to rock on its way to my gut. "Mom, don't."

"I'm just saying! You don't see her trying to make her plans around you."

I stared at the floor. The swirly pattern on the tile blurred in front of me. Never had I felt the way I felt right then. It was like my mom had taken out a bat and swung right at my chest as hard as she could. My own mother.

"Oh, hon. I didn't mean it that way," she said, reaching for me.

I slipped away from her. "No. It's fine," I said, my jaw clenched. "You're right. You don't see her trying to plan around me."

I snatched my backpack off the floor and barreled up the stairs. "Call me when dinner's ready."

I had just walked into my room when my phone beeped with a text. It was from Claudia.

I CAN STILL COME OVER AFTER BALLET TO HELP U W/ GENERAL APP! LET ME KNOW!

My fingers tightened around the phone, and I slammed the door. I swear, it was like between her and my mom, they were *trying* to get rid of me. I threw my bag and my phone onto my desk, then dropped onto my unmade bed, trying to breathe through the pressure. Once my heart rate calmed down, I rolled over and looked at the framed picture of me and Claudia on my nightstand. We'd taken it at the shore over the summer on what had pretty much been the best day of my life. We'd driven down at the crack of dawn and spent the entire day making out on a beach towel, running into the waves, eating greasy food, and napping under her umbrella. We both looked so tan and chill and happy. Like two people who'd never even thought about taking anything seriously. Back then, college hardly ever came up. It was just this sort of nebulous thing far off in the future. Now it was the only thing everyone talked about. Every day. Nonstop. Next year, next year, next year.

I just wanted to be that guy at the beach. The guy with no worries.

I'd almost told her I loved her that day, on the boardwalk, as the sun went down, but I'd chickened out. No. Not chickened out. *Decided* to keep it to myself. To not let things get too serious. To keep having fun. And it had worked out. We did have fun. For the rest of the summer. Until school started again and then, suddenly, *everything* was serious.

I grabbed the frame, hugged it to my chest, and stared at the ceiling. Maybe I didn't want to go to college. Did they ever think about that? Maybe I just wanted everything to stay the way it was.

CHAPTER FIVE

True

"Orion is here?"

My mother, the gorgeous and indomitable Aphrodite, stood at the open refrigerator with a bottle of Perrier poised an inch below her perfectly outlined, colored, and glossed lips. Her crisp white shirt was tucked into her form-fitting, black pencil skirt, her shimmering blond hair just grazing her chin. Her name tag from Perfumania, where she spritzed customers at the door, was still pinned to her left breast pocket, her name spelled out in gold script.

Unlike me and Hephaestus, my mother had refused to take on a more modern name when she had been relegated to human status. Just one of the many ways her stubborn nature had shown through since we'd been banished to Earth.

"Yep," Hephaestus said, looking across the wide kitchen floor at me as if he thought I might suddenly collapse against it in tears.

"Not only is he here, he was in most of my classes," I groused. If Zeus *had* sent Orion here to torture me, he'd done a thorough job.

"Why would Zeus send him here? What purpose does it serve?" She let the stainless-steel refrigerator door close with a bang.

"We were hoping you might have a theory," I replied, leaning back against the counter, feeling defeated, since it was fairly clear she hadn't a clue.

"And he doesn't remember you? He has no idea who either of you are?" she asked, placing the bottle on the counter.

"Not a one," I replied.

"But that is entirely un—"

She didn't get to finish her sentence, because we were suddenly blasted by an explosion of otherworldly wind. The lights in the room flickered, the fridge released an avalanche of ice cubes onto the floor with a harsh growl, and the coffeepot exploded, ricocheting shards of glass across the room. My mother was still screaming when I opened my eyes and saw my father standing not two feet away.

"Ares?" I gasped. "What are you doing here?"

"You couldn't have whirled into the backyard?" my mother complained, tugging a square of jagged glass from her hair.

"And risk the neighbors seeing?" he shot back. "Don't test me, woman. I don't have much time."

"Don't call me woman, *man*," she replied, eyeing him up and down with disdain. But then her gaze softened. She gripped the refrigerator's door handle, and an almost imperceptible blush appeared at the very crest of her cheeks.

My father looked different. Clean. As if he'd just bathed seconds before gracing us with his presence. Usually the God of War appeared sweaty and creased and stained from the field of battle, but as he stood in the center of our modern kitchen, his tan skin was so scrubbed it glowed. He wore the camouflage cargo pants often favored by today's warriors, and a green T-shirt, the sleeves of which were pulled taught by his massive arm muscles. His brown hair was wet and combed forward over his forehead in a way that altered his features from their usual squared-off growl.

Ares had always been handsome, but ruggedly, violently, almost off-puttingly so. For the first time I could see the god my mother had fallen for. Or maybe that was just my hankering for home.

"What is it you've come to tell us?" Hephaestus asked.

Ares turned abruptly, automatically assuming a fighter's stance. When he saw Hephaestus there, the deep furrow of his brow intensified.

"Hephaestus?" he blurted. "What are you—How is this possible?"

"The wonders of the universe never cease," Hephaestus replied with a Cheshire grin, wheeling around the end of the table and offering his hand. "It's been a long time, Ares."

"You haven't aged a day," my father said.

Hephaestus lowered his hand, realizing Ares was not about to shake with him. "I may be mortal, but I'm still pretty. Not sure why Zeus made it so, but he did, and I thank him for it. As do the bulk of the ladies I encounter. Plus, it makes it easier for me to help your daughter. This high school experience has been fascinating thus far."

Ares glanced over his shoulder at my mother. She shrugged like, *This isn't my fault.* There was clearly some communication passing among the three of them that I didn't understand.

"What's going on?" I asked.

"Can we speak somewhere in private?" my father demanded of me.

Hephaestus chuckled to himself. The tension in the air was palpable, the unspoken so thick I could have taken a bite out of it and tasted its sour heat.

"Why?" I asked, my eyes darting among the three of them. "What's your problem with Hephaestus?"

"Yeah, Ares? What's your problem with me?" Hephaestus asked merrily.

He was teasing the God of War. No one teased the God of War. Not unless they wanted a spear through the heart or an unceremonious beheading. His audacity was met with more silence. The kind that normally preceded a massive earthquake.

The fridge let out another groan and spat five more ice cubes onto the floor. They skittered down the pile already melting at its base and came to a stop near the pointed toe of one of my mother's stilettos.

"Ares, Hephaestus has been of immeasurable aid to me and to True—to Eros—over the past week. You can trust him," Aphrodite said, lifting her chin. "*We* can trust him."

My father sighed. "I haven't the time to debate you," he spoke at the floor. "Fine. I've come to tell you that Apollo and Artemis have learned of Orion's existence, and as you can imagine, they are none too pleased. With any of us."

My knees buckled. I stumbled toward the nearest chair, slipping and sliding across the ice and water and glass.

"How?" I asked. "How did they find out?"

"No one knows," my father replied. "Or if they do, they've yet to confess. Apparently, Artemis actually laid eyes on Orion in the royal palace, before Zeus had a chance to properly hide him. Now the witch wants nothing more than to get her claws into Orion. She and that bastard brother of hers have been causing chaos on the Mount."

"So this is the reason for Orion's sudden appearance," my mother said. "Zeus sent him here to protect him."

"And to insure your bargain," Hephaestus added darkly. "If Artemis were to steal Orion away for herself, you'd have no reason to complete your mission. But with him here, dangled before you, you have the motivation you need."

"That explains his lack of memory," Aphrodite said. "If he knew you when he saw you, there'd be no keeping the two of you apart. But if he doesn't remember you . . ."

"He gets to keep us apart even though we're so very close," I breathed. "Does she know it was I who rescued him from the stars? Does she . . . know of our love?"

Ares shook his head. "Zeus and I thought it better to keep that a bit of a secret. If the other gods found out you held such power . . . things could get complicated for you. For now, we've floated several rumors as to his reemergence."

"Thank you, Father."

"Don't thank me too soon. You know how word gets around on the Mount. It's only a matter of time before she discovers the truth."

I pitched forward and buried my face in my hands, my stomach clenched with pain. Artemis must have been livid, knowing Orion lived and she could not be with him. In her mind, Orion belonged to her. She was the one who'd loved him on the day he died those many centuries ago. She was the one who had set him among the stars so that his image might live forever. She'd been trying to bring him back to her for generations, but where she had failed, I had succeeded.

"If she ever finds out, she's going to kill me," I muttered through my fingers.

"She has not the power to take your life," my father scoffed. "At least not if you return to Mount Olympus with your full divine powers. You are both lower goddesses of equal merit."

My mother and I locked eyes, both of us recalling the same event—that day years ago when Artemis had appeared in my chambers and nearly ended me. She'd locked her hands around my neck and squeezed so hard I had felt the life force draining out of me. I had no idea how she'd developed the power, but she could have done it. She could have ended me. Would have, if not for the timely intervention of my mother.

It was the first time any of us had witnessed a god or goddess's power growing. Until that day, I hadn't known it was possible for our abilities to change.

"Do they know where on Earth he is?" my mother asked, choosing not to let Ares and Hephaestus in on our secret. But I could tell Ares had seen our silent communication. He knew that something was amiss.

"Not as of my leaving," Ares replied. "Zeus has all of you cloaked. But they are doing everything in their power to find out."

"But even if they do, they can't come here," Hephaestus put in. "They're lower gods. They can't come to Earth unless sent here by an upper god. Banished or set on a mission."

"And I'm sure Zeus has forbidden the upper gods to send them," my mother put in, though it was more of a question than an assurance.

"Of course," my father replied. "But that doesn't mean one of them won't be convinced to spite him. Neptune or Hades or Hera."

My mother rolled her eyes at the mention of the queen's name. There was no love lost between the two great goddesses.

He looked me in the eye. "You must complete your mission, my daughter, and you must do it now. When last we spoke, Zeus had no intention of breaking your bargain. He did not send you here for you to fail. He sent you here to teach you a lesson, to force you to refocus on your work. Of course the king wishes for love to succeed, for love to flourish in the world he so cherishes, but the situation is volatile and could easily change. Time is of the essence."

I wanted to groan, thinking of how I'd spent the day idly longing for Orion, willing him to remember me, when I could have been working to match my next couple. Somehow I held my tongue, not wanting my parents to mark my desperation, but my disappointment in myself burned hot beneath my skin. Self-pity was such a waste of time. I knew this. How could I have let myself indulge in it for an entire day?

"Why?" my mother asked. "Even if Artemis does get herself banished to Earth, there is no contest between her and Eros. Orion would choose Eros in a heartbeat."

"As always, you're thinking only of matters of the heart, and ignoring the logistics of the situation," my father said derisively. "If Artemis were to come here as a goddess while Eros remained human, Artemis could smite her with a blink of an eye. If Artemis were to come here as a human, and Eros remained a human, all Artemis need do is get her hands on any man-made weapon and she could end our daughter just as easily. The only answer is for True, as you call her, to complete her mission and have Zeus return her and Orion to Mount Olympus before Artemis and Apollo can get themselves to Earth. Then the two girls can face each other on common ground, with equal powers between them."

"And then what?" my mother demanded. "A fight to the death?"

"If need be," my father replied.

"How can you say that? How can you stand there and say that as if it's nothing? She's our daughter."

"He's right," I said flatly.

"What?" my mother gasped.

"He's right." I rose to my feet and pressed my sweaty palms

together. "I'm going to have to fight her. Eventually, that's what this comes down to. Whether it's here on Earth or back home on Mount Olympus, I'll do whatever it takes to keep Orion safe, to ensure our love."

"But Eros—"

I looked her in the eye. "Whatever it takes."

CHAPTER SIX

True

My father followed me as I made my exit out the back door, intent on walking into town to start trolling for some new lovers to match. The sun was just going down behind the wooden fence that surrounded our small but green yard, and birds chirped merrily in the dogwood tree off the patio. It was amazing how the world just went on, entirely oblivious to one's mood. Back on Mount Olympus, I would have had the skies swirling with black clouds and the sea roiling right about now. We might even be suffering a rain of toads.

"Eros, we need to talk," my father said, the wooden steps bowing under his weight.

"Do we? Now? Why now when we never have before?" I asked, barely glancing over my shoulder at him.

"Trust me. This, you'll want to hear," he said.

He glanced furtively at the kitchen windows. Hephaestus gazed out at us for a moment, before turning and moving out of sight. My interest was piqued, much to my chagrin. The very idea of giving my father the satisfaction of bending to his will made my skin crawl.

"Is this about Hephaestus?" I asked.

"Yes," he said. "And your mother."

My stomach twisted in a slow, prickling vortex. I stared into my father's dark eyes. "No. Please. Don't tell me—"

"They were lovers," my father said. "Many moons ago. In fact, they were once married."

"What?" I gasped.

"This was before your mother and I truly knew each other," he said. "Before you, your brothers and, of course, your sister."

My sister. Harmonia. A million images of her smiling at Hephaestus, standing by his side, accepting his gifts, his touch, his attention, flitted through my mind at once. Hot acid arose in the back of my throat and I turned around, trying to shake the visions from my mind. As long as I'd known Hephaestus, he'd been my sister Harmonia's constant companion. They'd never been more than friends, but I'd always expected their relationship to turn in that direction, until the day Hephaestus was flung out of Mount Olympus for good. It was the only way I'd ever known him—as my sister's almost-love. The very thought that he had ever been with my mother . . .

"How could I not know this?" I asked, facing Ares again.

"We swore we'd never speak of it," my father said. He walked over to a wooden swing that hung from an oak tree by two thick cords of rope. With a tug, he tested their might, then sat. The bough moaned, but held. I almost laughed at the sight of this hulking man, this legendary warrior, perched on a child's plaything. Almost. "I'm surprised that after the amount of time he spent with Harmonia, he never broke that promise."

He pondered this curious show of integrity for a moment, gazing off at the rose hedge near the fence, then fixed me with a serious stare.

"Hephaestus fell in love with your mother upon first sight and courted her for years. She wanted nothing to do with him, of course, Hephaestus being lame from birth and constantly smelling of the forge. He was never your mother's type."

He gave a wry laugh, but I wasn't amused. I had always detested how the upper gods insisted on branding Hephaestus as lame. He'd had a withered leg at birth but had forged himself a brace that allowed him to walk just like any other god (this, a part of his history he *had* shared with Harmonia and me). It was Zeus's fault that he was now confined to a wheelchair. He had flung Hephaestus to Earth so many times he'd shattered his legs irreparably.

"How did he win her, then?" I asked.

There was a glint in my father's eye as he answered this. "He forged a belt for her, made of gold and jewels. No one had ever seen anything like it. And you know your mother. She's easily distracted by anything"—he twiddled his fingers, searching for the word— "shimmery."

Now I did laugh. "That was all it took?"

"That was all it took," he said, tearing a bloom off a low branch on the dogwood and holding it between two fingers with a delicacy I didn't know he possessed. "They were married the following dawn. And they were happy. For a time."

"Until you came along?" I surmised.

My father stared at the flower, the deep pink at the center fading to white near the edges of the petals. "Yes. Until I came along. Your mother and I fell deeply in love with each other, but she didn't want to leave Hephaestus. She didn't want to break her vows. Then, one day, he . . . caught us together in their bed."

He crushed the flower in his mighty fist, and my stomach turned. "I think I might actually be sick."

"He had suspected something was going on and had set a trap—a golden net that no one, not even I, could tear through. It fell upon your mother and me and held us fast against the sheets. Then, while we were struggling to break free, Hephaestus gathered every god and goddess he could find—including Zeus, who had approved their match—and brought them to witness our shame."

My hand was at my throat. "That's . . . awful."

My father opened his fingers and looked down at the flattened bloom as if he'd forgotten it was there. He turned his palm sideways, and a stiff breeze tore the sticky, creased petals from his skin.

"We fled to Mount Etna for a time, and that's where we had the boys. I've always wondered if the reason they are the way they are is because of where they were conceived."

My older brothers, Deimos and Phobos, were the Gods of Fear and Panic, and the most paranoid, miserable, tetchy gods on Mount Olympus.

"We waited to return to the Mount before having you girls," he finished. "Which might be why you are the way you are."

He smiled slightly, and I detected a hint of pride in his eyes. As if that was even possible. The God of War had long made it known how little respect he had for the work my mother and I did. And I couldn't imagine he had any softer feelings for Harmonia, who was the Goddess of Communal Harmony. Her work directly rebutted his.

"Your mother was always wary of the friendship your sister formed with Hephaestus, concerned he might try to use her in some way to get back at us for our betrayal," my father continued. "She was never able to rest well until the day Zeus finally banished him to Earth for good. Which is why I was shocked to see him sitting so comfortably at your kitchen table. I'm surprised your mother even allowed him to enter your home."

"Well, as she said, he's been invaluable to us," I said. "Before he arrived, we could scarcely dress ourselves. If it wasn't for his intervention, I might not have made my first match."

"But you seem to have your footing now," my father said, rising. "What reason is there to keep him around?"

My jaw dropped. "Oh, I don't know . . . loyalty, gratitude, friendship?"

"Friendship? Loyalty? Have you heard anything I've just said? Or was your mind off in the clouds again, as always?" my father thundered. "Why can you never simply focus, Eros? The man cannot be trusted."

I felt as if I'd been slapped. "I *am* focused. I'm focused on finishing my mission! A mission I wouldn't be succeeding at if not for Hephaestus. A mission I wouldn't even be *saddled with* if not for *you*! You really think you're the god who should be telling me who to trust?"

"I am not responsible for you being here," he replied tersely. "It was your own bad judgment that got you into this mess."

I felt the sting of this and looked at the ground. "Perhaps you're right. Perhaps I should have gone straight to Zeus when I realized I loved Orion and asked him for his blessing—"

"Are you mad? Zeus would have smote him on the spot," Ares interjected.

"But you just said—"

"Your bad judgment was falling in love with him in the first place! Nay, saving him from his perch among the stars in the first place!"

"But I didn't do that on purpose! I had no idea I had such power!" I replied.

"Exactly!" my father thundered. He sucked in air, his chest heaving, and wiped his face with both hands. With a desperate look in his eye, he took a step toward me. I flinched when he reached for my hands, but he took them within his anyway, his touch absurdly cautious. "Eros, don't you understand what's going on here? Your powers have grown. They *are* growing. I've been watching you. I know you've regained your telekinesis."

I lost my breath. "What?"

"You were not supposed to have the power to return Orion to life, and you should not have the power to recall your abilities to yourself now that you're human. Zeus is baffled by you right now. Baffled and afraid."

"You're saying . . . you're saying that no one has gifted me with this ability? That I am somehow overcoming Zeus's magic?" I stammered. I had thought that one of the upper gods, perhaps even Zeus himself, had allowed my power to return as a sort of prize for forming my first couple. Had even hoped this was true, because it would mean that Zeus's anger at me was softening. But this . . . this was impossible to comprehend. "You believe Zeus . . . fears me?"

"He has always feared what he does not understand," my father said. "How do you think Hera keeps him in line? Women have always baffled him."

He smirked and I tried to smile, but I felt an awful, twisting ache of confusion inside me. "Why is this happening?"

"Love is one of the most powerful, audacious emotions in the universe," my father said. "And you harness it. I'm not surprised your powers have grown. I only fear they will lead you into peril."

I stared at my father. Never in my existence had he looked at me with such concern, such reverence, such . . . love.

"Eros, hear me now, because I might not be able to return to check on you after this trip. I want you to promise me you'll be careful," he said. "Zeus won't notice the odd use of telekinesis here or there, but if you must use it, keep it small. Do nothing to draw his attention or his ire. Of course, if Artemis comes calling . . ."

I gulped. "Yes?"

"If Artemis comes calling, hit her with everything you've got," he said, cupping my cheek with his calloused hand.

My heart, my throat, my eyes were full. Just to know my father actually cared about me, that he was keeping an eye on me, that he was protecting me, was overwhelming.

"I promise," I said throatily. "I swear I won't let you down."

After approaching a few random people in town, asking if they were looking for love, and having them back away from me as if I were a rabid dog, I realized I'd be better off concentrating my efforts at school as originally planned. I returned home at dusk feeling tired, discouraged, and on edge, expecting at every turn to find Artemis and Apollo around the bend. What I needed was a nice long bath. Something to refresh and invigorate me for tomorrow. But when I shoved open the door to the bathroom, my mother was kicked back in the claw-foot tub, encased in lavender-scented bubbles.

"Eros! You startled me!" she said, hand to her heart. Her short blond hair was pulled back in a bristly ponytail, and her face was covered in some sort of blue goop. "You musn't barge in on people when errant gods and goddesses could be on the loose."

She lifted a sponge and squeezed it out over one extended, willowy arm.

"So," I said, closing the door behind me. "You and Hephaestus? That's fairly disturbing."

Her arms dropped back into the tub with a splash. "I'm going to slaughter your father."

"At least he was honest with me!" I protested, sitting atop the closed toilet seat. "You should have told me the day Hephaestus showed up on our doorstep."

My mother sat up straight, sloshing water and bubbles onto the floor. "What would have been the point? We swore to keep it a secret. Not that that matters to your father. Besides, what Hephaestus and I had ended badly. And it ended badly thousands and thousands of years ago. It hardly matters now."

"But do you really think we can trust him?" I asked quietly, leaning forward. "Are you sure he doesn't want to use our situation to get back at you somehow?"

My mother clucked her tongue, and her blue eyes were almost pitying. "You have too much of your father in you. Not everyone holds a grudge, and even if they do, they don't necessarily act upon it. Hephaestus has been in love with your sister for several millennia. He would no more hurt her family than she would start a war."

I sighed and looked down at the blue-and-white tiles beneath my feet. "So it's true. He did love her."

"And she him, if I know anything about love. . . ."

We caught each other's eyes and laughed at the absurdity of the idea that Aphrodite might get something like that wrong.

"She never told me so, but I could see it in her eyes," my mother said. "Trust me, Eros. Hephaestus has nothing but our best interests in mind."

"If you say so."

I got up and pushed my hair back from my face. "Will you tell me when you're done?"

"Of course, but I wouldn't hold your breath." She sighed and sank down in the tub again, letting the water rise up to her chin. "I could be perfectly happy here for hours."

I left her to her solitude and went to my room, wishing I could channel some of her confidence, but feeling more conflicted than ever. What was I to do when my mother told me one thing and my father the exact opposite? How was I to know who to trust? Meanwhile, the top of the hourglass on my desk—once full of red sand—was already about a quarter of the way empty. The pressure was compounding around me.

The sand timer, Artemis and Apollo, my father, Hephaestus, Claudia, Peter, Zeus, Orion. I didn't know how to fix it. I didn't know if I could succeed.

If only Harmonia were here. She always knew what to do.

I took a deep breath, squeezed my eyes closed, and imagined Harmonia beside me in a room filled with roses. The scent of flowers always calmed me down and helped me think straight. Had I been in my chambers on Mount Olympus, I could have conjured thousands of blooms at a whim. I could have rolled in them, bathed in them, buried myself in them.

But I was here, and I was powerless. Or nearly so. The only thing I could do was keep my eyes closed, breathe, and use my imagination.

Harmonia's laugh. Her reassuring gaze. And roses. Roses

everywhere. I imagined the heady scent filling my nostrils and soothing away my fears and anxieties, helping me think. I breathed in and out, trying to see them. Roses upon roses all over my room.

Something pricked my palm.

"Ow!" My eyes fluttered open, my soothing vision obliterated. I looked down at my hand, and my heart stopped beating.

Clutched inside my fist was the stem of a gorgeous, plump, red rose.

CHAPTER SEVEN

Peter

"Sixteen schools? You really think I need to apply to that many?"

This was narrowing it down?

I stared at the stack of brochures. The one on the top had a picture of four smiling kids of different skin colors, laughing on a blanket as orange leaves fell. They were surrounded by books and a bike, a skateboard and backpacks. They all looked smarter than me. They looked like people Claudia would love to hang out with.

"Most of them take the general application," Mr. Garvey said, his forehead glistening. He'd been my guidance counselor since freshman year, and every year his hairline moved farther back on his head. He leaned forward in his chair and glanced at Coach Morschauser, who sat next to me.

"And most of 'em are looking for QBs."

"Yeah?" I said hopefully.

"Yeah. Now we just gotta get their scouts out here to take a look at you," he replied, like he wasn't entirely sure if it would even be possible. "Rutgers and the College of New Jersey are coming out this weekend to check out Ross, so if you put on a good show . . . well, you never know."

Mitchell Ross was our kicker, and had been All-State for the past two years. He'd have a lot of schools courting him.

"Oh. Right. Okay."

"Look, Peter. The point is, you've really gotta take your SATs again, and you've really gotta fill out at least the general application," Mr. Garvey said, pulling out a handkerchief to wipe his brow. "You can't put this off much longer. You're gonna be somewhere next year. If you don't decide where soon, the universe is gonna decide for you."

Coach Morschauser cleared his throat. I knew he was thinking the guy was cracked. That New Agey crap didn't fly with him. But me? I was feeling as if some huge hand was holding me unsteadily over the mouth of a big black hole.

Next year. I was gonna be somewhere next year. But where? With who? Would I have any friends? Would I ever get to see the guys? My mom? Michelle? And what about Claudia? Would I ever be with Claudia again?

My palms itched with sweat. I felt like I was having a heart attack.

I don't want to do this, a voice in my head said. *I don't want to do it.*

Garvey picked up the stack of brochures, which slid around, and clumsily dropped them in my lap. "Talk to your mom and see what she thinks."

"Okay," I said.

But I already knew what she was going to say. She'd approved these schools last night and had started filling out the scholarship applications for a bunch of them. My mom already had me halfway out the door.

The bell rang. At almost the exact same second, my phone beeped with a text. I somehow cradled the brochures in one arm while fishing the phone out of my pocket with my free hand.

"See you on the field!" Coach said, then disappeared.

The text was from Claudia.

MEET @ YOUR LOCKER! I WANT TO HEAR HOW IT WENT!

I swallowed hard. My throat was lined with dread. None of these schools were on Claudia's list, even though she could get into any of them. I couldn't even get into the Princeton Bagel Shop. I didn't reply to the text.

"Thanks, Mr. Garvey," I said, picking up my backpack and edging out of his cubicle.

"Anytime. Come to me with any questions and have your mom call me too, if she wants to," he said with a smile, pulling himself closer to his desk.

"I will."

As I passed the big gray garbage can near the door, I was tempted to toss the whole stack of brochures into it. I knew how much lighter I would feel. How much freer. But I didn't. Mostly because the secretary and two other guidance counselors were watching me. Instead I shoved my way into the hall, which was already packed with people.

"How's it going, QB? You gonna take down St. Joe's this weekend?" one of the guys from the basketball team asked as he and his friends hung near the drink machine on the opposite wall.

"You know it," I replied, feeling ill.

"Yo, Marrott? Can I get in on this city trip this weekend?" Jeffrey Norris asked, jogging up next to me. "Sounds like it's gonna be epic." Jeff was captain of the tennis team and constantly battling Claudia for the number one academic spot in our class. I had no clue what he was talking about, but this happened sometimes. My friends made plans, but everyone thought I was the one in charge.

"Yeah. Sure. I'll text you the details," I said.

We slapped hands and I kept moving, my pulse pounding in my temples.

A few girls in JV cheerleading uniforms blatantly checked me out, whispering and giggling before I even made it past them. A couple of teachers smiled at me as I passed them by. On the wall above my locker, Claudia's huge, glittery GO MARROTT! sign welcomed me. Suddenly I felt nostalgic for this. For now. Even though I hadn't left it yet.

This was my home. Everyone here knew my name. Some of them even wanted to be me. Or at least be *with* me. I looked down at the top brochure again, and my vision blurred. When I got to college—if I got to college—I wouldn't be me anymore. I'd be no one. And I'd be completely alone.

"So? How did it go? Lemme see! Lemme see!"

Claudia barreled into me from behind, wrapping her arms around me and knocking the brochures to the floor. One of the corners of the heavier ones hit me square on the top of my foot and I winced. Sandals. Not a good idea.

"Ow," I said through my teeth, starting to sweat under my arms and behind my ears.

"Oh God! Sorry!" Claudia stooped to pick up the brochures and quickly neatened them into a stack. Her smile was huge when she looked up at me. "Well? What did you think? Are any of these places *the one*?"

"I don't know." I spun my lock, then yanked on the catch. It didn't open. Claudia flipped carefully through the brochures, and as her eyes scanned the names of the schools, I wished more than ever that I'd thrown them out. I hadn't heard of half of them, and I was sure she hadn't either. But she was so excited. So excited to get rid of me.

"Bowling Green looks nice," she said finally.

"It's in Ohio."

"So? Ohio's not that far." She cracked open the brochure and flipped through the pages. "They have football."

I exhaled loudly and yanked on the catch again. This time it opened, and my locker door slammed back against the wall, loudly. Claudia jumped.

"What's wrong? Aren't you psyched? One of these places could be your school!"

She grabbed my wrist and sort of shook my arm. She was so bubbly it made me want to pop.

"God! Can we just drop it?"

Claudia's face fell and I immediately felt guilty, but my anger squashed it quick. I didn't want to talk about this. Didn't she get that? Didn't she care that going to school meant the end of everything? The end of us?

"Why are you always snapping at me lately?" she asked quietly, but angrily. "I'm so sick of it."

"Yeah? Well I'm sick of you being on me about this!" I shot back. "All you do is nag, nag, nag."

Her jaw dropped. "Are you serious?"

"Yeah, I'm serious! It's like you can't wait for this year to be over," I bit out, staring into my locker. Taped inside the door was a big blue #11 that she'd made for me last season, her first year as my booster. What I wouldn't give to be back there. To be a junior again. When none of this mattered.

"Well, yeah. I mean . . . it's college. Who can wait for college?

We're going to be on our own. We get to do whatever we want—"

I looked at her, my eyes flashing. "Yeah. Everything except be together."

I reached out and slammed my locker, but it was too hard and it ricocheted open again, so I had to slam it twice. It still didn't close, and Claudia flinched.

"It's like you just can't *wait* to move on and put me in the rear-view. Maybe it's *me* you're sick of," I spat, yanking my backpack straps over my shoulders.

Claudia glanced around. A few random packs of people were watching us and trying to look like they weren't. I felt like such an asshole, and such a dork, and such a whipped loser. Yelling at my girlfriend in public about her not liking me enough? Was this how low I'd sunk?

"What?" she said shakily. "Peter. Come on."

I glared down at her, my chest heaving angrily even as a tiny part of me withered and died. I didn't hear her denying it. She wasn't denying it.

"Whatever," I said. "If you're so psyched about starting your life without me, maybe we should just start right now."

What are you doing? a tiny voice in my head screamed. *What the hell are you doing?*

Claudia's face paled, then suddenly reddened. "Are you break-ing up with me?"

Take it back! Take it back!

But I couldn't. It was like I'd chucked a Hail Mary as hard as I could into the air and was powerless to stop it. I had to stand back and watch it fall.

And I was so angry. I'd never felt so angry. I just wanted time to stop, but it wouldn't. It just kept going and going and going. I had no control over anything anymore, and it totally pissed me off.

"Why not? It was going to happen anyway, right? Now you can go hang out with Lance as much as you want and practice for your big audition," I blurted. "Princeton calls!"

"That is so not fair," she said through her teeth. "You know there's nothing going on with me and Lance."

"Yeah. Not yet, maybe," I said. "But you can't tell me you don't think about it—what it would be like to go out with a guy like him. Somebody with a brain, somebody who likes the same things you do, somebody with a future."

"You could *have* a future!" Claudia shouted, holding the stack of brochures up. "You just don't want to be bothered. You're so pathetic sometimes, Peter. For the great big football star, sometimes I swear you're like some scared little boy."

And there it was. What she really thought of me. Pathetic. She thought I was pathetic.

A few freshmen laughed into their hands, and my face burned. She shoved the stack of brochures at me but stood her ground, lifting her tiny chin, which, I noticed with a pang, was quivering awfully. At that point, though, I was too pissed off and humiliated to care. If that was what she really thought of me, then maybe I was doing the right thing.

I took the brochures and threw them into the bottom of my locker with a clang. This time when I slammed the door, I made sure it stayed shut.

"Well, I know one thing for sure," I said. "My pathetic future is not with you."

As she crumbled into tears, I turned around and speed-walked toward the gym.

CHAPTER EIGHT

Claudia

What just happened? What just happened?

I couldn't breathe. I could barely see. Everything was a blur. The blue-and-white locker doors. The shred of paper on the floor. The yellowing caulk around the windows. I tipped my face up and tried to stop the flow of tears. The Marrott poster I'd toiled over yesterday afternoon glinted in the sun, mocking me.

Had Peter really just dumped me? Had he just called me a nag, accused me of liking someone else, said I couldn't wait to get away from him?

Had I just called the guy I loved pathetic?

Oh God, oh God, oh God. This couldn't be happening.

My hands shook. Slowly my gaze traveled along the faces around me. Most of them turned away as my eyes met theirs, as if that could make them invisible, erase the fact that my humiliation had come with an audience. The pulse in my wrists fluttered like the wings on a dying bird. Dying. I was dying. I was going to die. I wiped my face, then turned and slowly walked through the library entrance across the hall and over to the table where my chemistry notes were laid out neatly, ready to be organized into a lab report.

Are you breaking up with me? my tremulous voice repeated in my head.

Why not? he blurted in reply. *Why not? Why not? Why not?*

It was like I didn't matter to him one bit. Like breaking up with me was nothing. Did he really think I wanted someone else? Someone like Lance? Did he think that I thought I was too good for him?

"No."

I said the word so loudly I startled a girl reading a romance novel near the windows.

"Sorry," I said, shoving everything haphazardly into my leather backpack. "Sorry. I'm so sorry."

Tears filled my eyes, and I felt snot forming inside my nose. I took a deep breath and blinked rapidly. I had to get out of there. Now. My knees shaking beneath me as if I'd just done five hundred first-position deep pliés at the barre, I somehow made it out the door.

There had to be some kind of mistake. Peter wouldn't just break up with me out of nowhere. We were fine. We were happy. We were a perfect couple. We'd never fought in the fifteen months, three weeks, and three days we'd been together. Not once. Yes, he'd been snapping at me here and there, acting impatient, but that was different. That was a phase. Not a cause for a breakup. There had to be some kind of mistake.

I repeated this word to myself over and over again like a mantra as I walked toward the locker rooms just outside the gym.

Mistake mistake mistake.

Mistake mistake mistake.

Why not? Whynotwhynotwhynot?

No.

Mistake mistake mistake.

Mistake mistake mistake.

A twittering klatch of freshman girls stood near their lockers gossiping and messing with their hair. God, how excited they'd be when they heard that Peter Marrott was single again. I felt an ache in my heart that seemed unsurvivable, but yet, I kept walking.

Mistake mistake mistake.

Mistake mistake mistake.

I got to the door of the boys' locker room. Only then did I realize I could follow Peter no farther. Inside, I heard boy laughter, the kind that normally made my heart quicken because it was just so male, so mysteriously carefree. Now I wanted to slam my hand against the door and scream. Were they laughing at me? Was he telling them he'd finally dumped the bookish bitch they couldn't stand? I could see Lester doing a happy dance, whooping it up over my misery.

One humiliated tear spilled down my cheek, and then my teeth clenched. No. He loved me. He might never have said it, but he did. Or at the very least, he respected me. He wouldn't talk about me behind my back. He'd never do that. I turned and walked through the doors of the always ice-cold gymnasium, then out the back door, where the football players would eventually emerge from their locker room. The JV girls' soccer team was gathered into a huddle with their coach under a copse of trees, and that True girl sat on one of the metal benches, watching Gavin and Orion chat by the door with Mitchell Ross.

Well, at least if those three were out here, they weren't laughing at me inside. Part of me wanted to walk over there and talk to Gavin. To see if he knew anything about this. He and I had always gotten along pretty well, I thought. At least compared to me and Peter's other friends. Gavin was more mature than the rest of them. More intelligent. He actually listened when I spoke. Maybe he'd have an explanation for me. Maybe he'd even talk to Peter for me.

But I couldn't do it. I couldn't go over there and beg the best friend for information. I had my pride. I needed to talk to Peter myself. I had to explain. I didn't think he was pathetic. Not really. I understood that he didn't want to graduate. Leaving the world we knew behind was going to be hard for everyone, but everyone else was at least trying to figure out what came next. I just wanted him to wake up and smell the future. I didn't want him to get left behind.

That was what I would tell him. I would tell him that I was only doing these things because I cared about him. I just had to tell him and everything would be fine.

The heavy metal doors of the locker room finally opened, and half a dozen guys spilled out, consumed in conversation. They were just swinging shut when Peter stopped one of them with his hand and stepped through. He saw me as soon as he emerged. I opened my mouth to say something—I had no idea what—but he brought his helmet down over his head.

He might as well have kicked me in the gut.

"Peter, please. Just talk to me," I said quietly as he walked by. "You can't just unceremoniously dump me and then bail."

"I can't," he said. "Not now."

"But how could you even think that I want to move on so badly? After everything I've—"

He turned to look at me, but his eyes were shaded by the helmet. I could barely see them. "Claudia, don't," he said. "Not in front of the guys."

My eyes stung with tears. I was embarrassing him. Great. Could this get any worse?

"I'm—I'm—"

I wanted to say I was sorry, but I felt like if I tried to form the word, it was going to come out as a sob. And besides, Lester, Mitchell, Gavin, and Orion were walking up behind Peter now, and the last thing I wanted was for any of them to see me crumble.

"What's up, guys?" Peter said.

They started talking about holes in the offense and how Orion was going to fill them, and I was entirely forgotten. Just like that. Fifteen months, three weeks, and three days. Like it never even happened.

Peter did look back at me once as they walked away. At least I think he did. My eyes were a bit blurred, and I might have imagined it in my heartsick haze. I just stood there and watched them as they walked up the hill toward the football field. Until Coach Morschauser and his assistants drove by in their white golf cart. Until the girls' soccer team loaded onto their bus for their away game. I stood there for way, way too long, just waiting. Waiting for him to come jogging down the hill and tell me he was wrong. That he couldn't live without me. That it was some big misunderstanding.

I waited until I finally couldn't take my own wretchedness anymore. Then I finally turned around and bumped right into True.

"What are you doing, you freak?" I demanded.

Normally, I'd never talk to someone like that. But the girl was standing six inches behind me, watching my nervous breakdown like I was starring in an episode of *Real Housewives*. Also, I was a tad emotional at the time. Of course, being as weird as she was, she didn't flinch. She didn't even blink. She just said, "We should talk."

"You're a freak and a klepto," I snapped, every ounce of my misery and confusion and righteous indignation now directed at her. "Why should I talk to you?"

She smiled. I insulted her, and she smiled. "Because I can help you get him back."

CHAPTER NINE

True

"I don't even know what happened," Claudia said, staring down at a cup full of blue paint.

We had set up our art project a few feet away from the rest of the boosters on the hill. Lined up on the field below us were the football players, getting ready for another play. They'd given Orion the number 22, which was fitting since there had been seven stars in his constellation and fifteen in the scorpion constellation, which had hovered next to him those many centuries. Add them up and you get twenty-two. Somewhere, Zeus was laughing.

Zeus. I felt a shiver of fear at the mere thought of him. Had he been watching me last night when my conjuring power had returned to me? Every time I thought about that rose, I felt so anxious my vision crossed. I had to hope he had more important things going on in the universe than to notice the appearance of one tiny flower. There had to be wars, debates, famines, diseases that warranted his attention more than me.

Telekinesis *and* conjuring. My powers just kept on returning. It was too bad I couldn't use either of them to aid me in my mission. I was certain I could have found a creative way to put them both to good use. But I had to heed my father's warning. No using powers unless absolutely necessary.

I could deal with this whole power-growing phenomenon when I got back to Mount Olympus.

"And of course it had to happen on a day when Lauren had a dentist appointment," Claudia sighed.

"Lauren?" I asked.

"My best friend." She idly dipped her paintbrush into the paint, then gazed at it as it dripped. "No offense, but I'd much rather be talking to her."

"None taken." I leaned back on my hands as Peter yelled, "hike" and stepped back with the ball. He handed it to Orion, who ran forward and slammed into two guys the size of trucks. With a crunch, he hit the ground, but then popped right back up again and slapped hands with the boys who had leveled him.

Wow. This whole thing was just so brutal. I kind of loved it. Orion pulled his helmet off, and his sweaty hair fell around his face as he reached for a cup of water. I suddenly started to salivate. I wanted to be with him so badly. What I wouldn't give to lick that sweat right off his—

"You said you could help me?" Claudia prompted.

I shook my head to clear it. Right. It was time to focus on the task at hand. Namely, getting Claudia back together with Peter so they could realize true love. And so that Orion and I could take one step closer to freedom.

I had noticed these two around school before. I'd seen him steer her around a backpack on the floor so she wouldn't trip, pull out chairs for her, defend her to his friends. I'd noticed her watching him with starry eyes while he studied, oblivious to her admiring gaze, and heard her ask one of his teachers if there was anything specific she should help him focus on. They were obviously in love with each other. I had this gut feeling that what they were going through was a relationship growing pain or a misunderstanding of some sort. Something that if I could just help them move past, they would fall even more deeply in love with each other.

If I could successfully do that, I would chalk up my second matched couple. Two down, one to go. I slapped my hands together to clear them of the grass that had stuck there.

"Tell me what happened."

"I don't know. Everything was fine. I mean, everything was totally normal. I picked him up for school today and he kissed me hello, we ate lunch together as always . . . and then, out of nowhere, he dumps me."

"He gave you no indication of what the problem was?" I asked, trying not to be distracted by the action on the field. The guys were lining up again, and this time Orion was right behind Peter.

Claudia gave me this look like it pained her to say what she was about to say.

"He said all I do anymore is nag him." Her eyes fluttered shut, and I could practically feel her nausea. "Like it's so awful that I help him with his homework and I'm there for him when he needs me? That I want him to get his applications done so he can have a future? He didn't complain when I helped him get his first A in algebra last year. He took me out for ice cream."

I had a feeling I knew what was going on here. I'd seen it millions of times. Guys this age often started to feel like they needed space, like they'd invested too much in one person, like there might be something better out there. It was testosterone taking over, the need to spread the seed. Males were so primal.

Claudia's gaze flicked to the football field, watching Peter as he dropped back to throw. "I don't understand what I did wrong."

"You didn't do anything wrong," I assured her. "He's just being a guy. This is fixable."

But she kept staring into space as if she hadn't heard me. "When I asked him if he was breaking up with me, he said, 'Why not?'" she added, reaching up to touch a ring that hung from a chain around her neck. "Like it was no big deal. Was being with me really such torture?"

I glanced at Orion again, the word "torture" inextricably linked with him in my mind. At least he was happy right now, if oblivious to who he really was, running around down there with his new buddies. Little did he know that Artemis could suddenly plop down in front of me at any moment, slit my throat, and drag him back to Etna, where she could hide him among the volcanoes and ash, and I'd never find him.

Out of nowhere, Claudia's eyes widened.

"What? What is it?" I asked, glancing over my shoulder, half expecting to spot a leather-clad Artemis and Apollo flying at me in slow motion, their eyes wild, their teeth bared. Instead I saw that Wallace kid bent over his electronic pad thing, playing some kind of game.

What I wouldn't give to have my bow and arrows back. Not the gold-tipped arrows, of course, since they only breed love, but the leaden ones, which could breed hatred or cause death, depending on my will. I'd even take silver-tipped hunting arrows. Iron. Stone. Anything I could use to defend myself against a possible attack. If my powers were slowly returning to me, would my bow and arrows eventually appear in my room?

"His ring," Claudia said, lifting it slightly from her chest. "He didn't ask for his ring back. That has to mean something, doesn't it?"

I reached up and touched the silver arrow—Orion's silver arrow—that always hung from my neck.

"It means he doesn't know what he wants," I said, trying to keep the acidity out of my voice. "It means you still have a chance."

Her expression brightened, and she dropped the paintbrush onto a stack of paper towels. "So? What do I do? How do I get him back?"

Down on the field a whistle blew, long and shrill. A group of girls had gathered near the table full of water and sports drinks, and Orion noticed them as he pulled off his helmet. He and a few other guys jogged over to talk to them and I watched, frozen in horror, as Darla Shayne looked Orion, *my* Orion, up and down like he was a horse at the auction.

Envy surged through me and I felt not green, but white hot with rage. That was my man. Mine. She had no right to look at him like that.

"Hello?" Claudia said. "True?"

I snapped back to the now, and suddenly my skin tingled. Of course. Why hadn't I thought of this before?

"Make him jealous," I mused.

"What?"

I sat up a bit straighter as a cloud passed over the sun. "You have to make him jealous." It was the oldest trick in the book. If this guy was as primal as he seemed, he'd fall for the envy thing in seconds. "Guys always want what they can't have. Especially when they know what they're missing."

"So I . . . what? Flirt with other guys in front of him?" she asked.

"No, no, no," I replied. "That's for amateurs. You have to date someone else. Make it seem as if you've moved on entirely. That you have with this new person exactly what you had with him."

Claudia squirmed in her seat. She touched the ring again. My heart went out to the girl. The love of her life had just broken up with her. I was sure the very idea of being with someone new made her uneasy. But sometimes we had to do unpleasant things in the name of love.

"Like who?" she asked quietly. "I'm not interested in anyone at school. And besides, everyone looks up to Peter. They'd probably stay away from me out of respect or something."

"People do that?" I asked.

"Yep. Lauren couldn't get a date for, like, a year after she broke up with her boyfriend Todd. You know, Todd Ivanovic? The captain of the swim team?" I stared at her blankly. "Anyway, she finally got Chase Varone to tell her what was up, and *he* said that everyone still thought of her as Todd's girl even though Todd had totally been hooking up with a different girl, like, every weekend since she dumped him. So unfair."

"Brutally," I replied. "Well then, if none of the guys at your school will go out with you, we'll just have to go elsewhere."

CHAPTER TEN

Peter

I ducked my head as I walked past Coach. He was going over something with one of the assistants, poking at his iPad. I hoped to God he wouldn't notice me. I couldn't take a lecture right now. More than anything, I wanted to be home in front of the TV with a Big Mac and a monster soda. Actually, I wanted to be anywhere but here.

I still couldn't believe I'd broken up with Claudia. I pictured her crushed expression and my stomach clenched. Just like it had out on the field right before I'd thrown that interception. And right before I'd gotten sacked the first time. And the second. And the third.

Humiliating. The whole practice had been humiliating.

"Marrott! Where do you think you're going?"

I stopped and my head hung lower.

"Get your ass over here!"

I trudged up to him. Gavin, Mitchell, and Lester watched us from the bleachers, drinking their water. Great. An audience. This should be fun.

"What the hell was with you today?" Coach demanded, spit

gathering at the corners of his dry lips. "You looked like a freshman novice out there."

"Sorry, Coach," I said.

"Sorry? Don't tell me you're sorry. Tell me it won't happen again. Because we have our opening game against our biggest rivals this weekend, and we got scouts coming. Now is not the time to lose it."

"I know," I said quietly.

I saw Claudia's face again. My fingers curled tight on my helmet's grill. But I had to do it, right? I couldn't take her pushing me away anymore. I couldn't take the pressure. I couldn't live my life waiting for the inevitable day when *she* would dump *me* and head off into her perfect future. I'd taken control of the situation. I'd done what I had to do.

"Excuse me?" he shouted.

"I understand, Coach," I said more loudly, my chest heaving. I felt like I wanted to punch something, and he was standing so close I actually imagined doing it—punching him square in the jaw. But I didn't. Of course I didn't. Instead I said a silent prayer.

Get me out of here. Please just let me get out of here.

A stiff breeze rustled the leaves on the trees around the field and cooled off my neck. I took a breath.

"I swear it won't happen again," I said, looking him in the eye.

"Good," he said. "Now go shower and screw your head back on. I want to see the QB I know and respect back here tomorrow."

"Yes, sir."

I turned around and walked as fast as I could toward the school. Gavin, Lester, and Mitchell jogged to catch up with me. My heart pressed against my chest over and over and over again, and each time it felt as if something sharp was pressing right back, puncturing its outer wall.

"What the hell was that about?" Mitchell asked.

"What do you think?"

"So you had one bad practice," Gavin said. "Why're you so pissed?"

"I broke up with Claudia," I snapped.

"What?" Gavin stopped in his tracks. The rest of us kept walking, so that he had to run to catch up with us.

"Dude! That's awesome!" Mitchell crowed. "We are so gonna to party this weekend!"

"Shut up, man," I said, my brain racing. I wanted to call Claudia so bad right then it was killing me. I wanted to tell her how Coach had come down on me. Let her tell me it was no big deal, that tomorrow was another day (her favorite saying). Whatever she wanted to say. Who cared? It was her I wanted to talk to. Always her.

What had I been thinking, breaking up with her?

"What? This is great. Now you can take advantage!" Lester threw his arm out toward the girls hanging out behind the gym. The huge pack of freshmen, the JV cheerleaders, the smaller, sexier klatches of juniors. These girls were always, always waiting, like our own personal fan club. Normally, Claudia would have been there too, if Boosters got out early or she didn't have another club meeting. I scanned their faces, looking for Claudia's pale skin, her freckles, her thick hair. But of course she wasn't going to be there. Why would she be? I'd broken her heart.

You had to do it, a voice inside my head told me. *Why put off the inevitable?*

Because she'd be here. She'd be here right now.

"Wait a minute, wait a minute," Gavin said. "Are you sure about this? I thought you—I mean, I thought you and Claudia were like ..."

"What?" I demanded, really wanting to know. "We were like what?"

"Amish people?" Lester said.

"Repressed Amish people?" Mitchell supplied with a laugh.

I shook my head and kept walking.

"Look, the point is now you can be free," Lester said, jogging next to me. "Enjoy your senior year. Dude, we're going to the city this weekend. It's gonna be epic!"

He and Mitchell slapped hands. Gavin looked confused. Hurt, almost. Like I'd just told him I'd run over his dog. Seriously. The guy loved his dog more than anything. Even his mom.

Lester stopped walking and slapped my shoulder pad. "Just look at that, man. This could all be yours."

The JV cheerleaders were practicing some dance routine, looking right at us. One of the girls, a dark-haired hottie with an incredible body, did this bent-over move that was like something out of a porn video. She looked back at me past her butt and smiled.

I got hot behind my ears, feeling guilty for looking, but then I realized I didn't have to feel guilty. I was single. I was a free man. There was no one waiting for me. No one reminding me to study or forcing me to figure out my life. No one I had to worry about losing, because she'd already been lost. There was only this girl, dancing like she was dancing just for me.

"Seeing the beauty of your decision?" Mitchell said.

I said nothing, and the guys laughed.

"Hey, Pete!" Orion shouted. "A bunch of us are going to the diner. You guys wanna come with?"

He was standing with some other juniors, including our starting linebacker Josh Moskowitz; his girlfriend, Veronica Vine; and her hottie friend Darla Shayne, plus some of the other girls who always hung around with them. I glanced at my friends, and Gavin shrugged. I might not be ready for slutty cheerleaders, but I could hang with my teammates and their girls. Their admittedly hot, popular girls.

"Yeah. I'm in," I said, happy at least, for the distraction.

"It's the first day of the rest of your life!" Lester crowed as he kneaded my shoulder with one hand.

I smiled, but my heart felt heavy. The rest of my life, without Claudia.

CHAPTER ELEVEN

Claudia

"I don't get it," my sister, Casey, said, shoving a heaping spoonful of ice cream into her mouth.

"Don't get what?"

We were leaned back against my velvet headboard, watching *The Lucky One* on the big-screen TV hung on the opposite wall, with huge bowls of ice cream in our laps. My sister, only ten months younger than me, with the same red hair and fair skin, prescribed movies and ice cream as soon as I'd told her the story of my day, and she now sat cuddled into my side, her pedicured toes touching mine. Casey was a varsity cheerleader, a star of the track team, and one of the most popular girls in the junior class. Unlike myself, she'd gone through a string of boyfriends and breakups, so she knew exactly what to do in this situation. As I sucked some chocolate off my fingertip, Zac Efron grabbed Taylor Schilling by the face and laid a kiss on her like nothing I'd ever experienced. I'd always wanted Peter to grab me and kiss me like that, like his life depended on it, but he never did. And now he never would.

My stomach turned, and I set my half-empty bowl aside.

"I told you not to pick a love story." Casey shook her head. "We should be watching *Sucker Punch* or *Texas Chainsaw Massacre*. Not this crap."

I opened my mouth to automatically contradict her, but then I realized she was right. This was not making me feel better. I picked up the remote and pressed the all off button. The room went quiet and dark. Outside, crickets chirped, and I could hear the horn on the Lake Carmody commuter train blare in the distance. My father was probably on that train. In fifteen minutes he'd come striding through the door and ask about our day. I just couldn't wait to share the gory details of my afternoon again.

LOL.

"So . . . now what?" I asked.

"I always give myself a makeover," Casey suggested. "Showing up at school tomorrow looking as hot as humanly possible will make you feel so much better."

I sighed and glanced at my vanity table. Somehow, a makeover seemed exhausting.

At that moment the door to my room opened, and my best friend, Lauren, bounded in. Her black curls bounced around her face, and she wore baggy sweats with a wide-necked T-shirt from the Studio. She flicked the lights on, and I saw that she'd bitten her nails to the nub, the green polish we'd applied just yesterday jagged and chipped. We'd already spoken on the phone, so she'd heard the whole story.

"Ice cream?" she demanded.

"Don't judge. She's heartbroken," Casey said.

"I'm not judging!" Lauren replied, crawling onto the bed. "Gimme!"

I sucked off my spoon and gave it to her. Gross, I know, but we were besties. We shared food and drinks all the time. So far neither one of us had died. Casey wrinkled her nose, then rose gracefully from her side of the bed and walked over to my closet. She kicked aside the huge basket full of goodies I'd gathered so I could make the perfect basket for Peter for this weekend—such fun that would be, making a spirit basket for the guy who'd just dumped me—and started to flick through my clothes with her practiced fashionista eye.

"So? How are you doing?" Lauren asked, licking a bit of chocolate off her lip.

"She's fine," Casey replied over her shoulder. "She doesn't need a guy to complete her."

"But this is Peter we're talking about," Lauren said, wide-eyed. "You guys are soul mates."

My heart twisted, and Casey threw up her hands. "Lauren!"

"Sorry." Lauren took a huge bite of ice cream as if trying to shut herself up.

"Actually, I'm working on a plan to get him back," I said, biting my bottom lip.

"You are?" Lauren asked.

Casey turned around with her arms full of sundresses and narrowed her eyes. "What plan?"

"You know that new girl . . . True?" I said, squirming slightly, since I'd recently told them both I thought the new girl was possibly certifiably insane. "She had an idea."

"The klepto?" Lauren asked, her eyebrows popping up.

Casey tossed the clothes over the back of my chair and sat at the foot of my bed, one long leg crossed over the other, her posture perfect. "We're taking advice from the crazies now?"

I laughed. "Well, it turns out she's not that crazy. She thinks if I make Peter jealous, he'll come crawling back to me."

Lauren and Casey locked eyes. "How are you going to make him jealous?" they said at the same time.

"She's going to find me some guy to go out with. Someone from another school," I said, my nerves fluttering. I pulled my feet up under me.

"Who's the guy?" Lauren asked.

"We don't know yet. But in the meantime, she thinks we should float a rumor that I'm already, like, in a relationship."

Lauren grinned and whipped out her cell phone from the pocket of her sweats. "OMG, I *love* it."

She started to type at the speed of light.

"What're you doing?" Casey asked, leaning over her shoulder.

"I'm texting Mia."

Our sophomore friend from ballet, Mia Ross, had a brother on the football team and was a notorious gossip. If Casey told her something, half the team would know within ten minutes.

"What are you texting?" I demanded.

She hit send and turned her phone around.

DID U HEAR? CLAUDE & PETE BROKE UP!!! CLAUDE IS ON PROWL 4 HC DATE. SHE'S ALREADY GOT SOME PROSPECTS.

Casey and I giggled. "By the time we get to pep rally practice tomorrow, *everyone* is going to be talking about you."

My stomach clenched, and I had to shove aside the feeling that this was somehow wrong. We'd only just broken up. Would I really be "on the prowl" so quickly? But if I wanted Peter back, it was now or never. The text alert sounded, and Lauren quickly read it with a laugh, then showed it to us.

AWESOME! GO GIRL! PETES A JERK ANYWAY. :P

"This is perfect!" Casey said, grabbing the dresses off my chair. "Now we really have to find you a killer outfit for tomorrow."

"Fashion show!" Lauren crowed, shoving me off the bed. "Show me what you got, Claudia!"

I took a few options from Casey and headed into the bathroom that connected our two bedrooms. As I undressed, the stereo in my room flicked on, and I could hear the two of them chatting and laughing. For the first time in hours, I felt a real flutter of hope. I looked into my own eyes, squared my shoulders, and felt my confidence return.

Maybe True's crazy plan would actually work. Maybe this time tomorrow, Peter and I would be back together.

CHAPTER TWELVE

True

"Are you okay?"

I glanced up from my plate, where I was busy pressing my thumb into the chocolate crumbs. Tasha Montgomery, one of my coworkers at Goddess Cupcakes, pushed her square-framed glasses higher on the bridge of her nose. She had a comforting, open expression on her face, as if she was used to listening to other people's problems and solving them. Perhaps she was studying to be a therapist. Or a talk show host.

I lifted my thumb to my mouth.

"Yes. Of course. I'm fine," I replied, pushing the plate behind my hip. "Why do you ask?"

"You just wiped out the last of the triple chocolate stock," Tasha replied. "Last I checked there were half a dozen left. You do know you have to pay for those, right?"

The dry crumbs caught in my throat, and I coughed. "Of course." My eyes burned and I held my hand over my mouth. "I knew that."

Tasha quickly filled a plastic cup with water from the sink and handed it to me. I gulped it down, crushed the cup, and launched it toward the garbage can. It bounced off the rim and hit the floor. I suppressed a sigh. If I could have used my telekinesis, I never would have missed. But my father was right. I shouldn't use it unless I really needed it, and garbage-can b-ball didn't count.

"Want to talk about it?" she asked, leaning into the counter next to me. One of her two dark-blond braids fell forward, and the reflection of the fluorescent lights gleamed in the panes of her glasses.

Normally we never would have had this much time to chat. Goddess Cupcakes was the number one cool hangout for the kids from Lake Carmody High as well as several surrounding schools. But we were less than an hour from closing, and the crowd had thinned out considerably. The only tables still occupied were the big round one in the far corner, which was packed with cute boys in green-and-gold varsity jackets, the two-top where my first couple—Katrina Ramos and Charlie Cox—were splitting a red velvet, and a four-top where two girls in private-school uniforms pored over books on ancient Greece. I'd been peeking over their shoulders since they'd arrived to see if the writers had gotten anything even close to correct, but I'd had to stop when they'd complained to the manager.

From what I *had* been able to read, the writers knew nothing about history.

"It's my parents," I said glumly, avoiding the impossible topic of Orion. "I just found out some things about them that I definitely didn't want to know."

As soon as the words were out of my mouth, I pictured my mother and Hephaestus in bed together and almost heaved up every last cupcake. Did Harmonia know about their secret past? And if so, why had she never told me? She always seemed to trust Hephaestus implicitly, which was one of the reasons I hadn't even questioned his motives when he'd reappeared in our lives. Did she trust him in spite of knowing this, or had she been kept ignorant? Was her trust based on lies?

I wished I could talk to her for five minutes. How did Hephaestus communicate with her anyway? Was it really possible that their mode of communication only worked one way? Why hadn't he shared it with me? I realized now that it was possible that he wasn't in contact with her at all. That everything he'd told me was a lie.

But my mother trusted him, even with their history. That had to mean something, didn't it?

"Ugh. That sucks," Tasha said, resting her cheek in one hand. "Isn't it insane how parents always expect you to act like a little angel, but they're allowed to do whatever they want?"

"Exactly!" I blurted. "It's so wrong!"

"Preaching to the choir," she said flatly.

Just then Katrina and Charlie approached the counter to hand over their empty plate.

"We're heading out," Charlie said, entwining his fingers with Katrina's.

The mere sight of that gesture made my heart flip-flop with happiness. Katrina smiled and blushed and I felt a flutter of pride, followed by a quick thump of dread. I was supposed to be finding someone for Claudia to go out with to make Peter jealous, but instead I'd spent half the night obsessing about my mother and her former lover.

"See you guys tomorrow," I said to my pride-and-joy couple.

"Have a good night," Katrina replied.

But I was already looking past their shoulders at the laughing crowd in the corner. They were clearly from a different school, by the color of their jackets. And of the five of them, three were undeniably handsome. But I needed someone even hotter than Peter Marrott. Someone who would make him sick with jealousy. As I had the thought, a sixth guy returned from the bathroom, shaking water off his hands as he crossed to the table. He was distractingly large, but not in a bulbous kind of way, more in a broad, solid, I-could-lift-a-truck-with-one-hand kind of way. He had light-brown skin, close-cropped black hair, and laughing dark eyes. When he smiled at his friends, it almost took *my* breath away. He had a perfect smile. A big, welcoming, happy, carefree smile. The boy could have turned heads on Mount Olympus. As he sat, his left sleeve turned to me, and I saw the QB emblazoned on the leather.

QB. Those were the same letters on Peter Marrott's jacket. This could not be more perfect. Except a guy like him most likely had a girlfriend already. The truly gorgeous ones always seemed to. Which was why I was so concerned about Orion. With his perfect abs, deep-blue eyes, and thick dark hair, he wasn't going to stay single long.

But I wasn't going to think about that now. If I could match two more couples, this nightmare would be over and we'd be reunited. Then I'd simply have to deal with Artemis and Apollo.

More awfulness I wasn't thinking about right now.

My instinct was to simply walk over and ask this handsome specimen if he was interested in being set up, but the direct approach hadn't worked with Charlie. In fact, it had taken two weeks for me to realize the direct approach was never going to work with Charlie. So I decided to be more circumspect this time. I slipped a s'more cupcake out of the case, plopped it on a clean plate, and squared my shoulders.

"Excuse me for a second," I said to Tasha.

"You're gonna have to pay for that one too!" Tasha said need-lessly.

I rounded the counter and approached the boys. They stopped talking as I walked up, and one of them slapped another on the arm to get his attention. They clearly liked what they saw. After two weeks of being considered an odd troll at Lake Carmody High, it was a good feeling. But I wasn't here for me. I was here for Claudia. And there were a few things she wanted to know about a guy before she decided to use him.

I mean, date him.

I tossed my long black hair over my shoulder and smiled at my target.

"Congratulations! You're the winner of tonight's free cupcake!" I told him.

His brow knit. I saw that he had a tiny scar over one eye, and the clearest skin I'd ever seen outside Mount Olympus. Up there, skin was clear as a matter of course.

"Um, great!" he said. "Why?"

"Because you're our hundredth customer of the day!" I impro-vised, lifting my shoulders.

"But he didn't buy anything," a scrawny boy with plain features protested. "I paid for everyone. So technically it should be my—"

"Fine. Take it," I said, dropping the plate in front of him with a clatter. I slipped out my order pad and a pen from the pocket in my apron. "Now let me get your name."

"My name or his name?" the handsome boy said with a grin.

He laced his fingers together and sat back, and I realized he was that guy. That guy who's completely comfortable in his own skin. The one who seems to be born with confidence oozing out of his pores. The guy every girl fell for because he knew who he was, what he wanted, and what he was going to do with it when he got it. He was cocky, no doubt, and cocky boys were often players, but that was fine. In fact, it was perfect. If he was into the quick and casual relationships, then I didn't have to worry about him falling in love with Claudia and her breaking his heart when she got back together with Peter.

"Your name," I replied. "And age. And school affiliation."

"Why do you need his name?" scrawny boy asked. "I'm the one who—"

"Zach, shut up," one of the other guys said. Zach did.

"I'm Keegan Traylor," the handsome boy said. "I'm a senior at St. Joe's." He leaned toward me and smirked. "If you want to go out with me, you can just ask."

I smirked back. Definitely a player. "I'm not interested. But I do need to know a few things about you," I said as I made a mental run-through of the requirements Claudia had mentioned back at the diner.

"Such as?" he asked, straightening his jacket.

"What sport do you play?" I asked.

"Football," he replied, reaching for his soda cup. "I also run track in the spring."

I made a note of it. "What's your favorite subject in school?"

"History."

"Your religion?"

He raised his palms like *duh*. "Catholic."

"Do you like to dance?" I asked.

He and his friends cackled. "You know it."

"Got a job?"

"I work for my dad at his office some days," he said. "He's a PT, like I'm gonna be."

"Got a girlfriend?" I asked.

Keegan Traylor gave me a long, lazy, self-satisfied smile, like this was the question he'd been waiting for. He took a sip of his soda through the straw and looked me up and down.

"Not at the moment, no."

CHAPTER THIRTEEN

Peter

I sat down in the gym bleachers, near the end of one of the benches, surrounded by my teammates. Claudia, Lauren, True, and the rest of the boosters were sitting right across the aisle, behind the JV cheerleaders, and I tried my best not to be distracted by Claudia, but it was next to impossible. She looked gorgeous in a navy-blue dress, her hair down around her shoulders, and she was wearing more eye makeup than usual. She was right there and I couldn't touch her. Couldn't even talk to her.

"Okay, everyone! Listen up!"

The varsity cheerleaders stood in a straight line at the center of the basketball court, with their captain, Liza Verdanos, at the center, demanding our attention. Tall and curvy with wavy dark hair and a birthmark over her lip, Liza was the most untouchable girl at Lake Carmody High. Rumor had it she only dated college guys, and I believed it.

Next to her stood Casey Catalfo, Claudia's little sister, and she was looking right at me as if imagining the best way to murder me. I bent over to retie my sneaker.

"Let's pay attention so we can do our run-through and get

back to lunch," Liza shouted. "At the start of the pep rally, the football team will be gathered in the locker room, waiting for your entrance. . . ."

I tuned her out as Gavin loped down the bleachers to sit next to me, forcing me to jostle inward and everyone else in my row to move too. It wasn't like we hadn't done these pep rallies before. At this point, I was an expert. He nodded to Orion, Lester, and Josh Moskowitz, who were sitting behind me.

"How's it going, man?" Gavin put his backpack down between his feet and glanced over at Claudia. "You going over there?"

I cleared my throat. "Nope."

"You sure?" Gavin asked. "She looks hot today."

"Dude."

"Sorry."

I pressed my fist into my open palm, and my eyes darted to Claudia again. It was weird, being this far away from her. Weird that she hadn't been waiting for me in the Café that morning with her tea and my hot chocolate. Weird that she hadn't been waiting for me after class or at my locker. Weird that I'd taken new routes between classes this morning. This whole thing was just too frickin' weird.

"So, boosters? Why don't you come down here and line up like you will on Friday?" Liza shouted.

The boosters slowly rose from their seats and started down the bleachers, parting around the clump of JV cheerleaders.

"Come on, people! We're on a schedule here!" Liza called out, her voice ringing throughout the gym.

Claudia, Lauren, and True sidestepped right toward me and Gavin to walk down the aisle between our sections. Claudia's eyes caught mine and I immediately faced forward, my cheeks on fire.

"Please!" True said loudly. "Don't even worry about it. It is *so* right for you to move on. It's not like you owe the guy anything."

"I know. You're right," Claudia replied. "I mean, I'm a senior. I'm not gonna go become a nun or something."

"No, you're not," Lauren added. "And if guys from other schools notice you, that's not your fault."

My heart slammed against my ribs. What? What did they just say?

"Did you just hear that?" I whispered to Gavin.

He avoided looking me in the eye, hanging his head in a guilty way. "Um, yeah."

"What?" I said, my veins flooding with dread. "Did you hear something else? What do you know?"

"Nothing, man," Gavin said, shifting an inch away from me.

I slapped him on the shoulder. "Dude! What do you know?"

Suddenly Lester leaned in between us from behind, his black hair sticking straight up on top like a chicken. "Claudia's supposedly on the hunt for a homecoming date, man."

"On the hunt?" I repeated, disgusted. "What does that even mean?"

Lester shrugged. "Who knows? Talk to Mitch Ross. His sister was on it like white on rice. Told him she's got some guys from other schools after her or something."

I felt like I was going to be sick. Down on the court, Claudia was laughing with her friends. She tossed her hair back and smiled as she checked her phone. Was some guy texting her right now? Was it Lance? Someone else? Could she possibly have gone out last night and met someone new?

"Dudes! How awesome was last night?"

Mitchell tromped over and sat down next to Lester, reaching to slap hands with me and Gavin.

"Mitch, tell Pete about the text Mia got," Lester said.

"Something about her already having a homecoming date lined up. Or dates. Or something. But who cares, man? You dumped her ass."

Not a second too soon, either, I thought. If Claude already had potential dates lined up, that had to mean she knew these guys before we'd broken up, right? Was it possible she'd been cheating on me? The thought made me want to curl up and die. It couldn't be. That wasn't the Claudia I knew. But neither was this girl who was apparently trolling for prospects.

"Besides, you had the hotties licking your palm last night," Mitchell said, pounding my shoulder with his fist.

"Oh, yeah! What'd you end up doing?" Gavin asked. He hadn't come out with us because he had to get to a tutoring session with Tara.

"We hit the diner with these guys, plus the girlies they hang out with," Lester explained, gesturing at Josh.

"Yeah, Darla was pretty interested in you," Josh told Orion. "You gonna tap that?"

A streak of red spread across Orion's face. "I don't know. She seemed pretty cool."

"Yeah, but you should have seen how Caroline Policastro and Patty Flynn were practically fighting over our boy here," Mitchell said to Gavin, chucking his chin at me. "The second they heard Claudia was out, it was like a bad episode of *The Bachelor*."

"Like there are good episodes of *The Bachelor*?" Gavin replied.

They laughed as Mitchell turned purple. "Shut up, man," he muttered. "My mom watches it."

"Sounds like you had a great time," Gavin said, giving me some kind of meaningful look.

Down on the court, Liza counted the number of boosters against some piece of paper on a clipboard. I was staring at Claudia again, imagining her with some other guy and trying not to barf. She looked up and I glanced away as quickly as possible, but the deed was done. She'd caught me. And now Lester was staring back and forth between us, putting two and two together.

"And the fun's not over yet," he crowed, standing up. "Hey, girls? Why you wanna sit so far away? Come up and hang with us while Liza gets her crap together."

The freshmen and sophomores on JV giggled as Liza shot Lester a look that should have killed him on the spot. He pretended not to notice while the JV girls hesitated.

"Come on! We don't bite."

Finally one girl stood up from the center of the crowd and looked right at me. It was the girl from yesterday. The dancer. She was wearing a skirt that was so short I could practically see her underwear. Her thick dark hair hung down over her chest and a lollipop stick stuck out between her plump lips. She looked me up and down, smiled, and slowly pulled the lollipop out.

"Only if I can sit next to Peter," she said.

I kicked Gavin's foot. "Move."

Gavin's jaw dropped, but he got up. The way that girl moved her hips when she walked toward me should have been illegal. She paused next to the empty space on the bench and smirked.

"On second thought."

She sat down on my lap. Just wedged herself in there and put one arm around my neck. She touched the lollipop to her lips, looking me directly in the eye.

"I'm Josie," she said.

Then she rolled the pop around inside her mouth.

"Holy shit," Lester said, watching us.

"P-Peter," I stammered. "I'm Peter."

"I know that," she said with this laugh that filled the entire gym. Her butt pressed down firmly into my lap before she pushed herself up and took Gavin's spot on the bench. Which I could suddenly not imagine Gavin ever sitting in. Not when it was filled with that skin and that hair and those lips.

"Hey, football players!" Liza announced. "We're ready for you. Let's practice the player roll call."

While the rest of the team got up and tromped down toward the floor, Josie trailed her fingertips down my arm, and I did everything in my power to look her in the eye and not check out her body again.

"Hey, Marrott!" Liza shouted. "Way to be a leader, Captain!"

I glanced around and saw that Josie and I were the only people left on the bleachers.

"Oops," I said.

And everyone laughed. Everyone except Claudia, who was turning purple. Josie got up and we walked down together as I told myself there was no reason to feel guilty.

Claudia and I weren't together anymore. And apparently she was auditioning homecoming dates. The thought maybe made me want to strangle someone, but it also meant I could do whatever the hell I wanted.

CHAPTER FOURTEEN

True

"Did you know that you're the second-tallest girl in the junior class?"

I blinked up at the guy standing next to the lunch table Hephaestus and I occupied. It took me a second to focus. I had been so intent on watching Peter watch Claudia with a sourpuss look on his face that it was like waking up from a dream. That girl who had come on to him at pep rally rehearsal had been a momentary distraction, clearly. Peter was practically turning green while I watched. My plan was already working.

"Wallace Bracken, right?"

He was holding that electronic pad thingie he always had at Boosters against his chest and smirking at me. The boy wasn't bad-looking with his porcelain complexion, aquiline nose, and shiny dark hair hanging over his forehead. If only he wasn't constantly bent over his contraption, I might be able to find him a nice girl.

"Yep. You wanna know how I know you're the second-tallest girl in the junior class?" he asked excitedly.

He was already pulling a chair over to the end of our table

and sitting in it. I looked at Hephaestus, who seemed nonplussed. We hadn't been talking much, what with me watching Peter and Claudia and not having a clue how to talk to him—or whether I should—about my mother, so this was a welcome distraction.

"I know I'd like to know," Hephaestus said, leaning in.

"I created this app," Wallace said, putting the electronic tablet down and hitting the screen a few times. A picture of me came up, taken the other day while I was talking to Claudia, Peter, and Orion at Boosters. "I can take a picture of anyone, and the app will calculate their height, weight, and body mass index. Provided they're standing, of course. My margin of error is only three percent."

"Hey. That's actually pretty cool," Hephaestus said.

Wallace blushed pleasantly. "Thanks."

"Does it have any practical use?" I asked.

"True," Hephaestus said, somehow scolding me with one syllable.

"I'm just saying, what would you do with this knowledge?" I was genuinely curious as I leaned over his shoulder and bit into a carrot stick. "Why do you want to know everyone's height, weight, and whatever else you said there?"

"Well, aren't you glad to know you're the second-tallest girl in your class?" he asked plainly.

I lifted a shoulder. "I suppose."

"Here. Give me your phone." He held out his hand, which bore one thick purple band on its ring finger. "I'll download the app for you."

"I don't have a cell phone," I told him.

His whole face went slack. "You don't have a cell phone?"

"Nope."

His hand hit the table with a crack, and I winced. That had to hurt. But he didn't flinch. "How do you text?"

"I don't."

"How do you tweet? Update Facebook? Instagram? Play games? Listen to music?"

I sat up straight at this. "Wait. You can use them to listen to music?"

Wallace looked at Hephaestus as if I'd just dropped in through the ceiling from some far-flung galaxy.

"I know, dude," Hephaestus said, biting into an apple. "She's weird."

Wallace put his pad thingie away and took out his phone, which looked just like the pad thingie, only smaller. He placed his phone on the table and opened up a screen that had songs and bands listed with prices next to each one.

"You can buy any music you want," he said slowly, as if he was attempting to communicate with a dolphin. "You just need to open an account with a credit card number and you're in."

"Any music I want?" This was interesting. I scooted my chair closer to Wallace's and tentatively touched the screen. I had missed music since I had been on Earth. The stereo system at Goddess Cupcakes played a steady stream of current pop hits, but I was more of a classical connoisseur, and I'd heard nothing of it since my arrival here over two weeks ago. Perhaps these soul-sucking devices I'd so vilified had a positive purpose.

"Here." Wallace pulled out a pair of earphones and stuck one side in my ear, the other in his. "What do you like? Hip-hop? Hard rock? Country?"

"Mozart," I told him.

He glanced at me, obviously surprised and maybe impressed. "Mozart it is."

After hitting a few buttons on his phone, Mozart's *Requiem* flowed through the earpiece. I leaned back next to him and sighed, the music instantly working its calming effect on my frayed nerves. "Thank you."

He grinned. "You're welcome."

"Aw," Hephaestus said. "True's made a new friend!"

I picked up a carrot stick and chucked it at him. It bounced off Hephaestus's forehead and landed on Orion's foot as he was walking by. He froze. I froze. I couldn't believe I hadn't noticed him coming our way. For the past three days I'd had a sort of instinctive radar alerting me every time he was within a twenty-foot radius. Orion looked from me to Wallace and got this odd expression on his face—one I couldn't define. My heart pounded at his nearness.

"Your projectile?" he said finally, stooping to pick up the carrot.

I shoved myself up from the table, the earpiece ripping from my ear. "Hi," I said. "I actually need to talk to you."

"You do?" he said.

"You do?" Hephaestus echoed.

"Uh . . . yeah! About your spirit basket!" I improvised.

"Oh. Well, I was just going up to get something to drink." Orion smiled, and it nearly melted me. "Wanna come with?"

It was a simple invitation, but it made my heart dance. "Sure." I glanced at Wallace, who was wrapping up his headphones. "I'll be right back."

I wanted him to teach me more about the music purchasing system. If it was as easy as he made it seem, I might have to cave and finally get one of those cell phones for myself.

"So what's up?" Orion asked, rubbing his hands together as we walked. His strong, gentle, masculine hands.

I drank him in, even as I realized he wasn't looking at me. He was looking ahead, probably more interested in deciding what to drink than in me. My spirits began to sink.

I wasn't going to get what I wanted out of this. I wanted him to take me in his arms and kiss me like he had that day in the woods back in Maine when I'd saved him from that huge bloodlusting bear. Or the time we'd gone skinny-dipping in the stream just outside our house. The day he'd caught me singing to the birds in the trees while I searched for kindling. Or any of the hundreds of small, seemingly insignificant kisses—the wake-up kiss, the good-night kiss, the see-you-when-I-get-back-from-hunting kiss.

Any of these would have been fine. But none of them were going to happen.

I reached up to touch his arrow pendant, which was tucked under the collar of my T-shirt.

"Well, first . . . I wanted to apologize for the other day," I said, feeling as though my pulse was pounding in my skull.

He looked me up and down but kept walking. "Apologize for what?"

"For . . . you know . . . kissing you? I thought you were someone else."

You. With your memories. That's who I thought you were.

He glanced back over his shoulder at my table. "Oh, that."

He laughed and mercifully stopped walking. I wasn't sure I would be able to keep up with him with the room spinning and my brain weighing nothing and my heart slamming around inside my chest. I didn't understand how humans managed to make it through an average day, what with the way my body always seemed to be at odds with my intentions. I so badly wanted to play it cool, but just being this close to Orion was putting me in need of an oxygen tank.

"You don't have to apologize for that," he said. "There are worse things than getting randomly kissed by a hot girl."

I blinked, my face flushing with pleasure. "You think I'm hot?"

He grinned that grin that had stolen my heart. "Isn't that an accepted fact?"

That was the Orion I knew and loved. Confident and complimentary. Honest and playful. I wanted to kiss him so badly my lips hurt.

"So, you wanted to ask me about the spirit basket?" he said.

"Right. I want to make sure I fill it with things you like."

"Oh, you don't have to worry about it. I like everything."

"But everyone has favorites." I took a breath and held it, anticipating his reaction to what I was about to say. "Let me guess, you seem like a peanut butter cup kind of guy."

Orion's jaw dropped slightly. "How did you know?"

Because I brought them to you to celebrate your one-month anniversary back on Earth and your eyes rolled back in your head when you tasted them?

"Lucky guess," I replied with a smile. "I was also thinking raspberry cheesecake bars, pretzels, and maybe something with coconut?"

Orion actually took a step back and nearly leveled a pair of small girls walking by with vanilla cones from the frozen yogurt machine.

"That's crazy. What are you, a mind reader or something?" he asked.

"Nah. I just think it was meant to be, us being matched up."

He looked me over with a sort of pleased awe. "Yeah. Maybe it was."

My fingers twitched to take his hand. To press it against my chest so he could feel my heart beat. To do anything and everything to *make* him remember. But I could do nothing other than stare into his eyes, his incredible blue eyes.

This was so wrong. We were soul mates. We were each other's one and only. I knew him like the back of my hand. Shouldn't he have known me no matter what? Shouldn't our eternal connection be more powerful than any spell a god could cast on him?

I felt my blood begin to boil, even as I knew I was asking the impossible. Zeus was more powerful than any being in the universe. He could do anything, even erase true love, obliterate memories, alter souls. But still, I burned with anger.

Orion should have been able to overcome it. Our love should have been more powerful still.

"There's something about you," I said carefully, trying to tamp down my roiling emotions. "I feel as if we've met somewhere before."

He tilted his head and in a breath, something stirred inside his eyes. Some spark of recognition. My heart leaped, and I did reach for his hand.

"Hey, Orion!"

We both flinched. Darla Shayne stood behind me with Veronica Vine at her side, each wearing the same low-cut T-shirt in different colors. Darla's diamond D pendant hung right at the top of her serious cleavage, and I saw Orion's eyes dart there.

"Hey, D," he said, stepping toward her. "I didn't think it was possible for someone to look that gorgeous after staying up all night."

"I have my ways," Darla said flirtatiously.

"You were up all night?" I asked. "How would you know that?"

"They were texting," Veronica said with a sneer. "Not that it's any of your business, freak."

"I was just going to get a soda," Orion said to Darla, as if I hadn't spoken. "Want anything?"

"I'll come with you," she said.

"We're good, right, True?" he asked me.

"Sure," I replied quietly. "Yeah. We're good."

He lifted his hand in a wave, and the two of them walked off together to join the dwindling line near the soda machine.

"So many hot new guys and you seem to be going after every one of them," Veronica said, tilting her head. "First Charlie, then Heath, now Orion. Too bad not one of them looks like he's interested in you."

My jaw dropped open to reply, but I had no response, and Veronica slowly sauntered off. She was right. Not one of them was interested in me. Charlie had Katrina, Hephaestus had my sister and previously my mother (gag), and now, it seemed, Orion was moving on to Darla. As Orion ordered his soda, Darla placed her hand delicately on his arm, and I suddenly saw myself with my bow and arrow, drawing, aiming, piercing her through the heart.

I felt the cool, smooth shaft of a wooden arrow in my fist and looked down. I was holding an actual arrow. A straight, perfectly calibrated arrow with genuine feather fletching and a silver tip. My heart vaulted into my throat. Not again. Had anyone seen that simply appear in my palm? I glanced around, but no one seemed to be watching me. Then I spotted Claudia approaching, her eyes trained down on her phone. It gave me enough time to drop the arrow on the floor and kick it under the nearest table.

"True! Hey," Claudia said.

I glanced down at the arrow. The fletching was bright red and not entirely tucked away.

"Um, hi. How's everything?" I asked.

"Everything sucks," she replied plainly. "I think we need to step up our plan. Just gossiping about me and some fictional guy isn't going to do it. You said you found someone?"

Keegan Traylor's flirtatious smile flashed through my mind. "I did."

"Good. I want to meet him."

She turned to look back at the senior section. At Peter's table, specifically. The buxom girl from the pep rally rehearsal was kicked back in the chair next to his, her legs propped up on his lap while she did some kind of ritual with his hand. Massaging his palm? Cracking his knuckles? Counting his digits? It was impossible to tell, but whatever it was, it was clear by the hungry look on his face that it was totally turning him on.

"Jealousy is definitely a powerful thing," Claudia said, looking green.

I kicked the arrow that my own jealousy had conjured farther under the table and clenched my teeth at the sound of Darla's flirtatious laugh. "You have no idea."

CHAPTER FIFTEEN

Claudia

"This is crazy," I said to True, resting my "injured" leg atop the coffee table in front of us. It was covered with magazines for every audience, from *Vanity Fair to Highlights* to *Men's Fitness*. "I can't fake an injury."

"Why not? People do it every day," True replied. "Now pucker."

She'd already teased and fluffed my hair, applied more mascara to my lashes than I normally wore for a recital, and dotted my cheeks with berry-shaded blush. Now she was coming at me, wielding a pink lip-gloss wand like a sword.

"Yes, but what am I going to say?" I asked when she was done touching up my lips. I used my phone to take a picture of myself. I looked like a baby-faced prostitute. I hoped this Keegan person hadn't told True that this was the look he was into. I wasn't sure I could replicate it on my own, let alone get up the guts to leave the house like this. Or make it past my mother without getting grounded.

Keegan Traylor. His name sounded familiar, but I couldn't figure out why. True had told me the basics—that he was hot and he went to St. Joe's, but I didn't know anyone at St. Joe's. It was a boys' school, and as far as I knew, no one from there had ever joined my dance studio, so why would I?

"You're a dancer, right?" she said, capping the lip gloss and tossing it into my leather bag. "Tell him you felt something pop in your ankle at your last rehearsal. He'll check you out and tell you you're fine and then we're out of here."

"And how am I going to get alone time with his son?" I asked, glancing nervously at the woman behind the glass doors. She had teeny bifocals and a pig nose and kept looking over at us like she suspected something. Maybe because I was the only minor in the waiting room without an adult. Or because True was performing a rom-com-worthy makeover in her waiting room.

"Don't worry," True replied with a wave of her hand. "It's taken care of."

"What does that mean?" I asked.

"Claudia Catalfo?"

We both looked up.

"That's him," True whispered, turning away from me to hide behind her hair.

"No. Way," I said.

"Yes way," she replied.

The single most gorgeous guy I'd ever seen stood at the corner separating the waiting room from the exam rooms. He was tall and broad-shouldered with perfect posture and was wearing a light-blue polo shirt with a white doctor's jacket over it, which brought out the incredible cocoa-and-milk color of his skin. He looked like he'd just stepped off the set of some hot new medical drama. Emphasis on the "hot." If Peter ever saw me with this guy, he'd eat his heart out.

"Nice work," I said under my breath, feeling disloyal for my thoughts.

"I know," she sang.

But then, it wasn't disloyal. Peter and I were no longer together. At least, not for the moment. And he had a sophomore giving him lap dances in the middle of pep rally practice, not to mention what had gone on in the cafeteria. Every time I thought about the way that girl had just draped herself across him this afternoon, I wanted to kick something.

"Claudia Catalfo?" he said again.

"Go!" True whispered.

I got up, and she kicked my foot. Right. I was supposed to be in pain here. I limped toward Keegan Traylor, and he smiled at me. I swear my knees almost buckled. No one should be allowed to be that good-looking in real life. It simply wasn't fair to the rest of us normal humans.

"Claudia?" he said.

"Yes?" I breathed.

"I'm Keegan," he said. "Right this way."

He led me down a carpeted hallway and into exam room two. A man who had to be his father was sitting on a rolling stool near the counter, clicking through pages on a laptop. He looked up, smiling, when we entered. Yep. Same perfect teeth. Same friendly brown eyes.

"Hi, Claudia. I'm Dr. Traylor," he said, taking his glasses off and tucking them into the breast pocket on his jacket. "This is my son, Keegan."

"Nice to meet you both."

"Keegan is a senior in high school and plans on doing premed next year at Princeton."

"Princeton? Wow." Hot and smart? Even more unfair. "That's impressive. I'm applying there too."

"Oh yeah?" Keegan said.

"Yeah. I'm top of my class at Lake Carmody," I told him.

"He's second in his class at St. Joe's," Dr. Traylor said with a smile. "You two should talk."

"Maybe we should," Keegan said, and held my gaze for a long (possibly admiring?) moment. "Luckily, the number one guy wants to go to Yale for hockey, so . . . Anyway, Princeton's not a done deal," he said modestly, then loud-whispered, "My dad just thinks it is."

"I keep telling him I don't know why he thinks my pride in his success is an embarrassment," Dr. Traylor said, snapping on a pair of surgical gloves. "But on to the business at hand. Keegan's been shadowing me for a few weeks, and we'd like him to sit in on your evaluation. Is that okay with you?"

"Oh. Sure," I said. "No problem. It's not even that bad of an injury," I added, trying to preemptively cover. "But I have a big audition next week, so I just want to make sure it's okay."

At least that part wasn't a lie. And my stomach flip-flopped just thinking about it. The Lafayette School of Dance. Giddy shivers. But right now, I had other things to focus on.

"Well, let's take a look." He rolled his stool closer to me. "Why don't you have a seat on the table and tell us . . . how did you injure the area?"

I pushed myself up on the crinkly paper, feeling prickly and hot. I hated lying, especially when I knew for certain I'd get caught. The second this guy touched my ankle he was going to know I was faking it. He was an expert on the human body and could probably tell in an instant whether muscles or tendons or bones were intact. I glanced over at Keegan, who was watching me intently. He was sooooo beautiful. True was a genius.

"Well, I'm a dancer," I said.

"Oh yeah? What kind?" Keegan asked.

"Ballet is my focus," I said. "But I take jazz and modern, too."

"Cool," Keegan said.

"It is, indeed, cool," his father put in. "So what happened, exactly?"

"Um . . . well, I . . ."

My mind went blank. They both stared at me as my face burned brighter and brighter. What was I doing here again? Why was I wasting their time? I glanced over at the doctor's laptop, where the screen saver had started up, scrolling pictures of his children. An action shot of Keegan on the football field appeared, him pulled back in QB stance, ready to hurl the ball.

Holy crap. Keegan Traylor. Of course! He was the starting quarterback for St. Joseph's football team. Peter had mentioned him a few times—his stats, how he was probably overrated, how everyone was always talking about him playing ball at an Ivy League school.

Peter would die if Keegan and I got together. He'd seriously die. True Olympia was my new hero.

"Were you at rehearsal or . . . ?" Dr. Traylor prompted.

"Sorry," I said, looking at Keegan and feeling suddenly in awe. How could anybody be that good-looking, athletic, *and* smart? It seemed impossible. "Uh . . . yes. We were practicing leaps on Monday night, and when I came down on this foot I felt something pop behind my ankle." I cleared my throat and imagined the back of my leg throbbing. Tried to convey the pain through my expression. But acting had never been my thing. "I thought I could just walk it off, but over the past two days it hasn't gotten any better."

"I see," Dr. Traylor said. "Well, let's take a look. Scoot back for me."

I did, the paper crackling loudly, conspicuously, beneath me, my palms going slick with sweat. Dr. Traylor lifted my foot gently in his hands, and he and his son both leaned in for a better look. I hoped Keegan didn't notice my battered toenails and the calluses covering my toes. Side effects of spending hours a week in toe shoes.

Where was True and her diversion? I couldn't take this much longer.

"Okay, point your toe for me?" Dr. Traylor said.

Come on, True. What are you doing out there?

"Um, okay."

I pointed my toe.

"Does that hurt?" he asked, pressing the tendon on the back of my leg.

"Not . . . well, maybe a little. I—"

A door slammed out in the lobby, followed by a ridiculous crash. It sounded like a car had smashed through the wall or something. I gripped the table at my sides as Keegan and his dad looked at each other, alarmed. Someone was shouting and there were other random noises. Papers fluttering, a loud bang, people talking urgently.

"Dr. Traylor! Dr. Traylor! We need you out here!"

Both Keegan and his dad started for the door, but his father put a hand on his chest.

"Stay here. Let me see what's up." He looked at me. "I'll be right back, Miss Catalfo."

A nurse appeared just outside the doorway. "Dr. Traylor, there's a young man in a wheelchair who appears to be in some distress."

A young man in a wheelchair. Had True roped her friend Heath into helping us out today? If so, I could kiss them both.

The furrow in Dr. Traylor's brow deepened. "Bring him to exam room one."

Keegan peeked down the hall as his father and the nurse disappeared. I heard yet another slam and then he came back into the exam area, leaving the door open. Voices chattered in the next room, but the words were too muffled to hear. I tried to figure out if one of them was Heath's until I realized I'd never actually heard him speak. He was pretty new at school—even newer than True— and we didn't exactly hang out with the same crowd.

"Wow," I said. "What's going on?"

"I don't know, but that's the most exciting it's ever gotten around here," Keegan replied. "I feel like I'm working in an ER."

I laughed. This was my moment. It was time to try to snag Keegan Traylor. But this was not my strong point either—the flirting thing. It didn't come naturally to me like it did for some people, and it wasn't as if I'd had to wheedle my way into Peter's heart. He'd simply come up to me and asked me out.

My heart ached right now, just thinking about that day. Finding Peter waiting outside the dressing room. How awkward and handsome he'd looked in that sport coat and tie. The way my heart had fallen all over itself when he'd looked at me and I'd realized that he was, in fact, there for me.

Tears suddenly prickled my eyes. I coughed and looked down at my feet.

"Are you okay?" Keegan asked, gently touching my arm.

I glanced at his hand. If I wanted Peter back, Keegan was my ticket. I just had to go for it.

Confidence, I told myself. *Pretend you're about to go onstage for your solo. Lift your chin, elongate your spine, and dance.*

"Fine," I said, straightening my posture. "Just a little tickle in my throat. So, do you like working for your dad?"

"It's not bad. I get to take whatever I want out of the vending machine in the break room, I can roll in ten minutes late and no one cares." He crossed his arms over his chest and smiled. I couldn't help noticing how the fabric of his jacket sleeves strained as his muscles bulged. "I get to meet pretty dancers," he said in a leading way.

A warm blush spread across my cheeks. The silence dragged out for a long minute. I knew I should say something flirtatious back, but what? I thought of that waitress at Pizza City. That sophomore chick who had basically melded her body with Peter's this afternoon. Liza Verdanos. Even my sister, Casey. What would any of them say? It came to me in a flash, and I opened my mouth before I could lose my nerve.

"Well, when I came here I didn't expect to hang out with the doctor's hot son."

My words hung in the air, and for a split second I was sure I'd gone too far, said the wrong thing, totally turned him off. But then he smiled.

"We should hang out sometime," he said, pulling his phone from the pocket of his chinos and handing it to me. His attitude oozed confidence, like he knew there was no way I was going to say no. "Let me get your number."

I was trembling so violently I could barely enter the info, but somehow I got through it. Then Keegan lifted the phone to take my picture, and I couldn't wipe the proud smile off my face.

I'd done it. I'd flirted successfully, and now I was going to go out with a guy who was guaranteed to make Peter jealous. Step one of True's brilliant plan was complete.

CHAPTER SIXTEEN

Peter

"Would you like to declare a major?" I read out loud.

Were they effing kidding? Declare a major? Now? Who knew what the hell they wanted to do for a job when they were seventeen? Not me. I didn't know what I wanted to do tomorrow, forget the rest of my life. I rubbed my forehead with the heels of my hands, my eyes crossing. Part of me wanted to shove these applications into a drawer and deal with them tomorrow, but I couldn't. My mom had told me I wasn't allowed to come out of my room until I'd finished at least two of them. I groaned and looked at my cell.

Claudia. She would know how to fill these things out. If I hadn't broken up with her, she'd be here right now. Or as soon as her rehearsal ended. I reached for the phone and brought up her name. My thumb hovered over the call button.

What the hell was wrong with me? Couldn't I even do some paperwork without running back to my ex? Maybe she was right about me. Maybe I was pathetic.

I dropped the phone, and it clattered off the edge of my desk and smacked against the wall. The back popped off, and I was staring at the battery.

"Dammit."

I got up, grabbed the phone pieces, and lay back on my bed, trying to breathe. Coach was on my case about these two applications as well, because their scouts were coming to the game this weekend. College of New Jersey and Rutgers. I wasn't good enough to play at Rutgers, and I knew it. But I could maybe play, like, second string at CNJ. A couple of guys from last year's squad were playing there now. It seemed like it might actually be possible. It had to be. I didn't even want to go to college if I couldn't play football. I'd been doing it every fall since I was seven. I couldn't imagine life without it. If I had to go somewhere, maybe CNJ wouldn't be that bad. I could come home on the weekends easily. And if Claudia went to Princeton . . .

"Oh my God, you loser! *You* broke up with *her!*" I said through my teeth.

And it wasn't like she'd come begging me to take her back or anything. She was trolling for dates for homecoming right now, a thought that hurt like hell every time it popped into my mind, which was about every fifteen seconds.

I wanted to call her. I wanted to call her so bad. Which really pissed me off.

I sat up again and grabbed my Xbox controller. Eff it. Half an hour. I'd give myself half an hour to play. The applications weren't going anywhere.

I turned on the TV and muted it so my mom wouldn't hear the game. With her at the desk in her bedroom working on her blog and Michelle in her room reading her speech for her middle school council elections, the house was totally silent. Which was probably why I heard the car pull up outside and the doors pop. My friends' voices were insanely loud, and I realized my window was open. I went over to it and leaned my arms on the sill. Gavin, Mitchell, and

Lester were cutting across the lawn, which I really had to mow this weekend before it got completely out of hand.

"What are you losers doing here?" I whispered.

They stopped and looked up. "Kidnapping you!"

"Shh!" I said, glancing toward my mom's window. I hoped she was blasting Bon Jovi through her headphones like she did sometimes while she worked. "Where?"

"We're going to the diner to meet up with some cheerleaders," Lester whispered. "Josie's gonna be there!" He did a stupid dance, thrusting out his chest and butt like he was a girl. It just made him look more like a chicken.

But still, certain parts of me stirred at the sound of Josie's name. I glanced over my shoulder at the applications, then down at my busted phone. Suddenly there was nothing I wanted to do more than get the hell out of there.

"I'll be right down."

I grabbed my varsity jacket, tiptoed into the hall, and closed my door as quietly as possible. In five seconds I was out the front door and peeling out in Mitchell's car. The future could wait.

"So you don't know what you want to be when you grow up?" Josie teased.

I'd just told the table about the declaring-a-major question. Josie pouted her bottom lip as she tucked my hair behind my ear. She smelled like strawberry bubble gum and vanilla, and there was glitter dusted across her chest. Actual glitter. Like she was going clubbing in the city and not half sitting on my lap at the damn diner. It made not staring at her chest that much harder, but looking in her eyes was no picnic either. I kept expecting them to be green, not brown. Expecting to see the outlines of contacts in them.

For the last year and a half the only eyes I'd looked into this closely were Claudia's.

"I know what I want to be," Lester said, chewing with his mouth open. "A video game tester."

"A what now?" Gavin asked as he sucked down his second chocolate milkshake.

"That's not a real job," Josie's friend Jessa protested. She reached for one of Lester's fries and munched on it. Yes, Josie and Jessa. Their other two best friends, who thankfully couldn't make it, were named Jennifer and Jillian. Not confusing at all.

"It is so!" Lester replied, sitting up straight in his seat. "They hire people to test out the games and find the bugs. You don't even have to leave your house."

"I just got a flash-forward of you at forty years old sitting in your mother's basement playing Madden 2040 on a cracked big screen," Mitchell joked.

Everyone laughed.

"I got no problem with that," Lester said. "My mom makes a mean pot pie."

"You should be a writer," Jessa declared, gesturing at Mitchell with a french fry.

"I should?" Mitchell sat up straight.

"Why not? You're hilarious," she replied. "And that description was, like, so vivid."

Mitchell frowned. "Huh."

"So you're the only one without a thing," Lester pointed out.

"Thanks, man. That's real helpful," I replied flatly.

"Whatever. You're a superstar," Josie said, messing with my hair. "Whatever you do, you'll be a superstar."

I squirmed uncomfortably. Her fingers were too jabby, and I

felt hot everywhere and not in a good way. Maybe I was the shit this year at Lake Carmody High—emphasis on *this year*, because someone else would be next year—but I wasn't a superstar. I was the only loser at the table who had zero interests and zero talent. I mean, I could hurl a football, but so could ten million other dudes in America. What the hell was I going to do with my life?

The familiar pressure squeezed its way to life inside my chest. I cleared my throat and stole a fry off Jessa's plate, trying to ignore the feeling. I wished, suddenly, that Claudia were here. She probably would have changed the subject. Or come up with fifteen careers that I'd never thought of that I could totally do.

Why had I broken up with her again?

The door behind Lester, Mitchell, and Jessa opened and my heart completely stopped. It was Claudia. Her hair was up in a tight bun and she wore blue sweat shorts over her pink ballet tights. A gray sweatshirt with the collar cut out hung off one of her shoulders. She didn't see us. She was busy reading something on her phone. I moved closer to the window, as far away from Josie as I could manage. Which wasn't far.

"Hey, Claudia," Gavin said, when she was almost past our table.

She stopped. I shot him a look. She started to smile at him, but then she saw me. And Josie. And she went white.

"Hi, Gavin," she replied tightly. Then she looked me in the eye. "Peter." And around the table. "Other people."

Okay. She was definitely pissed. Claudia was the politest person I knew. She didn't say snotty stuff like that. She turned and walked up to the counter.

"Takeout for Catalfo?" she said to the waitress.

The silence at our table was bordering on painful. We heard

Claudia's phone beep, and she laughed as she read the text. The sound of that laugh sent chills right through me.

"I should probably go talk to her, right?" I said.

"Why?" Josie and Lester replied at the same time.

"Yeah. It's weird if you don't," Gavin said, sliding out of the booth.

I looked at Josie. She heaved a sigh before very slowly getting out so I could move. I shot her what I hoped was an apologetic glance and wiped my hands on my thighs. Even though I didn't know why I had to apologize. It wasn't like we were together. I barely even knew her. And I didn't want to get into a relation-ship two seconds after getting out of one. Plus, she was the one always throwing herself at me, not the other way around. Not that I minded. Technically.

I cleared my throat and slowly shuffled toward Claudia.

"Hey," I said to her profile. "What's up?"

She sent a text and looked at me, but for, like, a second. Then she stared straight ahead toward the kitchen. "Nothing."

Another text came in. She read it, giggled, and blushed. My chest felt like the entire team had just stomped on it with their cleats.

"Who're you texting?" I sounded mad, even though I hadn't meant to.

She texted back before answering me. "Oh, just this guy I met today before rehearsal," she replied. The waitress put her bag on the table and she took it, pocketing the phone.

She'd met *another* guy today? Where were these dudes coming from?

"What guy?" Definitely mad.

For a second it looked like she was going to answer, but then her mouth clamped shut.

"No one you know," she said with a tight smile, looking me in the eye for the first time. "Have fun with your cheerleader!"

Then she breezed right past me and out the door. Through the window, I saw her read another text and laugh again. I felt like I was gonna hyperventilate. So it was true, what people were saying. Claudia really was on the hunt, or whatever. We'd only broken up twenty-four hours ago. Practically. What the eff?

"Dude! What're you doing? Get over here!" Lester crowed. "Gavin just told us he wants to be an astronaut!"

"That's not what I said," Gavin grumbled. "I just think I'm gonna focus on science, that's it."

Outside, Claudia got into her white Prius and pulled out of the parking lot. Probably headed home to keep texting this tool while she ate her usual salad. I looked at Josie. She was putting on lipstick and made a kiss toward her pocket mirror, then smiled at me in the reflection.

Fine. If Claudia was already flirting with random guys, texting some other dude, and throwing it in my face, then fine. I wasn't going to feel guilty about moving on either. I shouldn't feel guilty. I was a senior. I was the star of the football team. I was out with my friends and two of the hottest girls in school.

Who cared if I didn't have a career mapped out or a major to declare or any applications done?

It was well past time to have some fun.

CHAPTER SEVENTEEN

True

I had been at work for about an hour when Hephaestus wheeled through the door. Instantly I tensed and started straightening the pretty, handwritten cards in the display case, bearing the names of each of the cupcakes. He rolled his chair to the counter and stopped directly in front of me. He was wearing an aqua-blue T-shirt under a brown leather jacket with the collar turned up, and he caught more than one admiring glance from our patrons. More than ten, actually.

"So that went well," he said.

"What did?"

"The thing at the physical therapist's office," he replied. "The guy thought I was insane, going off about tingling in my toes, but I kept him away from your girl for at least fifteen minutes. If she couldn't close the deal in that time, she's never gonna close it."

"Yeah. Great," I said, closing the case with a bang. "I'm actually kind of busy, so . . ."

"I don't get a thank-you?" Hephaestus joked lightly. "Why am I even helping you?"

"That's a good question, *Heath*," I said, glancing at the line of customers growing at the register. My coworker Torin was helping them, but it was only a matter of time before he asked me to jump in. "Why *are* you helping me, exactly?"

Hephaestus blinked, surprised. "You know why. Because Harmonia asked me to."

"Harmonia. Right." I crossed my arms over my chest. "Let's talk about you and Harmonia for a second. Are you two a couple or what? Are you in love? How did you two even become friends?" I asked, trying to push his buttons—trying to elicit a reaction. "When I think about it, I realize that Harmonia never really told me. It was just suddenly one day, there you were. There you *always* were."

Just tell me the truth. Tell me the truth and I'll know I can trust you again, I willed him silently.

Hephaestus wheeled himself to the end of the pink counter, far from prying ears, and I followed. He leaned toward me, his jaw clenched.

"It's a tad difficult to be in a couple with someone when the two of you live on different planes of existence," he snapped. "What's with you lately? Why are you so damn tense?"

"Oh, I don't know," I said, throwing up my palms. "Because the love of my life, the very person I've been banished to this hellhole for, has no clue I exist? Because my two worst enemies are doing everything in their considerable power to get sent here so they can rip me limb from limb? Because I am no closer to forming my second couple than I was two days ago?"

Because I have no idea who I can and can't trust, I added silently. If only he'd told me about him and my mother from the beginning. Or, better yet, if only he'd told me and Harmonia back in the day. But he hadn't, and now I didn't know if he was a friend or yet another insidious foe.

The door opened, letting out its signature tinkle of bells, and Claudia traipsed in. She was still dressed in her ballet gear and holding a brown bag that looked like takeout. Her eyes lit up when she saw us.

"True! You're here!"

"Hi, Claudia," I said, trying to smile.

"Oh my gosh, you're never going to believe what just happened," she said, popping up onto her toes. "I was texting with Keegan and I bumped into Peter. It was totally perfect. I'm ninety-nine percent sure he was jealous. Of course he was out with that awful balloon-lipped girl, and I was kind of rude to her and her friends, which I feel *sort of* bad about . . . but . . . anyway, he was definitely angry that I'd met someone else. That's good, right?"

"That's very good," I said, my heart expanding ever so slightly. Maybe I was closer to my second successful couple than I thought.

"Lauren's kinda freaked out, though. She said one of her sister's friends went out with Keegan last year and he's kind of a player." She pulled a concerned face.

"Yeah, well, that's not a big deal, right?" I said. "It's not like you want a long-term thing with him. You just want Peter to see you guys together."

"Well, that's true. I'll tell her that." Claudia's face lit up again. "Anyway, thank you so much." She looked at Hephaestus. "And you, too. Heath, right?"

"Yep. Nice to meet you," Hephaestus said.

"You too. Honestly. You have no idea how much this means to me," she gushed. "I don't know why either of you are doing it, but I'm *so* glad you are! I'll see you tomorrow!"

I lifted my hand in a wave, and Claudia practically floated back out to the street. Hephaestus opened his mouth to say something, but Torin chose that moment to save me.

"Hey, True? Little help?" he asked.

"I'll see you back at home," I told Hephaestus. Although I had every intention of avoiding him until I could figure out what his motives actually were for becoming my right-hand man. I wanted to believe that he was truly here out of the goodness of his heart, because he cared for my sister and she cared for me. But with each passing hour, my father's suspicions sank deeper into my mind.

No one did anything without an ulterior motive. Just look at me and Claudia. She was right. She had no clue why I was doing this. And as much as it was my job to help people find true love, as much as I truly wanted her and Peter to be happy, even I had a selfish purpose.

"Can I help you?" I asked the next customer in line.

Before the woman could even answer, the door opened again and in walked Peter, holding the door open for—as Claudia had called her—the balloon-lipped girl. He held her tiny waist between both of his enormous hands as he steered her toward the line, and the girl leaned back into him, clearly as comfortable as could be with the PDA.

"Two chocolate mint, please?" my customer requested.

I filled her order quickly and shoved her money into the register, never taking my eyes off Peter. He nuzzled the girl's neck. He looked at her with hungry eyes. And she was loving every minute of it.

I was going to have to put a stop to this. Like, now.

Four more customers came and went with Torin and I working in tandem. When Peter and his placeholder girl were up, it was Torin's turn, but I knocked him out of the way with my hip.

"What can I get you?" I asked.

"I'll just have water," the girl said, looking me up and down. "With lemon."

"That's it? Then why did we come to the cupcake place?" Peter asked her.

"I wasn't ready to go home yet," she said, resting her chin briefly against his chest as she batted her eyelashes up at him. "I'm going to the ladies' room. Try to get a window seat."

Then she twiddled her fingers and sauntered off. Her butt seemed to hang on its own hinge as it bounced back and forth on her way to the door. Peter couldn't take his eyes off it.

I couldn't help noticing she hadn't said please or thank you. To either of us.

Peter gave me this sort of suspicious look. "So. It's True, right?"

"Yep! True Olympia. That's me."

"You and Claudia seem like you're friends now," he said, squaring his sizable shoulders. "What's up with that?"

"Is that so strange?" I asked, leaning my hands into the counter.

"You tell me." He looked like he was on the verge of saying something else—my guess was he wanted to ask me about what he'd heard me saying at the pep rally practice—but then bit his tongue. "Can I get one Oreo cupcake, please? And water with lemon."

"Sure." I slowly took a cupcake from the case and went to get a plate. This was a great opportunity, getting Peter alone, but I wasn't sure what I should do with it. Should I stick to the plan and try to make him jealous of Claudia's new beau? Or should I try to find out what was going on with big-lips? When I turned around, Peter was staring down at his phone, checking the messages. "So . . . you've moved on pretty quickly."

"And Claudia hasn't?" he snapped.

I placed the plate on the counter, trying not to smile. So the jealousy plan *was* working.

"What do you see in that girl?" I asked, pulling a bottle of water from the fridge. "She's nothing like Claudia."

"No she's not," he mused, staring off toward the bathroom. Then he blinked. "Wait. What do you mean? How do you know?"

I shrugged and poured the water into a cup filled with ice. "Just Claudia's very mature. Very polite. Cares a lot about people. I don't exactly get that vibe from . . . what's her name?"

"Josie," he said, looking a bit green around the gills. But then his eyes flashed. "Not like it's any of your business."

"No. I guess it's not." I placed a lemon wedge on the edge of the cup just as Josie emerged from the bathroom. Peter tossed a ten-dollar bill on the counter.

"If you see Claudia, you can tell her I'm doing great," Peter said, jerking the plate and cup toward him. "And I hope she is too."

"Will do," I replied with a smile.

Together the new couple walked over to a table near the window and sat down across from each other. They made conversation for half an hour, but Peter checked his phone under the table at least four times a minute. Checking for calls, for messages, for tweets. And I knew exactly who he was hoping to hear from. At least I hoped I knew.

But Josie . . . she was completely focused on Peter in a way that was rare for kids these days. She wanted him, and I could tell she was the type of girl who wasn't going to stop until she got what she wanted.

I had to fix this situation, and I had to do it fast.

CHAPTER EIGHTEEN

Peter

I stared at my history notebook, the applications pushed aside. It was now after eleven and I still had to memorize these dates for my quiz tomorrow. A fact I had completely spaced on while making out with Josie at the park outside our grade school after Goddess.

My head hit the desk. What had I been thinking?

But then I remembered her lips, her hands, the glitter, and I knew. I hadn't been thinking. I'd been doing. For once. I'd done what I'd felt like doing instead of wondering whether it was right.

The door to my room opened. I lifted my head, and the notebook page stuck to it for a second before detaching itself.

"Where did you go?" my mother asked, crossing her arms over her stomach.

My heart thudded. So she'd checked on me while I was gone. She looked tired, the lines around her eyes deeper than usual. But she always looked tired. That's what being a divorced single mom of two kids did to a person, I guessed. Her blond hair was pulled back in a ponytail, and she wore a faded Lake Carmody High Football sweatshirt from my freshman year.

"Sorry," I said. "The guys came by and I just figured . . ."

"You figured you'd go out without telling me?" she asked, raising one palm. "That's not like you, Peter."

I felt this irrational stab of anger. "I know it's not like me," I snapped. "Maybe that's the point."

She blinked. "Don't yell at me. I'm not the one who did something wrong here."

I hung my head in my hands and stared down at my notebook, the words and numbers blurring. She was right. I was the one screwing up. I'd never snuck out of the house before. I'd never had to. My mom was the opposite of strict. So why had I done it tonight?

"What is going on with you lately?" she asked, putting her hand on my back. "You're so . . . tense."

"I just . . . I have so much to do," I told her. "Scouts are coming to the game this weekend, I have applications and homework and practice." I paused, knowing she wasn't going to like this next part. "And I broke up with Claudia."

Her mouth dropped open and she sat on the end of my bed. "You did? When?"

"Yesterday."

"Do you want to talk about it?" she asked, a crease forming between her eyebrows.

I kind of did, but I knew she had a million things to do. So did I. And I was already so exhausted my eyelids were heavy. "Not really," I told her. "Maybe later?"

"This weekend," my mother said, getting up. "I'll help you with those applications and you can tell me about it. Deal?"

I smiled. "Deal."

She kissed my head again and whispered into my hair, "I love you, kiddo."

As lame as it sounds, my heart felt warm. "You too."

She walked out and closed the door behind her. I stared down at the list of dates and tried to concentrate.

1952: Dwight Eisenhower elected president.
1953: Korean War ends.
1955: Rosa Parks refuses to give up her seat on a bus in Montgomery, Alabama.
1959: Hawaii and Alaska become states.

This sounded somehow familiar, but impossible to remember. Especially when I was dying to put my head down on the desk and pass out.

"Make it into a song," I heard Claudia say in my ear. "Sing it to the melody of the ABCs. It'll help you remember, I swear."

I saw her in the corner of my room, doing a little dance as she sang the periodic table of elements last year. I'd cracked up and grabbed her, unable to resist throwing her down on my bed and kissing her until she stopped singing and started laughing. Back then I'd wanted more than anything to be as close to her as possible. What the hell had happened? When had everything changed?

I looked at the clock again and groaned. This was getting me nowhere. I was not supposed to be thinking about the girl I'd dumped. The girl who had moved on to some lame-ass texter. She didn't care about me, so why should I care about her?

But still, I saw Claudia. Dancing.

"Focus," I said to myself, pulling the notebook closer. "You can do this. You don't need her."

I started to hum the ABCs and got down to work.

CHAPTER NINETEEN

True

Laughter. I walked into my house that night after eleven p.m., and the first thing I heard was laughter. I froze with my hand on the brass doorknob, and then closed the big creaky door as quietly and slowly as I possibly could. It clicked shut and I held my breath, then turned the lock silently.

Another laugh. Hephaestus's laugh. And it was coming from his first-floor bedroom. Thick, black, unctuous dread filled my body from head to toe. The laugh sounded flirtatious. Possibly passionate.

If he was in there with my mother, I was seriously going to set them on fire.

Clenching my fists, I crept through the parlor and down the hallway behind it on my toes, cursing the warped floorboards of this decades-old house. The door to Hephaestus's room was closed. I leaned my ear toward it, and he laughed again.

"You have no idea how long I've been waiting to hear you say that," he intoned, his voice throaty. "No idea."

My lips pressed into a tight, angry line. I thought about walking right through the door so I could catch the two of them in flagrante, but then I imagined what that might look like and I paused. Better to knock. Better to not have that image burned on my brain for eternity. I lifted my fist and pounded on the door.

Silence, followed by a slam. Was it a window? A door? A drawer? I couldn't tell. Too bad I couldn't conjure up a hole in the wall so I could see inside. Well, I could have, but I wouldn't.

"Hephaestus, it's me." My voice sounded like it was going to shake apart.

He dropped something. Cursed under his breath. I imagined him trying to get dressed and back in his chair before I opened the door.

Ugh. I had already vomited once since becoming human, and I didn't want to have to do it again.

"Are you well?" I reached for the doorknob, figuring that if I barged in I could explain it away with my supposed concern.

"I'm fine. Come in."

I shoved the door open. Hephaestus sat not five feet away at his desk, his cell phone held to his ear. Hung on the wall in front of him was the large mirror he'd brought with him when he'd moved in, about the only personal item he had other than clothing. He'd clearly worked his magic on it. The glass was rimmed by an intricate frame, thousands of thin slivers of various metals woven together to look like a tangle of grass and leaves. I bent forward to check the rest of the room. His queen-size bed was perfectly made, not a throw pillow out of place, but the doors to both the attached bathroom and the closet were closed.

"What's going on?" I asked, taking a tentative step into the room.

Hephaestus held up one finger to me as he listened to whoever was on the phone. I took the opportunity to edge to the closet. I opened the door quickly and peeked inside, expecting to see my half-dressed mother standing there, but instead I was greeted by perfectly organized shelves of T-shirts and a low bar hung with a couple of leather jackets and jeans. Hephaestus glanced over his shoulder at me as I closed the door. I tried to look casual.

"Yeah, I understand," he said into the phone. "Of course. I'll be there."

I backed toward the bathroom and shoved that door open too. The light was out, but the room was empty. The glass door on the shower stall was pristine enough to tell me there was no one hiding inside. The window was closed and locked from the inside. Nothing amiss.

Oddly, my spirits sank. I didn't want to not trust Hephaestus, but I suppose the thrill of the hunt had gotten into my veins.

"What're you doing?"

Hephaestus had wheeled his way over to the door, and now sat looking at me like I might be in need of a lobotomy.

"Nothing," I said, sashaying past his chair and back toward his desk at the foot of his bed. "Just making sure everything's okay in here. You are our guest."

"Is that what I am?"

I glanced at his cell phone, which rested atop his right thigh. "Who were you talking to?"

"Guy from work," he replied, lifting one shoulder. "He needs me to cover for him this weekend."

My brow knit. A guy from work? That wasn't what it sounded like to me.

"True." He fixed me with a steady gaze. "What the hell is going on?"

I hesitated, my hand on the footboard of his bed. Part of me wanted to tell him what I knew and give him a chance to explain, but I talked myself out of it. If he was here to find a way to get back at me or my mom or dad, then he couldn't know that I didn't trust him. He would just try even harder to hide whatever it was he might be hiding.

And if he wasn't hiding anything, I didn't want him to know I suspected him. Because then I'd just look like a jerk. Gods, I hated my father. If he'd just kept his mouth shut, I wouldn't have to worry about any of this.

"I'm fine," I replied. "I'm sorry about before. There's just a lot going on."

"I know," he replied, looking relieved over my apology. "But it looks like the Claudia and Peter plan is starting to come together."

"Yeah," I said lightly. "Hopefully."

He nodded. I looked around the room again. If he wasn't talking to my mother, and I knew he wasn't talking to some dude from work, then who the hell had he been talking to?

"Well, I was going to turn in," Hephaestus said suddenly. "Unless there was something else?"

I sighed. "No. Nothing. Have a good night."

I walked out and closed the door behind me, feeling like a suspicious nutcase. Like a failure. And somehow, even more certain that Hephaestus was keeping secrets from me. Big, fat secrets.

CHAPTER TWENTY

True

"So then he gets up on the stage and reads this poem asking me to homecoming. . . ." Katrina beamed as she trailed off and looked over at Charlie.

"Pretty much the most humiliating moment of my life," he said, shaking his head at the french fries on his plate.

"No! It was sweet! Everyone loved it." Katrina rubbed his back, then leaned in to kiss his cheek. "*I* loved it."

"As long as *you* loved it," he said. "But I guarantee you I'm not going back to open mic poetry night at the library anytime soon." Then he glanced up at Katrina. "Unless you're reading, of course."

I beamed across the lunch table at them—my big success story. It was just the three of us today, since Hephaestus had discovered this morning that the school had a functioning metal workroom in the arts wing and I was pretty sure I was never going to see him again. The good news was, being around Charlie and Katrina made me feel more confident that I would find a way to bring Peter and Claudia back together. It was just a matter of time.

Unfortunately, I didn't have too much of that. Just ask the rapidly emptying sand timer on my desk and the ever-looming threat of the AA twins.

"I got you a present."

Wallace announced his arrival by tossing a wrapped gift on the table in front of me. He wasn't one for hellos and good-byes, this one. I looked up as he grabbed a chair and sat at the end of the table. He was wearing a faded Star Wars T-shirt and plaid shorts along with battered flip-flops, and totally making the look work. Geek chic, I believe it was called.

"What's this for?"

Wallace lifted a shoulder. "My mom always says, 'When you see a need, fill it.' That's why she's the CEO of a major multinational food chain," he said matter-of-factly. "This is something you need, and I had one I didn't want anymore, so now it's yours."

Charlie raised his eyebrows at me, intrigued. I tore open the package. Nestled into layers of tissue paper was a phone that looked exactly like Wallace's, with the earbuds already attached.

"You're giving me a cell phone?" I asked.

I didn't know whether to laugh or cry. For my first couple of weeks on Earth I'd considered cell phones my enemy—the insidious monster that kept teens everywhere from experiencing actual interpersonal communication. But then I remembered the music. And I knew after watching Peter with his phone last night as he pined for Claudia, and hearing how mere texts between Keegan and Claudia had sent him over the edge, they might have some purpose in my mission. Slowly I was coming around to the idea that cell phones weren't so bad. And now I had one of my very own. I was going to have to ask my mother to set up the account, but I was sure she would. She'd just gotten her own credit card, and if the shopping bags strewn throughout her room last night were any indication, she loved using it.

"It's the last generation, so it's not as cool as mine, but yeah. You can do everything you want with it," Wallace said. "And I already downloaded some classical."

"Wallace! This is too much!"

"What're friends for?" he replied.

I got up to wrap my arms around his shoulders and planted a smacking kiss on his cheek, moved by the generosity of this person I barely knew. "Thank you, thank you, thank you."

He was blushing by the time I sat down again.

"I'm Charlie Cox, by the way," Charlie said, lifting a hand.

"Oh, hey. Wallace Bracken." He lifted his chin at Katrina. "Hey, Kit Kat."

"Hey, Wall-E," she replied.

Charlie and I shared a confused glance.

"Day camp nicknames," Katrina explained. "We had a counselor who couldn't remember anyone's names, so he made up nicknames for us. It was like a million years ago, but you don't forget an entire summer being named after a chocolate bar."

"Or a robot," Wallace put in. "He probably woulda called you Chuck E. Cheese," he said to Charlie.

"And you would have been True Dat," Katrina added with a laugh, biting into an apple.

I laughed and unwound my earbuds, feeling relaxed for the first time in days.

"Hey, guys."

My heart took a twisting, flipping dive into the depths of my stomach. Orion was hovering behind Wallace's shoulder, holding his lunch tray. He wore a dark blue T-shirt that clung to his biceps, and had a bit of stubble on his chin and cheeks that reminded me of his first few days on Earth. The days when we were just getting to know each other.

"'Sup, Orion?" Charlie said. "Why don't you sit with us?"

"Yes!" I could have hugged Charlie for suggesting it. And the closest empty chair just happened to be next to me. I pulled it out and grinned. "Please, sit with us. I need to get to know my football player better."

Orion's smile widened, nearly breaking my heart. "Okay. Sure."

He glanced uncertainly at Wallace as he skirted past him and took the chair next to mine. As he sat, our knees touched, and a shot of attraction zoomed up my leg so hot and fast I almost passed out. Orion froze for a second. Had he felt it too?

"Sorry about that," he said, clearing his throat.

"No, it's . . . I'm fine." I put my new phone back in its box and then suddenly didn't know what to do with my hands. My stomach was in knots, so eating the macaroni salad in front of me wasn't an option. Finally I placed them awkwardly in my lap, folding them together like some nineteenth-century student at a convent school in Italy, elbows out, back straight, ready to listen and learn.

"How're your classes?" Charlie asked Orion, reaching for his iced tea.

"Pretty good," Orion replied. "I don't know why they stuck me in art ninth period, though." He glanced over at me. It was one of the many classes we shared. "Mrs. Fabrizi's kind of out there, right?"

"I like her," I said. "She says what she thinks."

"Saying what she thinks is one of True's special talents," Charlie said with a laugh.

"Oh yeah? What do you think of me?" Orion asked confidently, leaning his elbows on the table.

I gulped. My throat suddenly seemed the size of a drinking straw. *I think you're incredible. I think there's no one in the universe like you. I think I want to spend the rest of my existence by your side.*

But instead of gushing, I shook my hair back and narrowed my eyes at him. "I think you're cocky, but in a good way. I think you're going to get everything you want in life. And I think you're going to find true love."

"That's her other special talent," Katrina said, reaching for Charlie's hand. "True's a matchmaker."

"Bonus," Orion said, his eyes sparkling. "So who do you think I should—"

"What about me?" Wallace interjected.

I turned to look at him. He sat straight in his chair, his dark bangs shoved back from his forehead.

"What about you what?" I asked.

"Do me. What do you think of me?"

I smiled. "I think you're sweet and giving and caring and very smart."

To my right, Orion shifted in his seat and shoved a fistful of french fries into his mouth.

Wallace's eyes widened. "Yeah?"

"Yeah," I replied.

"I'm gonna go get you some ice cream." Wallace pushed his seat back and stood.

"That's really not necessary," I told him. "You've reached your gift quota for the day."

"No. It really *is* necessary. No one's ever said anything that cool to me before," he replied. "Anyone else want anything?"

"I'm good!" Katrina and Charlie said as one.

"No, thanks," Orion mumbled.

"Be right back."

Wallace took off for the front of the room and I faced forward, trying as hard as I could to act natural when Orion's skin was mere inches from mine. I reached for my new phone and realized that I was smiling. Here I was, with my friends and the boy I loved, eating lunch, playing with my new cell phone. For five whole seconds, I felt like a normal teenage girl.

And I kind of liked it.

CHAPTER TWENTY-ONE

Peter

Nothing. I knew nothing. I was the dumbest dumb-ass in the history of dumb-ass Lake Carmody High. I tossed my quiz paper onto Mr. Flannery's desk, walked out into the hall, and punched the first locker I saw. It made an awful, loud clanging noise, and my hand exploded in pain as if every one of my fingers had just been blown to bits.

"What the hell was that?" Gavin asked, coming up behind me.

"I thought the quiz was on the 1950s, not the sixties!" I shouted. Up and down the hall, people were staring in my direction. Of course they were. I'd just dented some poor kid's locker and probably looked like a maniac. Near the doors to the stairwell, some dude in a Superman costume was hugging his girlfriend. Another happy couple going to homecoming. "I studied the wrong effing decade!" I said through my teeth.

"We already took the fifties quiz last week," Gavin told me, grabbing the arm of my varsity jacket to turn me around—away from the spectators and the Man of Steel. "How did you study the same shit again?"

I squeezed my eyes shut as I shook my head. "I don't know. I usually study with Claudia. She would never've let me do that." I stopped near the end of the hall and leaned back against the wall, smacking the back of my skull against the hard brick. It hurt, but I didn't care. "I'm such an asshole. I completely flunked."

Gavin sighed and looked back toward Flannery's room. "Maybe you should tell him what happened. He might let you retake it."

"Then I'll look like an even bigger idiot," I protested. "Who doesn't remember that they already took a quiz on something?" I pressed the heels of my hands into my eyes hard enough to pop them into the back of my skull. "I was just so tired. . . . I knew it sounded familiar." I banged my head into the wall again. This time I saw actual stars. "I'd rather just fail."

With a groan, I rounded the corner and saw Claudia standing at her locker with Lauren. I froze. She looked so beautiful in a red dress with short sleeves and a wide collar that showed off her long neck. Suddenly I needed to talk to her more than anything. I had to. There was no getting around it.

Without giving myself a chance to double-think the decision, I walked right up to her, leaving Gavin in the dust. She turned to stone as she saw me coming and tried to keep talking to Lauren, but I knew she'd seen me, because her cheeks turned bright red. My heart was in my throat.

"Can I talk to you?" I asked.

Lauren gave her this look like *What do I do?*

"It's okay," Claudia told her.

"I'll be right over there," Lauren replied.

She shot me this unreadable stare before walking over to stand by Gavin. The two of them just hung out by the corner and watched us, like we were about to burst out singing. Claudia turned to her locker and started rearranging books.

"Hey," I said.

"Hi." Her voice was strained.

"Um . . . hey," I said again. God. This was not going well.

"That's what you came over here to say? Hey?" she asked.

I cleared my throat. "Um, no. I just . . ." The scent of her flowery perfume was making my head fuzzy. "Can you just look at me, please?"

She hesitated a second before looking into my eyes, then she nervously looked away.

"This is how it's gonna be now?" I asked. "You can't even look at me?"

Her jaw dropped. "You're the one who broke up with me."

Yeah, but I take it back, I wanted to say. *I take back every word.*

But when I opened my mouth, the words choked in my throat. Because if we got back together now, we'd just have to break up again in a few months. Besides, she'd already moved on. And so had I, I told myself, trying to up my spirits.

"I know. I know. But can't we . . . I don't know . . . be friends or something?" My heart was desperate. I wanted more than anything to just reach out and touch her. Take her hand, pull her into me, kiss the top of her head. But I couldn't. I wasn't allowed to anymore. And it was my fault.

She made this soft but sort of strangled noise, then slammed her locker. Her eyes darted past my shoulder, and she paled. I glanced over and saw that Josie, Jessa, and a couple of their other girlfriends had joined Gavin, and they were watching us with a disgusted kind of glare.

"How would that work, exactly?" Claudia said. "You've always had your friends," she added, nodding over at the cheerleaders.

"And I've always had mine. At least now we don't have to make them pretend to like each other anymore."

She started to walk away.

"Claudia," I said. "Come on."

"Friends is not something we were before, Peter," she said quietly, looking at the floor. "And it's not something I want to be now."

Then she walked over to Lauren, grabbed her arm, and steered her around the corner, before I could even come up with another word to stop her.

CHAPTER TWENTY-TWO

Claudia

I could feel my cells bouncing around inside my veins and under my skin as I waited for Liza to announce Peter's name at our last pep rally run-through before the real deal. The whole football team was out on the basketball court in one long line, facing the bleachers, having already heard their positions and names announced. Now they were just waiting for their leader. The boosters stood behind them, between the locker room and their backs, lined up to face each other, since we'd be holding pom-poms and pennants and signs for the players to run through tomorrow. Flanked out on either side of our two lines were the cheerleaders, a few varsity and JV on each side. My sister was behind me. So was Josie the Big-Lipped Girl. I held my breath as Liza called him out.

"And now, the moment you've been waiting for!" I looked at Lauren across the way, and she rolled her eyes. "Number Eleven, your starting quarterback and senior captain, Peter! Marrott!"

Everyone on the court cheered, and it was pretty loud considering it was just boosters, players, and cheerleaders. Peter bounded out of the locker room with a big smile on and jogged down the center aisle created by me and the other boosters. Watching him in his element, so larger-than-life and happy and carefree, made me want to cry. He was my boyfriend. Mine. I wanted to reach out and grab his hand, or throw myself into his arms so he'd pick me up and twirl me around and kiss me. But I couldn't.

Because he *wasn't* mine. Not anymore.

He did look at me as he jogged by. A passing glance. It felt like death.

Then he was with the team, huddled up, bouncing up and down on their toes doing their throaty-voiced chant.

"Rams! Rams! We are the Rams!

Who's gonna win?

Rams! The Rams!

Gooooo, Rams!"

The cheerleaders screamed like some celebrity had just walked into the room. I glanced over my shoulder at Casey, and she was shaking her blue-and-silver poms in the air.

"Perfect!" Liza shouted. "After we're done with this, you'll all sit down. Football players in the front row, boosters behind them."

I made a move for the bleachers, but everyone else stood there watching her.

"Go! Bleachers! Now! Sit!" she ordered, waving her hands at us. She shook her head as everyone did as she said, then turned to the cheerleaders. "This is where we do our dance routine, girls. Everybody ready?"

Lauren and I came together as we headed for the bleachers. The players had already sat down, taking up the first two rows, and Peter was right at the center of the middle, watching the action on the court. His eyes were trained on something, and I was sure it was Josie, but I refused to turn around to check.

"How're you doing?" Lauren whispered to me as we shuffled across the bleachers.

"Fine. Don't ask," I said. We both knew she was asking about that encounter with Peter earlier. The whole thing had been so awkward and devastating. Friends? He wanted us to be friends? "Where's True?"

"She had to work right after school," Lauren explained. The line of boosters reached the end of the bleachers, and everyone started to sit. I looked down. Perfect. I was almost directly behind Peter. Now I could spend the next ten minutes pining for him and wishing I could touch his hair.

As soon as my butt hit the bleacher seat, my phone beeped. I whipped it out and my heart skipped a startled beat. It was a text from Keegan.

JUST GOT OUT! NO PRACTICE TODAY. WANT TO MEET UP?

He wanted to get together. With me. The insanely hot quarterback from St. Joe's. How was this even happening? I tilted the phone toward Lauren. Her eyes lit up.

"Perfect!" she mouthed.

I could tell what she was thinking and I grabbed her hand, suddenly nervous beyond belief. *"Don't!"*

But it was too late. When Lauren decides to do something, she does it.

"He wants to meet up with you now?" she asked giddily. She didn't even say it overly loudly. It was as if we were having a real conversation.

Out on the basketball court, the cheerleaders gyrated through their number. Peter cocked his ear ever so slightly toward us. My heart thudded in my chest in time with the crazy dance music.

"Um ... I guess," I said.

"So are you gonna go?" Lauren asked.

"I can't. We're not done for another twenty minutes or so, and we have rehearsal tonight," I replied through my teeth. I felt guilty somehow, participating in this charade. It seemed hurtful, suddenly. And wrong.

Then one of the cheerleaders popped up into the air, momentarily distracting me, and when I looked up, Josie was bent over with her butt in the air, looking over her shoulder at Peter.

Why did I feel guilty, exactly?

"I'll text him back," I said. "Maybe we can do something tomorrow."

Lauren gave me a thumbs-up, her hand against her thigh. I cleared my throat and typed back.

CAN'T TODAY. SRY. PEP RALLY PRACTICE THEN HOMEWORK, DINNER, REHEARSAL. FUN FUN FUN! BUT HOW ABOUT TOMORROW?

I sent the text and held my breath. He responded in about two seconds. When my phone beeped, I swear Peter flinched.

TOMORROW NITE GOOD?

I grinned. "He says tomorrow night," I told Lauren, looking at the back of Peter's head. His ears were a very deep shade of pink. I texted back.

DEFINITELY.

COOL. TXT ME UR ADDY & WILL PICK U UP @ 7.

I showed the phone to Lauren and we both giggled. Although mine was more nervous than excited. With shaking fingers I texted him the info he needed, then pocketed my phone.

The dance routine ended and Peter jumped up, clapping and whooping, so of course everyone else did the same. I stood up for my sister's benefit and clapped for her, a satisfied smile on my lips. He could cheer for his JV girl as much as he wanted. I had my own hottie up my sleeve, and tomorrow night I was going to pull him out.

CHAPTER TWENTY-THREE

True

The Studio. It had an oddly self-important name, this place where Claudia spent half her free time. *The* Studio. As if it was the only studio on the face of the planet. Or at least the only one worth mentioning.

I glanced at my watch. I was early. Claudia's class didn't start until seven o'clock, and it was only 6:50. Rolling up onto my toes, I looked up and down the lazy side street on which the Studio was located. A woman walked her four large dogs along the opposite sidewalk, each of them so perfectly behaved their leashes weren't even touching. A few doors down, several children let out a loud "hi-ya" in unison, working their way through tae kwon do drills. Then the clouds shifted and the setting sun glinted off a blue-and-silver sign near the corner, almost blinding me. When I could see again, I read the sign. MURDOCH'S OUTDOORS: THE HUNTING AND FISHING SPECIALISTS.

My heart gave a flutter as my father's warning rang in my ears. If Artemis showed up here with her temper on, she would be a serious threat to my existence, especially in my weakened human state. I thought of the arrow I'd left on the floor of the cafeteria and how useless it would have been anyway, without a bow. Perhaps it was time I armed myself. Just in case.

I tossed my hair behind my shoulder and strolled over to this Murdoch's establishment. There, displayed proudly in the window, was a tremendous hunting bow, so tall it would have come to my chin with its base resting on the ground. Next to it, a crossbow was propped against a fake rock, its loaded arrow facing the ceiling. There were bear traps and bludgeons and even a slingshot. I couldn't believe my luck. How much did these things cost? Could I afford one with the paycheck I had coming to me tomorrow night? I felt a prickling sensation inside my mouth and realized I was salivating. I reached for the door.

"True?"

My hand fell and I turned. Claudia and her best friend, Lauren, stood before me, Claudia sporting pink tights, gray leg warmers, white slip-on sneakers, and a tiny black sweatshirt, and Lauren in black tights, a black leotard, gray shorts, and black sneakers.

"Oh. Hello," I said.

Claudia's eyes flicked over the camouflage netting strapped to the inside of the glass door.

"Um, what're you doing?" she asked, letting out a short laugh.

"Shopping," I replied.

Their jaws dropped.

"In there?" Lauren asked, stunned.

"Do you, like, go fishing with your dad or something?" Claudia asked, slowly starting up the hill toward the Studio. Lauren and I fell into step with her.

I snorted a laugh, imagining me and Ares sitting on a dock somewhere, peacefully letting our lines hit the water as we chatted about our lives. The sky suddenly falling in on top of us was far more likely.

"No, I hunt," I told her. "I was just going in to look at the bows and arrows."

"Omigod, no way," Lauren said. "You, like, actually kill things?"

I shrugged. "Yeah."

"Omigod, I could never do that," Lauren said, her brown eyes wide. "Like, kill Bambi?"

"I don't hunt fawns," I said, screwing my face up.

"But still. Hunting is so un-PC," Lauren told me, flattening a hand in front of her. "Maybe you should find a normal hobby. Like soccer or something."

"We do have an archery team," Claudia offered. "You could try that. The only things they shoot at are standing targets."

"Really? I didn't know that." We paused on the wide sidewalk in front of the Studio. A minivan pulled up and spewed out three more girls in tights before speeding off.

"Yeah, it's mostly guys, but it's supposed to be a coed team," Claudia said, lifting her hand to wave at the three skinny girls who trailed by. "You should try it. It's good to be involved."

"Why?" I asked.

Lauren and Claudia looked at each other and laughed. "I don't know. It's fun," Claudia said.

Through the floor-to-ceiling windows of the Studio, I could see Claudia's friends warming up their muscles, stretching, and then pirouetting across the room. I could see how they might enjoy this group activity, the camaraderie, the sharing of talent, the endorphins released by physical activity. But I was here to do a job. I didn't have time for extracurriculars.

"I actually came here just to see how it's going," I told Claudia, leaning against a blinking parking meter. "Have you gotten anywhere with Keegan?"

"Um, totally!" Lauren said. "They're going out tomorrow night."

"You are? That's great!" I enthused. "We have to figure out a way for you to bump into Peter. Where're you going?"

"That's the thing. I don't know yet," Claudia replied. "And besides, after we made the plan, I realized it's not gonna happen. Not on a Friday night before a game. Peter has this whole ritual. We used to order in pasta so he could carbo-load, and then we'd watch some action movie to get him pumped up for the game the next day. There's no way he's going to be out anywhere."

"Well, if he loves you—and I'm pretty sure he does—it can't hurt to try," I said. "I just got a phone, and I'm gonna go to the mall to get it activated. Tomorrow I'll give you the number, and you can text me when you get where you're going. Then I'll find a way to get Peter there."

"If you say so." Claudia shook her head. "This is so crazy."

"Crazy, but effective," I replied.

"I'm kind of starting to like you," Lauren said, holding up her palm.

I high-fived her, a ritual I'd seen happen countless times, but didn't quite understand until I felt the satisfaction of my skin slapping against hers, like a punctuation of our mutual achievement. "Thanks."

"I don't know if I can do it," Claudia said. "What if it doesn't work? What if he's already, like, in love with that Josie girl?"

"He's not," Lauren and I said at the same time, in the same assuring tone.

"What makes you so sure?" she asked. "I mean, they're always together and I—"

"Hey, guys!"

An adorable boy with lanky limbs and curly blond hair paused on his way into the Studio. He wore black tights and a blue zip hoodie and had a large battered duffel bag on his shoulder.

"Hi, Lance!" the girls sang as Claudia pulled him in for a hug.

"Ready to perfect our piece?" Claudia asked him.

"You know it," Lance replied. Then he tilted his head at me. "I'm Lance Turska."

"True Olympia," I replied. "Nice to meet you."

"You as well. Anyway, I heard Madame Helene is handing out tickets for the recital so we can start selling them. We want a sold-out show next weekend! Are you inviting Peter? It'd be cool if he came to one of these things."

"He doesn't usually?" I asked.

"He always has a practice or a game or something," Claudia replied. "I'm guessing he'll be busy again," she hedged. Clearly she hadn't told Lance about the breakup and wasn't about to do it now. Maybe she'd never have to, if my plan did the trick.

Lance sighed a sigh of the world-weary, which made no sense considering how fresh-faced and energetic he was. "That's what happens when you go out with a football star. See you inside."

"He's really never come to one recital?" I asked as Lance trotted off.

"He came to *The Nutcracker* last Christmas," Lauren offered.

"Besides that, it was just the first one. The day he asked me out," Claudia said, her eyes shining with nostalgia. "But that was in the spring, and his little sister was dancing. Then last spring he was at some football clinic. But I don't mind. I would never expect him to miss a game to come see me dance, just like he'd never expect me to miss a recital to come see him play. It's fine."

"Still. It would have been cool if he'd found some other way to support you, like you did for him by joining Boosters," Lauren said.

"Yeah, I guess. But ballerinas don't have boosters. And he supported me in other ways." She looked at me and lowered her voice. "Boy gives a killer foot rub."

She fell silent suddenly, obviously caught up in the memories and the emotions. My heart went out to her. It was clear she was in love with this boy. We needed to make him realize he loved her back.

Claudia took a deep breath and sort of shook out her limbs like she was a wet dog shaking out her coat. "How did this get so negative? We have a plan, and the plan is going to work. Right, girls?"

Lauren and I looked at each other and nodded. "Right."

I imagined Claudia and Keegan ensconced at an intimate table at some romantic restaurant when Peter burst in, grabbed Claudia, and kissed her like no one had ever been kissed.

I rolled my shoulders back confidently. "Tomorrow night, we seal the deal."

CHAPTER TWENTY-FOUR

True

I was getting better. I was. I had just sat through ninth-period art for forty-two minutes and had not once looked at Orion. Not once. Not even when the girl next to me had turned her easel toward the boy next to her with the word "Homecoming?" spelled out inside the shape of a big red heart and everyone had applauded. Of course, the easels had been set up in such a way that I couldn't have seen him even if I'd craned my neck so far I'd fallen off my stool, but that was neither here nor there.

When the bell rang, I pushed myself out of my seat, shouldered my bag, and speed-walked toward the hallway. I had to get to the gym for the pep rally, but before that, I wanted to find Claudia and give her a final pep talk (ironically) about tonight. The sand in my sand timer was getting close to the halfway mark, which meant we didn't have that much time to make Peter Marrott wake up and smell the love. I didn't need to sneak a peek at Orion to see if he was, by chance, sneaking a peek at me. I was focused. One hundred percent focused.

It wasn't my fault that I had to take a small detour and walk past Orion's easel as he bent to gather his things into his backpack. Some girl had left her tennis bag in the aisle, so I really had no choice. As I passed behind him, I inhaled as deeply as I possibly could, longing for a whiff of his scent. Then my eyes fell on his easel and I froze. My throat went entirely dry.

It was a painting of his arrow. The arrow pendant I had given him months ago inside our cabin in Maine. The arrow that now hung around my neck.

Slowly, casually, I reached up and tucked the pendant under the collar of my white sweater. At that moment, Orion sat up and our eyes met.

"Oh, hey!" he said with a smile.

I searched his eyes for some spark of recognition. Surely if he remembered the arrow, he remembered me. There was nothing.

"Hi." My gaze darted past him to the painting.

"Oh, don't look at that," he said, blushing deeply. "It sucks."

"No, it doesn't," I told him as he rose to his full height, shouldering his backpack. He was wearing his blue-and-white football jersey, the number twenty-two outlined in silver, and somehow the uniform made him even hotter. Maybe I really was becoming a human girl. Every last one had seemed to stop and almost faint every time a football player passed by in a jersey today. "Why did you . . . I mean, what made you paint that?"

I rested my hand just below my collarbone, flattening it against the arrow beneath the cotton weave of my sweater. Orion's brow knit as he looked at his own painting.

"I don't know," he said slowly. "It's weird. I'm always seeing that arrow in my mind for some reason." He stared at it until someone dropped a tray of paintbrushes, and the clatter seemed to awaken him. "Who knows? Maybe I was a Native American warrior or something in a past life."

My heart lurched at the words "past life." He had no clue how close he'd come to hitting on the truth.

"Or maybe you've seen it somewhere before?" I suggested. "Does it maybe have some significance to you?"

He frowned and lifted a shoulder. "I don't think so."

As he turned away from me, I grabbed his arm to stop him. He looked down at my hand first, before meeting my eye.

"Because some people say that a true artist paints what's in his heart," I said, my own heart slamming so hard against my rib cage it had to be bruising itself.

Orion turned to fully face me. He looked deeply into my eyes, searching, searching, his face looming closer. I could scarcely breathe. He was remembering. Finally! He was remembering. I hooked my finger around the silver chain on my neck, ready to pull the arrow out.

"Wow," he said quietly. "That is the cheesiest thing I've ever heard."

And then he laughed. My face burned brighter than the hot sun in the midday Death Valley sky. Anger burbled beneath my skin. Anger at him for not remembering and for mocking me. Anger at Zeus for sending him here to torture me. Anger at myself for continuing to put myself out there when clearly, I was only going to get rebuffed.

But that was what love was about, right? Taking chances. Baring one's soul. Too bad it hurt so damn badly.

"Hey, True!"

Wallace walked up to me, his backpack securely strapped to both shoulders. He looked handsome in a gray T-shirt with the word FRINGE across the front, and a pair of well-cut jeans.

"How's the phone working out for you?" he asked.

"Good! Oh, I got the number activated last night. Let me give it to you," I said.

He whipped his own phone out of his back pocket. "Go."

I recited the digits. He typed them in, then snapped my picture and looked at it. "You are very photogenic," he stated.

I blushed. "Thank you."

"We'd better go. Gotta get set up for the pep rally."

"Oh. Okay." I looked at Orion reluctantly. "Want to come?"

"That's okay," he said stiffly. "I'm meeting someone anyway. And there she is now."

Then, without so much as a look over his shoulder, he turned and sauntered off down the hall, where he joined Darla Shayne. She ran her hand over his shoulder and down his arm, looking him over in an appraising, covetous way.

Get off! I thought. *Get away from him!*

They headed for the stairs together, and I narrowed my eyes, imagining the heel of her red shoe breaking, seeing her plummet down the stairs. As they reached the top step, she wobbled and I took in a breath, looking away. For a moment, I'd forgotten I could actually make it happen. I grabbed Wallace and stomped off toward the gym.

Enough was enough. It was time to find Claudia and get this show back on the road. Before I slipped up and accidentally killed Darla Shayne.

CHAPTER TWENTY-FIVE

Peter

The entire team was gathered just inside the door to the locker room, listening as the gym filled up with voices. Sneakers squeaked on the polished floor. There was a peal of feedback. People laughed and talked, and a couple of chants broke out. I grinned at my teammates. This was it. The first pep rally of the season. I couldn't help it. I opened the door a sliver and peeked out. The bleachers were jam-packed, wall-to-wall.

Gavin leaned in and whistled. "Man. This never gets old."

I closed the door and rubbed my hands together. "I know, right?"

"I can't believe we're seniors," Lester said, shaking his head. "This is our last first pep rally of the year."

The smile fell from my face. My heart thunked. "Way to be a downer, dude."

"Pete! You're never gonna believe this!" Mitch Ross shoved his way through the crowd and stood panting in front of me.

"What?" I asked.

"Claudia's going out with some guy from St. Joe's," he said, delivering the news as if he was half-pissed to know it and half-psyched to be the one to tell it. "Tonight."

"What?" Gavin blurted.

"Now *that's* a downer," Lester pointed out.

Out on the court, Principal Peterson brought everyone to attention and started his opening speech. I swallowed hard, feeling as if I hadn't had a thing to drink in days. "Do you know who it is?"

Mitch shook his head. "Apparently, she's keeping it on the DL or whatever. But what the eff, man? She's dating the enemy? The night before our game?"

The energy drained right out of me. What the hell was Claudia doing? And why? Did she hate me so much that she had to make me look like a total tool in front of everyone? Every single member of the team was staring at me. I had to keep it together. If I broke down right now—if I showed any weakness—they'd think I was a total loser.

"Whatever, man. Claudia can do whatever the hell she wants to do," I said. "I dumped her ass."

A few of the guys laughed. I saw them exchanging glances, and I knew I'd said the right thing. But inside, I was boiling. A guy from St. Joe's? I couldn't even imagine Claudia looking at someone else, let alone sitting at a table with someone else, laughing with someone else. . . .

Kissing someone else.

God. I was gonna hurl. I was gonna hurl right on Gavin's new kicks.

"And now! Your starting lineup!" Liza announced into the microphone.

Was he on the team? Was he good? Was he good-looking?

"First, your defensive line, starting with number fifty-six, junior linebacker Josh Moskowitz!"

Josh broke through the crowd, yanked open the door, and disappeared. The roar of the crowd was deafening. I imagined Veronica Vine cheering for him. Him finding her in the crowd and smiling. That kid was so lucky. He had his girl. He knew where he stood. And he wasn't thinking about how this was his last first pep rally, because it wasn't. At that moment, I would have killed to be Josh Moskowitz.

As Liza announced each member of the team, the crowd around us thinned out. Finally it was just me and Gavin left. He clapped his monstrous hand on my shoulder.

"Don't think about her right now, man," he said. "This is our thing. Enjoy it."

"And now, the captain of the defense! Number sixty-seven, senior defensive end Gavin Dunnellon!"

Gavin gave me a tight smile and ran out. Suddenly I was alone in the locker room, and my head was filled to bursting with images of Claudia. Claudia standing out there waiting to cheer for me when she was really thinking about some St. Joe's tool. Those pitying faces on the guys a few minutes ago when Mitch had made his announcement. My fingers curled into fists. I wasn't some loser whose girlfriend went out and dated other guys. I wasn't some dork who got left behind. I wasn't pathetic.

"And now, the moment you've been waiting for! Number eleven! Your senior quarterback and captain of your Lake Carmody Rams, Peter Marrott!"

I yanked open the door and jogged out, grinning as widely as humanly possible. I ran right by Claudia and didn't even give her a glance. Then I did something that surprised even me. I took a left, grabbed Josie out of the line of cheerleaders, and kissed her in front of the entire school.

Josie let out this surprised squeak before she sank into me, and the crowd went freaking crazy. The whole thing took about five seconds, but it felt like the best five seconds of my life. I was Peter Marrott. King of the school. And I was living in the moment.

Later that afternoon, I lay on my back on the weight bench, pressing, pressing, pressing. Sweat poured down my temples and puddled behind my ears. I clenched my teeth. My muscles quivered. Just five more reps. Four. Three. Two. I let out a huge grunt and hit the last one, then dropped the weights on the ground, gasping for air.

It was already after six, and most of the guys had bailed hours ago. Coach had told us not to work too hard. He didn't want to wear us out before tomorrow's game. But I couldn't go home. Not yet. I was too pent up. Too pissed off. I crooked my arms and lay the back of my hands against my forehead, staring at the lights sunk into the ceiling while I tried to catch my breath.

I wondered what Claudia was doing right now. Was she really out with some guy from St. Joe's, or was that just a rumor? Maybe she was actually at home with Casey, baking something for my spirit basket. If she was even still making me a spirit basket.

I laughed under my breath. Who was I kidding? Of course she was. Claudia would never back out on something she said she'd do. Even though I'd broken up with her, I couldn't imagine her dissing me like that. She was too good for that. Unless maybe she was busy baking for this new guy she was going out with.

The idea made my fists clench and I bit down on my tongue. "Sonofabitch!" I shouted, sitting up. Josh Moskowitz and Trevor McKay looked over at me from the corner, where they were spotting each other. "Sorry," I said. I couldn't believe that the second I'd stopped working out I'd started thinking about Claudia. It was like there was some kind of malfunction inside my brain.

"Everything okay?"

I glanced at the door. Josie had just walked in, wearing the tiniest cotton LCH shorts imaginable and a white tank top. Her hair was in a ponytail. She'd clearly just come from cheerleading practice, her chest shimmery with sweat. I was instantly turned on.

"Yeah. M'fine," I said, reaching for my towel. I wiped off my face and tossed it aside.

"Good." Josie straddled the weight bench in front of me. Our knees touched. "Because some of the guys were saying you'd had a bad couple of days. I thought I'd come in here and see if you needed some cheering up."

Her eyes traveled up and down my body as she said this, then over my arms and down to my hands.

"That was some kiss at the pep rally," she said.

"Uh, we're gonna go get some Gatorade. You want anything?" Josh asked, hightailing it for the door with Trevor on his heels. McKay stared at Josie's breasts the whole entire way.

"No thanks, man."

They slammed the door to the weight room—the door that was always propped open—behind them. Josie and I were very, very alone.

"So." Josie took my hand and placed it on her thigh. Very high up on her thigh. Then she did the same with the other hand. "Do you need some cheering up?"

My pulse pounded in my ears. My lips throbbed. "Um, maybe."

She slid forward onto my lap in one motion so quick I never even saw it coming. Just like that, her legs were wrapped around my waist and her breasts were pressed up against me and thoughts of Claudia were obliterated from my mind.

"I'm gonna take that as a yes," she said.

And then she kissed me. And it didn't matter who Claudia's new guy was or what I would do to him if I ever met him. All that mattered was the hot girl in the tiny shorts with the grabby hands who clearly wanted no one but me.

CHAPTER TWENTY-SIX

Claudia

"Do you think he'll come to the door?" Casey asked, leaning sideways to peek out the window while letting only a very minimal part of her body show. "Peter always came to the door."

"Of course he'll come to the door. He's a gentleman," my father said, still in his shirt and tie, though he'd lost the suit jacket. He cast me a sidelong glance, his blue eyes teasing. "He *is* a gentleman, right, Claudia?"

"Very polite," I replied. I looked around at my family, remembering the first time Peter had come to pick me up. They'd hovered that night too. They were pretty good at hovering in general.

"I don't know about this," my mother said. "Going out with some boy so soon after breaking up with Peter. I don't like it."

"It's just one date, Tanya," my father said in a placating way. "It is just one date, right? Not planning on running off and marrying the boy."

I rolled my eyes and laughed. "No, Dad."

"Now, Peter. He was marriage material," my mom said, fiddling with her pearls.

"Mom!" I blurted.

"Bet you wouldn't say that if you'd seen what he did at the pep rally today," Casey said under her breath.

My stomach turned just thinking about it—Peter's tongue shoved down Josie's throat for everyone to see—but I pushed the image away as quickly as it had come. This was going to work. Somehow or other Peter was going to see me with Keegan tonight and remember what we had. What it meant. How good it was. That plus the insane spirit basket I'd left in front of his house earlier today were going to do the trick. He was going to dump Josie Big Lips on her perky butt and come running back to me.

"What?" my mother asked Casey.

"Nothing!" we both replied.

"Does your heart actually break when you get dumped?" my brother asked, looking up from his iPad, his red hair sticking out like he'd shoved a fork in an electrical socket as he sat on the bottom step of our curved staircase. "And like, how much does it break? Do pieces fall off? And how many pieces are there? Can it break so much that you up and die?"

"It feels like it can," I replied.

"Corey, go upstairs and wash your face," my mother said, dragging him up by the elbow. "You look like you've been rolling in ketchup."

My brother barreled up the steps, tripping once before making it to the top.

"There he is!" Casey squealed, then flattened herself against the wall so he wouldn't see her. She widened her eyes at me in a meaningful way. "Killer car."

"Really?"

I glanced out the window and saw a black Mustang with a double royal-blue stripe painted from its nose to its windshield, across its top, and down to its tail. It shone in the waning light of day as if it had just been washed and buffed, and the engine made a deep growly noise as he eased it toward the curb in front of our house.

For a long moment no one moved. I looked at my mom. She looked at my dad. He stood in front of the tall skinny window next to the door and pushed the curtain aside.

"He's not getting out of the car," my father said. "If he's one of these kids who thinks it's perfectly acceptable to honk the horn—"

Then the engine died, and we heard the door open and close. Relief flooded through me. It didn't really matter what my parents thought of Keegan, because it wasn't as if I was going to go out with him forever, but it would make this one night easier if they approved.

"Everyone get out of here!" I whispered. "You can't be waiting by the door when he rings the—"

The doorbell rang. My mother and sister scurried toward the kitchen. I was surprised by how nervous I felt when I knew this was not a real date. What if he didn't like me? What if we had nothing to talk about? But there was no going back now. My dad waited a couple of seconds, then opened the door.

"You must be Keegan!" he said, offering a hand.

"Yes, sir, Mr. Catalfo." Keegan sounded completely confident and at ease. "It's nice to meet you."

"You too. Come on in."

My mom and Casey peeked out from the kitchen as he entered, then disappeared the second he turned toward me. When my eyes met Keegan's, my nervousness swelled, closing off my throat and prickling my palms. I swear it was like somehow, between Wednesday afternoon and Friday night, he'd grown exponentially better-looking. And he'd already been gorgeous on Wednesday. He was wearing his St. Joe's varsity jacket over a button-down shirt and jeans, and green was 100 percent his color. He was clean-shaven, and when he smiled his teeth were so straight it was almost wrong.

"Hi! Good to see you," I said, feeling awkward in front of my dad.

"You too," he replied. "Ready to go?"

"Oh, um . . . yeah."

We stepped outside together and it was weird, just doing that with someone who wasn't Peter. Everything about this was weird.

"Where're you two off to?" my father asked, leaning against the doorway.

"Dad!" I hissed.

"I thought we'd hit Dave and Buster's at the mall, if that's cool with you," Keegan said, smiling my way.

"Definitely! Sounds like fun."

I'd been to Dave & Buster's with Lauren's family once, and we'd had the best time challenging each other on the random video games. Plus, they had good salads there, unlike most of the other chain restaurants. I could rank the salad selection of every establishment within a twenty-mile radius of my house.

Keegan led me to his car and walked around to the driver's side. Peter always opened the passenger door for me, but it was no big deal. I slipped into the seat and took a deep, calming breath. The inside of Keegan's car smelled like leather, fresh-cut grass, and french fries. I knew instantly that I was always going to associate those scents with this moment. My first date with someone other than Peter. As Keegan got in next to me, I whipped out my phone and texted True.

GOING TO DAVE & BUSTERS @ THE MALL

I hit send and shoved my phone back in my bag, saying a silent prayer that True would come through and find a way to get Peter out of his house.

"Have fun!" my dad called out with a wave. When I looked up, I was mortified to see my entire family, even Corey, gathered around him.

"Sorry about them," I muttered, buckling my seat belt.

"Eh. They're not so bad," he replied.

I smiled as he gunned the engine and started down my block. If everything went according to plan, by this time tomorrow— maybe even later this evening—Peter and I would be getting back together. As Keegan started to ask questions about my family, I tried not to feel guilty over misrepresenting myself as someone who was on the market. Keegan wouldn't mind that we'd have only one date. It wasn't like he was invested in this. He barely knew me. For him, tonight was just about having fun.

For me, it was about so much more.

CHAPTER TWENTY-SEVEN

True

That night I was at the mall with Wallace and Lauren as we waited for Claudia's text, discovering the hands-down coolest thing about cell phones—the huge variety of pretty cases. We had rounded the kiosk at the center of the wide marble hallway fourteen times as I pondered which of the many colors, patterns, and materials I wanted for my new phone.

If someone had told me a week ago that I'd be on this particular shopping errand, I would have exterminated them on the spot, but after countless millennia of the same old routine, I was starting to think that change was good.

"I don't know," I said, musing over my top three choices—a red-and-pink stripe, a purple plaid, and a blue with white polka dots. "I'm not sure any of them are me."

"Oh my God, will you just pick one already! I'm starving!" Lauren groused.

"This is a very important decision," Wallace told her calmly. "The case your cell wears means everything."

Lauren widened her eyes at him, then let her arms and head slam into the top of the glass case dramatically. She turned to the side, so that her cheek was pressed into the surface. "This is my least favorite trip to the mall ever."

I glanced up at the proprietor of the stand, who was busy texting on his own phone. "Do you have anything with a heart on it?"

He finished his text and then, silently, opened a cabinet and pulled out a white case. He dropped it in front of me and I gasped. It was decorated with a fat pink heart made out of glittering rhinestones. I whipped out my wallet.

"I'll take it."

"See? When you know, you know," Wallace said with a satisfied smile, pushing his hands into his pockets to draw out his own phone. His case was gray-and-black argyle—the only two colors the boy ever wore.

As the proprietor rang up my purchase, I took the case out of its plastic wrap and snapped it onto my phone. Right then, the screen lit up with a text from Claudia.

GOING TO DAVE & BUSTERS @ THE MALL

"They're coming here!" I said, my heart starting to race. This was a sign. It had to be. "What's Dave and Buster's?"

"It's this huge place with tons of video games and prizes and awesome desserts. Only the perfect place for a first date," Wallace replied. "This guy is good."

"And they have the best fries in the world." Lauren grabbed Wallace's hand and my arm and started to drag us toward the escalator, nearly tripping a woman with a walker on her way. "Let's go!"

"Wait! Wait! Wait! We have to text Peter and get him over here," I reminded them. I yanked my arm out of her grasp and paused by the fountain in the center of the mall. "It's kind of the whole reason we're here?"

"Oh. I guess I forgot during the marathon case-browsing session," Lauren sniped, rolling her eyes as she sat on the edge of the fountain. Then she grimaced. "Sorry. I get bitchy when I'm hungry."

"Understood. Let's get this over with, and then the fries are on me," I said.

"Sah-weet!" she sang, perking up considerably. "Okay. What's the plan?"

"Wallace? Can I borrow your phone?" I asked.

"What for?" he said, actually angling the pocket that held his phone away from me as if I were going to pickpocket him. Perhaps my reputation as a klepto had swelled. A pair of kids with wheels on their shoes parted to scoot around him.

"I'm going to text Peter, and I don't want it to be traced back to me."

"Well, maybe I don't want it to get traced back to me," he replied. "Peter Marrott could pound me into oblivion with his pinky toe."

Lauren and I exchanged a glance. "Wallace, let me explain," Lauren said patiently, rising from the stone frame of the fountain. "If this whole thing works and Claudia and Peter get back together, then Peter is eventually going to program True's number into his phone, because True and Claudia are friends. Once he does that, he'll be able to tell that tonight's text came from her, and he'll realize that this whole thing was one big setup. But if the text comes from you . . ."

"He'll never trace it back to me, because there's no reason that the great Peter Marrott would ever get the number of a dorkus like me," Wallace finished flatly.

"I wouldn't have put it that way, but . . . yeah," Lauren said.

Wallace shrugged and handed me his phone. "Makes sense."

"Thank you!" I cried. "What's Peter's number?"

Lauren read it to me and I dialed it into the text box, which took way longer than I expected, since every number I hit came up as another number. I groaned in frustration. The one thing I couldn't stand about this damn phone was the touch-screen keypad. If I could only use my powers . . .

"It takes a little while to master it," Wallace said, patting me on the back. "Patience, Luddite."

I gave a tense laugh, turned away, closed my eyes, and pictured the number. When I opened them again, the digits had appeared on the screen. It was just a small thing. Nothing Zeus would ever notice. I hoped.

"Okay. Here goes. Let's pray he has his phone on." I typed in my message.

AY SACE AMD VIDTWS. VLAIDOA HETR WORG AOE GIT HUT.

My lips pursed. Screw it. Sometimes a girl just had to use her powers. And until I had time to practice with this thing, this was a necessary evil. I kept my back to Wallace and Lauren, closed my eyes again, and pretended to text. When I opened them, the message was clear.

AT DAVE AND BUSTERS. CLAUDIA HERE WITH SOME HOT GUY.

I hit send and turned around. The three of us gathered close and stared at the screen, awaiting a reply. Finally the phone vibrated in my hands, startling me so much I almost dropped it into the fountain. Wallace gasped and grabbed it from me.

"I got this." He read the text to us. "He wants to know who I am."

"Say 'A friend,'" I instructed.

Wallace typed it in and hit send. Peter texted back.

"'Is she with that Lance dude from Ridgefield?'" Wallace read.

Lauren sighed. "He is *so* paranoid about Lance, and I'm, like, ninety percent sure the guy is gay."

"Type, 'No. Someone from St. Joe's'—"

"Say he's wearing a varsity football jacket!" Lauren instructed. "That'll get him."

"But don't tell him who it is," I added. "We need the shock value."

"Nice," Lauren intoned, and we slapped hands. Wallace typed and hit send. We stared at the phone and waited. And waited. And waited. People shuffled around us and chatted, tossed coins into the fountain, tried to calm their overtired babies. The phone remained silent.

"He's not texting back," Wallace said finally.

"Do you think it worked?" Lauren asked.

"Definitely. He's not texting because he's on his way over here," I said, crossing my fingers behind my back for luck. I hoped that maybe, just maybe, since we were at the central gathering point of the mall, Harmonia would smile down at us and nudge things in the right direction. I looked up at the ceiling and smiled. "Guaranteed."

CHAPTER TWENTY-EIGHT

Claudia

"So how long have you been taking dance lessons?" Keegan asked before biting into a huge bacon cheeseburger. Nearby the video games dinged and clanged and exploded as people shouted and laughed. It was Friday night, and it seemed as if every twentysomething in a fifty-mile radius had decided to unwind here.

"Since I was three," I replied, spearing a dainty bite of my salad. "My mom took me to see *The Nutcracker* at Carnegie Hall, and I thought I was in heaven. I wore a tutu everywhere I went for, like, a year after that."

"Really?" He laughed and wiped his mouth with his napkin. "I bet you look cute in a tutu."

I blushed. "Cuter then, probably."

"Yeah. Now you probably look hot."

I laughed nervously, feeling flattered. "Well, maybe you'll come see me dance sometime, and then you can tell me."

He sucked some ketchup off his pinky. "Yeah. Maybe."

The waitress came by to refill my water glass and brought Keegan a new soda.

"Thanks," I said as Keegan reached for his drink.

"Anytime," she replied. "Let me know if you need anything else."

"So, big game tomorrow," I said.

He grabbed a couple of fries. "Yeah, I guess."

I stared. He casually chugged some soda, then picked up his burger again. Keegan was 100 percent Peter's opposite. He'd never casually shrugged off a game in his life, and there was no way he'd be eating this much grease before a start.

"You're not nervous?" I asked. "Thinking strategy . . . ?"

He tilted his head. "We have a game plan," he said. "We stick to it, we'll be fine."

I wished I could have been so chill about my upcoming audition. Every time I thought about it, nervous butterflies started to mosh around my stomach. Even now, I felt guilty for being here instead of in the studio rehearsing. But there were other things in life besides dance. Important things. Like Peter.

"What about you? You coming to the game?" Keegan asked.

"Um . . . yeah, I guess."

Keegan lifted his arm to wave at a pack of guys on the other side of the room, huddled around some shooting game. I tensed, waiting for him to beckon them over to join us, but he didn't. Thank goodness. I wasn't exactly interested in meeting Keegan's friends. If this was going to be a one-and-done scenario, it would be easier for everyone if we kept it between us.

"You guess?" he said. "What if the quarterback of the opposing team personally invited you? Then would you come?"

I rolled my eyes. "Then it might be impossible to resist."

Keegan smiled and my skin prickled. Had I really just said that? When had I become this expert flirt? Maybe he just brought it out in me. Which was odd, considering he was *not* the guy I liked.

From the corner of my eye, I saw True, Lauren, and Wallace enter the restaurant, slinking along the walls by the basketball games like they were on a spy mission. Suddenly my phone, which was on silent, lit up at my side. It was a text from Lauren.

PETER IS PARKING HIS CAR OUT FRONT.

Ho. Lee. No way. My insides instantly felt hot and sick and throbbing, even as my heart fluttered around with happiness. He was here! He did still care! But then the dread took over. I sucked down some more water and glanced at the door.

This was really going to happen. It was happening right now. I looked at Keegan, who was obliviously shoving fries into his mouth, and suddenly felt so guilty I wanted to run. He had no idea what he'd gotten himself into—what True and I had dragged him into. And then Peter walked through the door, his varsity jacket open over a T-shirt patched with wet, his hair matted with sweat as if he'd just come from a workout. When he spotted us, his whole face crumbled, then, just as suddenly, turned to stone.

It looked like Keegan was about to find out.

CHAPTER TWENTY-NINE

Peter

I saw them the second I walked through the door. They'd snagged one of the few two-person booths near the center of the restaurant, the ones so small that your knees pretty much had to touch under the table. Somehow I registered that before I realized whose knees, exactly, were touching Claudia's. And when I did, I almost died.

Keegan Fucking Traylor?

I couldn't move. For a second, I saw double. This was a nightmare. An actual, waking nightmare. The guy was my nemesis. The quarterback of our crosstown rivals. Not to mention an infamous dick who, if the rumors were true, had already had sex with half the girls in the senior class at Holy Cross School for Girls and had recently moved on to the public schools. Someone had to shake me awake from this. Please, God, let me wake up.

Then a stroller rolled over my foot. I doubled over in pain and knew that I was awake.

"Sorry," the saggy-faced mom said, still moving toward the door.

I bit my lip and stood up. I was going to kill someone. And that someone was Keegan Traylor.

Somehow I made my way through the crowd, around the loud-as-hell games and screaming kids, past the cheering packs of guys at the NFL simulation machines. Before I knew it, I was standing next to their table, and as much as I wanted to grab Keegan Traylor by the collar and pull him out of his seat and pound him for moving in on my girl, I found I couldn't even look at him. Instead I glared at Claudia.

"Are you kidding me?" I heard myself say.

"Peter!" Claudia looked up at me, surprised. "What are you doing here?"

Then Keegan smiled this big-ass smile that looked about as genuine as the framed copy of the Declaration of Independence my dad had left behind in our basement. He wiped his fingers and got out of his seat.

"Peter Marrott, right?" He offered his hand. "Nice to meet you. I'm Keegan Traylor."

"I know who you are." There was no way I was touching him unless it was to punch him across the face.

"Oh, so my reputation precedes me," he said, like the cocky bastard I'd always heard he was.

I glanced at Claudia. She looked at the table.

"You guys know each other?" he asked Claudia.

"Like you don't know," I snapped. "What are you doing with this tool, Claude?"

"He's not a tool," she replied. "Don't be rude."

"You really think you can tell me what to be or not be?" I demanded. "When you're out with the quarterback of the opposing team?"

"Oh, wow. I'm . . . wow. Are you guys, like, together?" Keegan asked.

"We were," Claudia said. "Until Peter decided to end it."

"You broke up with this girl?" Keegan asked, like he couldn't believe it. He whistled under his breath. "I wouldn't break up with this girl if you paid me."

Claudia beamed. My stomach churned. I hadn't eaten in hours. In fact, until about twenty minutes ago I'd been making out with Josie in the weight room, breaking about every rule possible. Why had I left her to come here? Why was I standing here letting myself be humiliated?

Why could I think of nothing other than grabbing Claudia's hand and getting her the hell out of here, away from this jackass? And worst of all, why couldn't I make myself do it?

I stared at her, waiting for a sign. Waiting for her to show me that this was a bad joke. That she didn't want to be here. That she wanted me to save her from this jerk. But she didn't move.

"Well, have a good game tomorrow, man," Keegan said. "May the best man win." He sat down across from my girlfriend and looked up at me. "If you don't mind, I'd like to get back to my date."

For a long moment, I stood there, hovering. Waiting. Praying. Wishing. And then, finally, finally, finally, she looked up at me. My heart soared.

"Good luck tomorrow, Peter," she said.

And just like that, I was dismissed. My worst fear had come true months before I'd ever imagined it would. Claudia had moved on with someone else.

CHAPTER THIRTY

True

When Lauren dropped me off in front of my house, I practically skipped up the flower-lined walk. Tonight could not have gone more perfectly. It was obvious that Peter was green with envy, realizing what he'd thrown away, coming to the conclusion that he had to have it back. I wouldn't have been surprised if he showed up at Claudia's door tonight and begged her to forgive him. Plus, we had just dropped off Orion's spirit basket on his front porch, and even though he hadn't been there when I pressed the bell, I knew he was going to get it and I knew he was going to love it. If the way to a man's heart really was through his stomach, those raspberry cheesecake bars I'd been up half the night baking were going to make him mine.

Things were good.

Until I saw Hephaestus sitting in the foyer, waiting for me.

"The shit has officially hit the fan," he said darkly.

I closed the door with a final-sounding click. "What shit are we talking about?"

"Artemis and Apollo," he said, earning my full attention. "They found a way to bust through Zeus's cloak, and they know where Orion is. Where you and Aphrodite are."

He turned around and wheeled himself into the parlor, a small, octagonal room stuffed with velvet couches and settees, carved wooden tables, and a stone fireplace. If he expected me to get comfortable for this discussion, he'd severely miscalculated.

"How do you know this?" I asked, so dizzy I had to lean against the doorway.

"Harmonia. How else?" he said, his hands gripping his wheels. "They're on Mount Olympus right now, doing everything they can to piss off the upper gods so that one of them will banish them here. She says she hasn't seen this much chaos since the fall of Troy. This is not good, Eros."

"You think I don't know that?" I demanded, pacing to the fireplace and back again.

I had lived on Mount Olympus with these gods throughout my existence. We knew how these things worked. Every last one of us had some ancient quarrel or another with everyone else. Every last one of us harbored feelings of resentment, competitiveness, jealousy, guilt, anger, unrequited love. If Artemis and Apollo truly wished to be banished to Earth, they simply needed to anger the right god, someone who had a bone to pick with Zeus and therefore felt the need to flout his authority. Some of them would have banished Artemis and Apollo to Earth just for entertainment, to see how it would all play out, to place bets on which one of us would win. A cage match between gods and goddesses.

My elders could be so childish.

"How close are they to getting here?"

"I don't know," he said.

"Well, are the upper gods committed to Zeus's decree that they not send them?" I asked.

"I don't know," he repeated.

"Well, what *do* you know?" I shouted, frustrated tears filling my eyes. "That's it. I want to talk to Harmonia myself. How are you communicating with her?"

He looked me dead in the eye. "I can't tell you that."

"Why not?" I thundered.

"Because Harmonia and I swore we'd keep it a secret," he replied through his teeth.

"You and your secrets," I spat. "I'm sick to death of you and your secrets."

"What does that mean?" he demanded.

"I know about you and Aphrodite!" I blurted. "I know you were married to her, that you loved her, that you probably love her still. Tell me I'm wrong!"

Hephaestus's visage hardened. His eyes seemed to flatten. He curled his fingers around the wheels of his chair, clinging to them until his knuckles turned white. "Ares told you."

"Yes, Ares told me. He was worried about me," I cried, feeling disloyal even as I said it. I didn't want to take Ares's word over Hephaestus's, but it was true that one of them had been honest with me and one hadn't, so what was I supposed to do?

"Worried about you?" Hephaestus repeated. "Seriously?"

I took a deep breath, bracing one hand against the intricate wood frame of the settee closest to the window. "Why are you here, Hephaestus?" I asked quietly. "Does Harmonia know about you and our mother?"

There was no way she knew. She would have told me. We told each other everything.

"Yes," he said quietly. "She's known for generations."

I felt as if I'd been slapped. It wasn't possible. It simply was not possible.

"And as for why I'm here, it's because I care about your sister and she cares about you," he said, his voice growing louder and more vehement with every word. "I'm here to help you."

I turned to fully face him. I thought of his sudden departure from school the other day when he had to "work." I thought of the conversation I'd overheard in his room two nights ago and how, again, he'd brushed it off as work. But worst of all, he wouldn't tell me how to get in touch with Harmonia. He was keeping my sister from me, the one person who could soothe my fears, the one person who could convince me that everything was going to be okay.

He was keeping her for himself.

"Tell me why. Why must you keep your communication with Harmonia a secret?"

Hephaestus rubbed his face with both hands, frustrated and seemingly exhausted by my impertinent questions. "If anyone knew that the two of us were communicating, the repercussions could be disastrous," he told me. "It's a miracle we haven't been discovered yet. If we told you how it worked, not only would we be in danger, but so would you."

"But I wouldn't tell anyone, I swear," I promised.

"You know that's a promise you might not be able to keep," he said wearily. "Zeus could torture you until you told."

I crossed my arms over my chest. "I'd never break."

"What if he tortured Orion in front of you?" he asked. "Or Harmonia. What then?"

I swallowed hard. The prick in my chest gave me the answer. I could never watch either one of them suffer.

"You see? We can't risk it. I'm sorry, True. You have to trust me. This is what's best for all of us."

CHAPTER THIRTY-ONE

Claudia

"Sorry it's so early," Keegan told me as he put his car in park in front of my house. The lights in my parents' upstairs bedroom were on, and I saw the curtains move ever so slightly. "I was supposed to be home an hour ago. Football curfew."

"Well, thanks for breaking the rules for me," I replied, reaching for the door handle.

I wanted to get out of that car more than anything. Every time I blinked, I pictured Peter's devastated face when he'd caught sight of Keegan, and every time I pictured it, my heart split farther down its center. I'd wanted him to be jealous, not suicidal. I felt like I'd made a huge mistake, and I didn't know how to fix it. Everything inside me ached to get to my room, put on my pajamas, and cry into my pillow.

I wasn't a manipulative person. I didn't know how to do this.

"Wait. You don't have to go yet," Keegan said, touching my arm.

As soon as his skin brushed mine, every cell in my body hummed, and my mouth went dry. It hadn't occurred to me until that very moment that he might want to kiss me. Ever since Peter left, I'd been too busy silently brooding over what had happened to consider it.

But now . . . yes . . . there was a definite charge in the air and that telltale hopeful-slash-sultry look on his face. Did I want to kiss him? No. I was in love with Peter. Whether or not we were together, I couldn't just go around making out with other guys. That wasn't how I worked.

Still, I settled back in the seat, not wanting to offend the guy who'd paid for my dinner and made me laugh throughout the night. Instead I tried to think of a good excuse not to kiss him. It was too bad I hadn't ordered garlic bread. Unfortunately, the heavy dessert I *had* ordered now sat like a brick at the bottom of my stomach.

"Pete Marrott seemed nice," Keegan said, looking down at his knees.

I felt like I had a huge breadstick lodged in the back of my throat. Pete Marrott had seemed pissed off, but I knew he was only saying what he thought he should say. "Um, yeah."

"Did you guys break up recently?" he asked, casting a quick sidelong glance at me.

The breadstick swelled into a whole loaf. "Um, kind of."

He nodded. "I had a feeling. I thought the guy was going to upchuck on your feet when he saw me."

I pressed my lips together and looked at the front door, half hoping my dad would come storming out and demand that I come inside. Why were we talking about Peter?

"So, which one of us are you going to root for in the game tomorrow?" Keegan asked, shifting his weight, the white leather of his jacket sleeves squeaking against the black leather of the seats. His smile was so charming, my gut reaction was to say, *You! Of course, you!* But I controlled myself.

"Well, I go to Lake Carmody and I'm on the Boosters, so . . ."

"Maybe this'll change your mind, then."

And before I could even process what he'd said, he kissed me. No. He didn't just kiss me. He slid his hand along my neck, cupped the back of my head, and pulled me to him, like if he'd waited to do it for one more second, he might have died. It wasn't exactly like the Zac Efron/Taylor Schilling kiss, but it was as close as I'd ever come. Just like that, the lips of a person who was not Peter Marrott were on mine and it was . . .

Mind-blowing. My pulse thrummed quick and shallow in my wrists. My skin flushed outward from my chest to my neck to my arms and legs, to every last inch of my body, as if my heart was radiating heat with each and every beat. The pressure of his lips was so insistent, so searching, that in the back of my mind an unbelievable thought began to spark to life.

This guy really liked me.

And also? I should really start kissing him back.

And so I did. And we stayed out there kissing for twenty minutes, until the front lights flicked on and I had to gigglingly say good-bye. Then I tripped up the walk, fumbled through the door, and closed it with a sigh behind me, realizing one thing as I bit down on my swollen bottom lip.

Minus the whole devastating-encounter-with-Peter part of the night, I hadn't had that much fun in a really long time.

CHAPTER THIRTY-TWO

True

I waited for Hephaestus as the lift outside his van lowered his chair to the asphalt parking lot, silently watching the football players and their families stream into and around the school, headed for the locker room or the field behind the building. Once the lift had replaced itself inside the van, I slammed the door, and we were off. Hephaestus's wheels crunched over the first fallen leaves of autumn as I toyed with the arrow pendant around my neck.

The silence between us was deafening.

"So. Are you psyched for your first football game?" Hephaestus asked.

"Very," I replied, relieved that he was the first to speak. "There's something so primal about the whole battle-for-territory theme. I quite like it."

"Oh, so you *are* talking to me," he chided.

"I thought you weren't talking to me!"

We looked at each other, and we both laughed. For the moment, the tension between us lifted. But there were still so many unanswered questions, and I was still angry at him for putting up a wall between me and Harmonia. As sound as their logic for the secrecy

might be, I still longed to talk to my sister, with a borderline patho-
logical vengeance.

"True!" The sound of my name shouted in Orion's voice made
my heart leap like a gazelle. I turned around to scan the crowded
parking lot. "True! Wait up!"

He broke free of a klatch of people and jogged over to me, wearing his tight white football pants and his jersey, carrying a packed
duffel with his shoulder pads slung over it. The smile on his face
sent my spirits and hopes soaring. It was familiar, confident, over-
joyed. He had remembered me. He had remembered us. I could
feel it.

"Orion!" I shouted back, ready to throw myself into his arms.

"Down, girl," Hephaestus said under his breath.

It was only at his words that I realized Orion was not reaching for me. Instead he was stopping a few feet in front of us, his
hands on his hips. I cleared my throat and looked at my feet. That
was almost seriously embarrassing. Once again, Hephaestus had
saved me.

"I'm glad I caught you!" Orion said, still smiling. "Thanks for
the spirit basket. It was out of control."

Oh. That was what this was about. "Please. It was nothing," I
said modestly.

"Are you kidding me?" He started to walk toward the school,
so Hephaestus and I fell in next to him. "Did you really bake that
stuff from scratch?"

"She did," Hephaestus said. "And she didn't let anyone else in
the house sample any of it. I have the slap marks to prove it," he
added, holding up one hand. There *was* a tiny black-and-blue mark
on his middle knuckle, but I couldn't imagine that I had actually
been responsible for it.

"Well, thank you. Really," Orion said. "Because of you, I'm one hundred percent ready for this game."

We had reached the front door and he paused, looking me in the eye. Suddenly I couldn't breathe. I was surprised my body didn't totally give out from the anticipation. Then Orion opened one arm, clinging to his bag with the other, and reached for me, pulling me into a hug. I wrapped my arms around him and hugged him back, my face pressing into his shoulder. Our bodies fit together so perfectly, it was as if we'd been made for each other. When he pulled away, tears of regret sprang to my eyes. I could have stayed in the crook of his arm forever.

For a blissful moment, Orion hesitated. He searched my face. His fingers trailed down my arm and squeezed my hand. I thought I might actually faint.

Kiss me, I thought. *Kiss me. Kiss me. Kiss me.* They were the only two words left in the world. There was no other thought in my head.

"See you after?" he said.

I pressed my lips together to stop their insane tingling. "Sure," I breathed.

He smiled, turned, and disappeared inside the school. A cool breeze lifted the hair off the back of my neck, and I reached for Hephaestus's shoulder to keep myself from buckling to the ground.

"That was intense," Hephaestus said.

"So I didn't just imagine it?"

"Nope. If I were a betting man, which I'm not, I'd put my money on him asking you out by day's end," Hephaestus told me. "He's obviously attracted to you."

"I knew it!" I cried happily, watching the door as if Orion would return any moment and claim me as his own. "I knew we were meant to be!"

"What about Zeus?" Hephaestus asked, lowering his voice as a crowd of guys in the St. Joe's green and yellow walked by.

"What about him?"

"Aren't you worried he'll be displeased by this development?" Hephaestus asked. "He sent you here, at least partially, to split up you and Orion."

I laughed sarcastically. "And then he sent Orion to my side. He can't blame me if the boy falls in love with me again. It's not my fault I'm so irresistible."

Hephaestus smirked. "Just tread lightly, True," he said, starting around the side of the school with the rest of the burgeoning crowd. "I speak from experience. When it comes to Zeus, you never know what's going to happen next."

CHAPTER THIRTY-THREE

Peter

"You guys are ready for this," Coach said, stepping away from the whiteboard in the locker room after his last-minute strategy session. It was covered in *X*s and *O*s, arrows and numbers. "Now let's get out there and beat these bastards!"

The team cheered, rising from the benches, smacking helmets together, slapping backs, bumping chests. This was usually my favorite part of the pregame. The adrenaline, the team spirit, the confidence. But today I felt sick. Sick and angry and, annoyingly, tired. I'd been up half the night replaying that crap with Claudia and Keegan Traylor over and over in my head. Seeing his shit-eating grin. Wishing I'd coldcocked him in the face. Wondering what they were doing while I writhed in my bed, frustrated and helpless.

Just to make everything worse, there were scouts coming today. No sleep and scouts in the stands. Plus, I'd never finished those applications. Not that it mattered. I was sure I was going to be totally unfocused out there, eat dirt a couple dozen times, and neither one of the schools would want me anyway.

How the hell had Claudia met Keegan Fucking Traylor? That

was the question. And why? And didn't she know how screwed up that was, going out with the QB of St. Joe's? Didn't she care about me even a tiny bit? Or how it would look to everyone?

How about when you dumped me in front of half the school? I heard her say in my mind. *How much were* you *caring about* me *then?*

And of course, she'd be right. But still. Keegan Fucking Traylor? And at Dave & Buster's, where half our school hung out every weekend? That was just wrong. And he was the one who was going to pay for it.

Coach Morschauser and the assistants led the charge out the locker room door for the field, but I grabbed Moskowitz and Gavin and held them back.

"WTF, dude?" Josh said, shrugging me off.

"Carson! Frangipane! Get over here!" I half shouted to the other key members of the defense.

They stopped and loped toward me while the rest of the team trotted out after the coaches. The four biggest guys in school formed a semicircle around me. I waited until the door squealed and slammed. Then I looked them each in the eye.

"What's up, QB-one?" Frangipane asked in his raspy voice.

I loved when they called me that. That was when I knew they had my back.

"I need you guys to rip Keegan Traylor's head off," I said, through my teeth.

They laughed. "Of course we will," Moskowitz said good-naturedly.

I slapped Gavin's chest plate with the back of my hand as he started to turn away, stopping him.

"No, guys. I'm serious."

The vibe in the room shifted to all business. "What's up, Pete?" Gavin asked, chucking his chin.

"That asswipe took Claudia out last night," I told them, barely able to bite out the words. Their eyes widened as they exchanged shocked, appalled, furious glances. "I need you to cause him pain."

CHAPTER THIRTY-FOUR

Claudia

As soon as the St. Joe's Saints ran out onto the field, I started to scan their ranks for Keegan. Unfortunately, the players looked alike in their green and yellow uniforms with their helmets on, and there were no names on their jerseys. Plus, they were lining up on the far side of the field in front of the away bleachers, which were packed with fans in green and yellow. The sun glinted off the gold helmets, as if each player had a tiny gleaming star attached to his head.

"Oh, they're one of those teams," Lauren said wisely.

"What teams?" Mia Ross asked, plucking a kernel of popcorn from her bag on my other side. Her long blond hair was up in a bun, and she wore a blue LCHS sweatshirt over skinny jeans. Her best friend, Rhonda, and two other sophomores giggled next to her, checking out some boys across the way.

"The ones who are like, 'It's not about the player, it's about the team,'" Lauren replied, putting on a snooty voice. "Don't they get that we want to know whose cute butt we're looking at?"

"Lauren!" I scolded, looking behind me at the group of players' moms on the riser above. They wore their usual jeans, T-shirts, and blazers, with blue and white ribbons pinned to their lapels—

the definition of athlete-mom chic. The most ardent mom, Mrs. Moskowitz, had blue-and-white streaks painted on one cheek, and her son's number—56—on the other. Which was odd, because she wasn't like one of those tomboyish moms. Her nails were done, her hair perfectly shellacked into its ponytail, and she was dripping in gold jewelry. But still, the face painting. Sometimes people defied pigeonholing.

"Please. You ladies know what I'm talking about," Lauren said, turning around to face them. "Am I right?"

They narrowed their eyes in unison, a movement that would have inspired awe over at the Studio.

"Or maybe not," Lauren said, facing forward again.

"Can you tell which one he is?" Mia asked, leaning into me as she munched.

One of the guys at the center of the line started to bounce up and down, shaking his arms out and stretching his neck from side to side. I recognized the perfect posture and the kinetic energy right away, and felt a surprising flutter inside my chest.

"There he is. Number thirteen," I said, pointing.

At that moment, he turned and looked at our bleachers. I could have sworn he was looking right at me. My skin flushed red.

"Oh my God, you're smiling like an idiot," Lauren said, sounding appalled.

"No, I'm not!" I replied.

But even though I tried as hard as I could, I had no control over my muscle function. I was, in fact, a smiling idiot.

"Do you *like* him?" Lauren demanded.

"And now, your Lake Carmody Rams!" the PA announcer shouted, his deafening voice blasting through the speakers.

Our team ran out onto the field, flanked by Casey and the

cheerleaders and their huge flags and pom-poms, and I jumped to my feet with the rest of the crowd, saved from answering. Saved from telling her that Keegan and I had texted that morning and decided to meet up by the gym after the game, which I kind of still couldn't believe I'd agreed to, since it used to be my ritual with Peter. But, I'd reasoned, if there was any locale tailor-made for Peter to spot us together, it was next to the gym after the game. And his friends would see us too, which would make the jealousy that much more potent. So I'd agreed. Me and Keegan. Together. For everyone to see.

We jumped up and down and shouted as the cheer squad launched into the fight chant. I raised my fist and screamed along with Mia and her friends, but I could feel Lauren eyeballing me the entire time. Silent. Just watching.

Which, of course, made me blush even harder.

"And now, please join the Lake Carmody marching band as they play our national anthem," the PA announcer said, suddenly somber.

The trumpet began its tune, and everyone sang at a whisper, like they always do at these things. I scanned the team in front of us and found Peter instantly, the MARROTT spelled out in big white letters across his back. His hair stuck out over his ears from removing his helmet for the anthem, and the back of his neck looked red, as if he'd already been working out for an hour. My heart pounded as my eyes flicked from him to Keegan, and I wondered what he was thinking. Was he angry at me for last night? Angry at Keegan? Probably not. Knowing him, he was probably 100 percent focused on the game. He'd think about me and Keegan later. If he even bothered.

And then I had the most horrible thought. Maybe True's plan

wasn't working. Maybe what had happened last night hadn't made him jealous, but irrevocably angry. Maybe he was never going to speak to me again.

Right then, Peter turned around and scanned the bleachers. My breath caught with anticipation, hardly daring to hope that he was looking for me, hardly daring to think of anything . . . and then he found me. And he stared. He stared right at me for the whole rest of the song.

"He totally still likes you," Lauren said as soon as the anthem ended and everyone began to cheer. "Or likes you again. He re-likes you."

"Guess that True girl isn't as crazytown as she seems," Mia added.

"Maybe not," I replied, my heart slamming around inside my chest like an out-of-control wrecking ball. "See? Peter and I will be back together in no time," I said, looking Lauren in the eye.

She arched one eyebrow and I looked away, feeling nervous and hot, guilty and confused, as Keegan and a couple of his teammates walked to the center of the field to shake hands with Peter and some of his teammates before the coin toss. Sometimes having a best friend who knew me as well as she did was not entirely cool.

CHAPTER THIRTY-FIVE

Peter

I was supposed to be watching the game, but I was watching Claudia. It didn't seem like she was rooting for Keegan, but it was hard to tell. I mean, she was sitting with the Lake Carmody fans, wearing her booster ribbon, so even if that asshole was the new love of her life, it would have been awkward for her to cheer for him. But still. Every time our defense came up with a big play, she cheered, and they were playing awesome. It was almost halftime and we were up 24–10. They hadn't killed the guy yet, but then the game was only half over.

She was so pretty, Claudia. Sitting there with the sun on her face, her skin practically glowing. Hands down she was the prettiest girl I knew.

"Go, Peter!"

My eyes flicked to the track around the field. Josie was waving her pom-poms with the other JV cheerleaders, who were flanking varsity since it was a big game. I shot her a look through my helmet like, *WTF?* I wasn't even on the field.

"Blitz!" someone shouted in my ear.

I whipped around to watch the action. Traylor had dropped

back with the ball, and his offensive line had crumbled. Dunnellon and Moskowitz came at him from either side, and there wasn't a single soul to stop them. Traylor dropped back even farther, trying to scramble away.

"Get him! Get him!" I shouted.

He searched desperately for an open receiver, but there was no one. The dude was about to get nailed. I saw his eyes widen. Saw him try for one last bob-and-weave, and then Gavin and Josh sandwiched him. Everyone in the stands gasped as he went down under five hundred pounds of linebacker. The fans on their side of the field went silent. The fans on our side of the field went nuts. I turned around and looked at Claudia. She was cheering and jumping up and down with Lauren and Mia, clutching her hands.

That was pretty much all I needed to see. And what I felt inside was all I needed to feel. It was like my heart had swelled up to fill my entire body. There was apparently nothing in the world like watching the girl you liked cheer over the guy you thought she *might* like getting flattened.

Right then and there I decided. I was going to win this game, and then I was going to find Claudia and ask her out again. She didn't belong with Keegan Traylor. She belonged with me. By the end of the day, everything would be back to normal.

CHAPTER THIRTY-SIX

True

"And now, your Lake Carmody High School marching band!"

There was a smattering of applause across the depleted crowd in the bleachers. The band had formed the letters *M* and *J* out on the field, and now launched into a barely recognizable version of Michael Jackson's "Thriller." Fortunately, I was hardly paying attention. I couldn't stop thinking about Orion.

Orion, who had run over the other team's defense throughout the first half, leaping and spinning and slamming through guys twice his size. Orion, who had never looked hotter than when he'd pulled off his helmet on the sidelines and dumped a cup of water over his head. Orion, who I swear had almost kissed me before the game. He'd been thinking about it. I was sure of it.

I took a deep breath and gritted my teeth. That was it. After the game I was going to find him and ask him out on a proper date. Why not? What did I have to lose? I'd already been forced to give him up once. If he said no, I could handle it.

Maybe.

But he wouldn't say no. He was my soul mate. He couldn't say no.

"So, you're friends with Lauren, and Lauren is friends with that girl Mia Ross . . . right?"

I glanced at Wallace, who had materialized as if from nowhere. He was standing next to my bench, wearing an LCHS T-shirt over a white thermal, trying to act casual. Instead he looked kind of like the Tin Man in need of a good oiling. His right hand leaned into the bleacher's railing, the arm perfectly straight, his legs crossed at the ankle, and he was tilting sideways. Definitely trying too hard.

Out on the field, the marching band moved through their formation changes as they stumbled their way into their next Michael Jackson song, "Black or White." I narrowed my eyes as the drum major moonwalked across the pockmarked field.

"Why? Do you like Mia Ross?"

"She's the fourth-shortest girl in the sophomore class," he said, dead seriously.

"And that appeals to you?"

He looked across the bleachers, where Mia sat gossiping with some friends. She had a pretty face. Light-blue eyes, soft features, and a melodious laugh.

"She's like an elfin princess," Wallace said with a sigh.

I grinned. This was perfect. If I could hook Wallace up with his elfin princess, and Claudia and Peter could get their act together, then Orion and I could be out of here before next weekend.

"I'll see what I can do," I assured him.

"Hey, True. Can we talk?"

I turned to squint up at Lauren, whose curls were framed by the sun. "Actually, we were just going to come find you," I said. "What do you think of introducing Wallace to Mia?"

Lauren eyed Wallace, who stood up straight, shoulders back like an Elizabethan-era butler awaiting his lady's inspection.

"Later," Lauren pronounced, shoving her hands into the pockets of her denim jacket. "Right now I need to tell you about how your brilliant plan is backfiring."

She cast a glance over her shoulder at Claudia, who was standing near the Snack Shack with Casey, watching something on a phone screen. Instantly my shoulders went tense. My plan could not be backfiring. I'd kept an eye on Peter Marrott throughout the first half, and he'd spent a good 80 percent of his time on the sidelines blatantly longing for Claudia. My plan was as good as gold.

"Wallace, will you excuse me for a second?" I asked.

"Sure."

As Lauren and I walked down the bleachers, he pulled out his own phone and fired up a game of Angry Birds. If he wanted to meet Mia Ross so badly, why didn't he just go over there and introduce himself? If only I had my golden arrows. That coupling would be done and done.

I wondered if I could conjure them. Not that I would have ever tried. If I started shooting people in the heart with magical arrows, Zeus would definitely notice. Not to mention everyone in a ten-mile radius and their camera phones.

"What's going on?" I asked Lauren as I leaned against the guardrail at the bottom of the steps. A group of rowdy guys in football T-shirts jostled by, looking us up and down.

"Put your tongues back in your mouths, frosh," Lauren griped at them. She rolled her eyes, then sighed. "Look. I know my best friend pretty well, and I'm, like, ninety-nine percent sure that she's falling for Keegan Traylor."

My heart dropped, seeing my grand plans for couple number two go up in smoke. Keegan the cocky player was not worthy of Claudia's love, and I could tell just by looking at him that he wasn't the type to get serious in high school. Lauren was right. This was not good.

"No. She wouldn't," I said. "She knows that Keegan isn't for her. She knows he's just a means to an end."

"I'm not so sure. You should see the way her face lights up when she talks about him. He's going to break her heart. That boy is a player with no conscience, who plows through girls like he's harvesting them for grain."

We were both silent for a second, pondering whether that metaphor made any sense. I shook my head.

"Well . . . maybe it won't end badly. Maybe he'll fall in love with her," I suggested hopefully. "There's a first time for everything."

"Not for this guy," Lauren said, shaking her head glumly. "Last year, my sister's best friend, Felicity, went out with him, and he told her he loved her, then hooked up with her other best friend before dumping her because she wasn't, quote, 'Keegan Traylor material.'"

Okay. Even I knew there was no reforming a person like that. "Well why didn't you say any of this when I set her up with him?"

"Because! She was supposed to be using the asshole. I didn't expect her to *like* him! She's usually too smart to fall for a guy like that."

We both turned and looked at Claudia. She scanned the far sideline, as if she was waiting with bated breath for Keegan to appear once more. She looked so hopeful and guarded at the same time. So open and so timid. And just like that, I realized what was happening. I'd been too intent on helping her to see it before, but now it was crystal clear.

Claudia was rebounding. Maybe on a normal day she'd be able to see through a too-perfect boy like Keegan Traylor, but Wednesday hadn't been a normal day. It had been the day after the love of her life had dumped her. Clearly she would have fallen for the first non-troll who happened to look her way.

And I'd set her up with a troll in prince's clothing.

CHAPTER THIRTY-SEVEN

Claudia

Standing outside the visiting team's locker room after the game, I checked my reflection with my phone. Ugh. So pale. Too many freckles. And what was I thinking with the braid? Was I trying to look like I'd stepped out of the pages of *Little House on the Prairie*? I quickly reached back and untied it, fluffing my hair over my shoulders. It fanned out in silky auburn waves.

Huh. Pretty. But there was so much of it. Now I looked like I was trying to be sexy at five o'clock on a Saturday afternoon. Too much. I shoved my phone into my bag and shakily pulled my hair back into a ponytail. The band was just snapping into place when Keegan emerged from the back door and I smiled, trying not to appear as self-conscious as I felt.

But how could I not? Because look at him, and then look at me. I could already sense people watching us curiously. Skeptically. But I'd been Peter Marrott's girlfriend for over a year. Was it that much of a stretch that Keegan Traylor could be interested in me?

"Hey," Keegan said with that ridiculous knee-melting smile. I looked at his lips, and suddenly it was last night and I was experiencing his kiss again. His lips, his hands, his tongue . . .

"Claudia?" he said.

"Oh, sorry. Hi!" I replied brightly. "How's it going?" Then I remembered his team had lost, and my smile faltered.

He stopped a couple of feet in front of me. "You came."

Wait. Didn't he remember we'd made a plan? Or maybe he'd only made a plan to be polite. Crap. Did he even want me here?

"Um, yeah. Of course I came," I said, trying to think of a way to cover. "I go to school here, remember?"

I made a lame gesture at my booster ribbon and glanced around for Peter, wondering briefly what he'd think if he saw Keegan and me together right now. Whether he'd care.

"I know. But you came to see me," Keegan said, his smile widening. "I wasn't sure if you would. You know, fraternizing with the enemy and stuff."

I smirked and tried to relax. Tried to focus. "I don't take football that seriously. No offense."

"None taken." He shrugged.

"Sorry about the loss."

A couple of his teammates came out behind him, and he lifted a hand as they shouted their "See ya laters!"

"Their defense was on fire today and my offensive line basically crumbled," he said casually, holding the strap on his duffel bag with both hands. "What're you gonna do? You win some, you lose some. It's a cliché for a reason."

And he laughed.

Really? That was it? Whenever Peter had lost a game last year, he'd walked out of the locker room angry, stormed to my car, and brooded the entire way home. Then he'd spent the rest of the day in stony silence, occasionally blurting out something else he should have done differently or some bonehead move he'd made that could have changed the whole game. This was a whole new world. And maybe, just possibly, a better one.

Or was it bad that Keegan wasn't taking any responsibility for the loss? Somehow I had a feeling that was what a quarterback and captain was supposed to do.

Then Keegan took a step closer to me, so close our toes were almost touching. My pulse went low and quick, making it hard to breathe.

"Besides, how can I be depressed about some game when I have you here to cheer me up?" he said.

He was going to kiss me. It was blatant to the entire world. And I had a million thoughts at once. Where was Peter? Would he see? What had I eaten for lunch? How gross was my breath? Did everyone think he was too hot for me? Oh God, he really was so insanely hot.

And then he did kiss me, and I no longer cared. About any of it. Because when he kissed me the only thing that mattered was the kissing.

CHAPTER THIRTY-EIGHT

Peter

Everyone was still whooping and shouting and laughing when I got out of the shower. I felt like some kind of actual hero as my team-mates clapped me on the back and tossed their towels at me. I slapped hands and did everything I was supposed to, but what I really wanted to do was get out of there and find Claudia. She was going to take me back. She had to. It wasn't like she actually liked Keegan Traylor. They'd only gone out once. And besides, he'd just had his ass handed to him. Publicly. That couldn't have been attractive.

I yanked on my jeans and pulled a blue Rams T-shirt over my head. It stuck to my skin on the wet patches left over from my shower, and my hair was dripping on my shoulders, but I didn't care. I jammed my feet into my sneakers and headed for the back door, hoping I could still catch her. Hoping that maybe she'd even be waiting back there for me.

"Marrott! Wait up!"

I stopped, my heart sinking. It was Coach. Anyone else I would have ignored right then, but I couldn't ignore Coach Morschauser.

"What's up?"

When I turned, I almost dropped my bag. Coach was standing

inside his small office off the locker room, and with him was a man with tan skin wearing a blue polo and visor. The visor had the New Jersey Lions logo on it. The scout from TCNJ.

"Peter Marrott, I want you to meet Justin Crouch, the scout from the College of New Jersey," Coach Morschauser said as I stepped into his office. He put one hand on each of our shoulders as if it was draft day and he was the commissioner, posing for the camera.

"It's nice to meet you, sir," I said, shaking Mr. Crouch's hand.

Outside the office windows, lockers slammed, my friends shouted to one another, something crashed, but it was like I was existing in a different space. One where college was possible. Not just possible, but standing right in front of me. It was not just a far-off thing I would one day have to deal with. It was here. And it was smiling.

"Pleasure's mine," Mr. Crouch replied. "You showed some skills out there today, son."

"Thank you!" I said, my pulse racing. I felt so hot, suddenly, it was as if I'd never showered.

"Have you gotten your application in to admissions?" he asked.

I gulped, glancing at Coach. "Um, no. Not yet. I've got it on my desk, though."

Coach Morschauser picked up on my panic and clapped Crouch's shoulder. "I'm sure he's just putting the finishing touches on it, right, Peter?"

"Right. Yes. That's it. Trying to get it perfect."

"Good. That's good," Mr. Crouch said. And I sighed in relief. "There are some people in our athletic department who might be interested in meeting you."

"Wow, really? Um, thank you," I stammered, my palms starting to sweat. "Yes, definitely."

Coach Morschauser and Mr. Crouch chuckled. I felt like the butt of my own joke.

"I'm not making any sense, am I?" I asked, running my hand over my wet hair. "Sorry, I'm just . . . thanks, yes. I'm definitely considering TCNJ."

"Well, we'd love to move to the top of your list," Mr. Crouch said. "Why don't you come down for a tour of the school and give me a call while you're there? I'll set up a meeting with some of the players, and they can tell you what it's like to be a Lion."

Coach Morschauser beamed. Mr. Crouch handed me a card, and my hand shook as I took it. TCNJ. Me at the College of New Jersey. It was a great school with an up-and-coming team. And they wanted me.

This was really happening. I felt nauseous and excited at the same time, like I'd just gotten strapped into a roller coaster I wasn't totally sure I wanted to ride. I needed to talk to Claudia.

"Thank you, sir. I'll definitely do that."

"Good. It was great meeting you, son," he said, reaching for my hand again. "Keep up the good work."

"Thank you. I will. Have a good day," I said, sounding like some random guy behind the counter at McDonald's. I turned around and walked slowly out of the office toward the back door. I felt like my insides were vibrating, and I thought for sure I was gonna throw up, but when I shoved open the door and stepped into the sunlight and the fresh air filled my lungs, a huge smile spread across my face.

College. They wanted me. And TCNJ wasn't that far from Princeton. Maybe next year wasn't going to be so bad. For the first time this year I felt a huge weight lift off my shoulders. I felt like the old me. I'd been so worried about not getting into school, about being separated from Claudia and my family, and now, suddenly, none of it had to happen. If I went to TCNJ, I'd be able to drive home to see them whenever I wanted. I'd be able to drive to Princeton in less than an hour.

Suddenly I felt better about everything. Every. Last. Thing. It was going to be okay. I was going to have a future. Now I just needed to figure out how to fix things with Claudia and make her a part of it.

There were a few groups of people hanging out behind the gym. I didn't see Claudia right away, but I did see her friend Lauren with True and a couple of guys, standing a few yards off. Lauren looked kind of sick when she saw me, and then her eyes darted to the right.

Automatically, I turned in that direction, and suddenly everything that scout had said, the excitement I'd wanted just seconds ago to shout to everyone in sight, faded to nothing.

Claudia was standing ten feet away with Keegan Traylor, and it looked like she was trying to swallow his face.

Suddenly it became totally clear that everyone around me was staring at me. Pitying me. Or waiting to see if I would pound the guy to a pulp. And I was angry. I was. But even more I was disgusted. Sad and disappointed and confused. I'd thought Claudia loved me. This time last week we'd still been together, and now there she was, humiliating me with the opposing quarterback outside my gym.

Maybe she'd *never* given a crap about me.

"Dude, you cool?"

I glanced up to find Gavin hovering near my shoulder. He was looking at Traylor like he would have done the pounding for me, if I'd asked. I stared as hard as I could, as if I could somehow make what I was seeing different. Change the fact that her fingers were digging into his sleeves, that his hand was touching her face, that their bodies were pressed so close together you couldn't have slid a playing card between them.

"Yeah, man," I said through clenched teeth. "Let's get the hell out of here."

We turned around and walked away, headed back for the field where Gavin had parked his car. I clutched my card from the scout in one hand, my duffel in the other, and decided right then and there that it was time to move on. For real this time.

"I need to do something, man," I said to Gavin. "I need to get out of here."

"The city thing's still on. You wanna go?" Gavin asked. "Tiquan said he'd drive."

"Yeah," I said, feeling a rush of freedom. A rush of rebellion. Screw Claudia. She didn't give a crap about me, then I didn't give a crap about her. "Let's do it."

I took out my phone and brought up Josie's number.

"What're you doing?"

"Texting Josie to see if she and her friends want to come," I said, pissed off that my fingers were trembling.

"Wow, when you rebel, you rebel big," Gavin said.

"Go big or go home," I recited.

And from what Claudia was doing back there, it was pretty damn clear, there was no going home.

CHAPTER THIRTY-NINE

True

"Well. That happened," Lauren said wryly as Peter stormed past us.

"He's clearly jealous, so that part's working," I replied.

Lauren rolled her eyes at me, then flounced off to break up Claudia and Keegan's lip-lock. It was too bad the guy was such a jerk. The two of them made a stunning couple.

"Things aren't going so well for you today, are they?" Hephaestus said, his tone sympathetic. He dexterously pushed his chair through the grass, and Wallace and I walked alongside him, Wallace checking his phone for whatever might have changed in his world in the last ten seconds, me trying not to spontaneously combust.

"I'll figure it out."

I lifted my chin as we passed by Claudia, Lauren, and Keegan and rounded the corner to the front of the school. What I needed to do was talk to Peter. I had to find out what he wanted. Why he'd really broken up with Claudia. He was half this equation, and I'd largely ignored him until now. That was my new plan for the afternoon. Track down Peter and convince him to fight for Claudia. I was certain that if he made some grand gesture for her love, Claudia would forget about this temporary attraction to Keegan and true love would be born.

"Everything's going to be fine," I said.

And I believed it for half a second, until I practically tripped over Orion and Darla Shayne, who were latched together by their lips. Flashes of bits of their bodies assaulted me like harsh slaps to the face. His fingers in her hair, her hand on his ass, their pelvises smashed together. I staggered backward, my vision going gray at the edges.

"No. Wrong. No. Wrong."

I had no control over my tongue. Words were spilling out of me at will. My brain seemed to be spinning a kaleidoscope of horrifying images over and over in front of my face. A flash of tongue, a half smile behind pressed lips, and groping fingers. Groping, needing, wanting fingers. I shook my head and closed my eyes.

"Can't. Don't. Can't. Wrong."

"True? Are you okay?" Wallace asked.

"Wow. Things aren't going so well on an Olympian scale," Hephaestus deadpanned.

Orion was not supposed to be with Darla. He was supposed to be liking me. Wanting to kiss me. Hephaestus had even said so. He'd bet on us getting together. What had gone wrong? What had I done wrong? I tripped backward over a rock or a curb and my arms flailed out. Wallace caught me before I could break my ass on the ground and make this moment even more horrifying than it already was.

"True?" Wallace's face loomed over mine. His grip was tight on my arms. "True? Are you having a psychotic break?"

Jealousy.

The word reverberated inside my mind, and I did the only thing

I could think to do. I grabbed Wallace's head with both hands and kissed him. I kissed him deeply, with tongue, hoping that Orion would see and miraculously recall how much he loved me.

"Um, True? They're gone."

I yanked my mouth away from Wallace's, a string of saliva connecting us for two seconds more before it snapped. Wallace wiped his mouth with the back of his hand as I watched Orion and Darla walk off toward the parking lot, each with a hand inside the back pocket of the other's jeans.

"Um . . . True? I'm sorry, but . . . I don't like you that way," Wallace said, turning ten shades of purple. "I like Mia. Remember?"

I pressed the back of my hand into my lips, shaking with horror and disgust, with jealousy and anger and sorrow.

"You're right. I'm sorry," I said. "I don't know what got into me."

"Psychotic break?" he offered in a gentlemanly way.

"Psychotic break," I confirmed.

Yards away, Orion and Darla got into some sleek red car and sped off. I imagined the two of them ensconced inside the cocoon of the car's cabin, music blaring, fingers entwined as he drove with one hand. She had him all to herself. *My* love. She was able to touch him whenever she felt like it. To kiss him, hold him, listen to his voice. If anyone was going to be dying of envy around here, it was me.

How could I have been so wrong about what he was feeling, what he was thinking? How could both Hephaestus and I have been *so* wrong?

"I'm sorry, True," Hephaestus said. "I really thought that he—"

Suddenly he flinched. His gaze shifted, and he stared past me so abruptly that I turned around, the tiny hairs on my neck standing on end.

"What?" I asked, scanning the blue sky, the green trees, the rooftops of the houses on the street below. Apollo and Artemis. Were they here? "What is it?"

"Nothing." He turned his chair and headed for the parking lot. "I have to get home."

"Since when?" I asked, throwing my palms up. "I thought we were going to the diner."

"I'll drop you there if you want," Hephaestus called over his shoulder, pausing to let a herd of students traipse by.

And then it hit me like a meteor to the cranium. I knew that look—the wide eyes, the frozen features—as if he'd been shocked with a couple hundred volts of electricity.

Similar to the way it felt when my mother used to summon me back to Mount Olympus from Earth at the end of my Valentine's Day sojourns each year. Was that what he was doing? Was he running off to be alone so that some upper god or goddess could whirl him back to the Mount? Was that who he'd been talking to in his room the other night? And if so, who the hell was it? Who was he plotting with?

The herd finally cleared the sidewalk and Hephaestus forged ahead, crossing the driveway for the parking area beyond.

"I don't suppose you're going to tell me why!" I shouted after him.

His response was to yank open the door of the van with a loud creak. "I'm leaving in five minutes whether you guys are in the van or not!" he shouted, lowering the lift.

"Come on," Wallace said, loping past me toward the van. "I'll buy you some pie."

Pity pie. That was what he was thinking. He thought I liked him, and he needed to buy me pity pie. Could this day get any worse?

I sighed and followed after them. I didn't want to let Hephaestus out of my sight. If he was whirling out, I wanted to catch him in the act. But it couldn't be now, when he knew my interest was piqued. Right now he was going to be extra careful. No. It would have to be at a moment when he wouldn't expect me to be watching.

I was going to have to bide my time.

CHAPTER FORTY

Peter

"I want to try the key lime cupcake," Michelle said as I opened the door to Goddess Cupcakes for her on Sunday afternoon. "And the salted caramel. Oh! And the gingerbread."

"But you hate gingerbread cookies," I said through a yawn. Every muscle in my body ached, and I felt like I was about to pass out. It had been a long night and an even longer day. I'd been daydreaming about my pillow for a solid couple of hours.

Half out of it, I glanced around the shop to see if anyone from school was there. A couple of sophomore friends of Josie's waved, and I nodded back. I felt hot around my collar suddenly, wondering if they knew what Josie and I had gotten up to after we'd dropped them off last night. Even I wasn't entirely sure. The whole thing was a messy, headachy blur.

I knew I'd seen a lot of skin. That I could remember. And I knew that I'd woken up at five a.m. on her basement couch, alone, and had to blearily find my way home before my mom and my sister woke up. Not my finest moment. When I'd trudged into church that morning, I honestly thought I might get zapped by a bolt of lightning.

"Well, maybe I'll like it in a cupcake," Michelle replied, bouncing on her toes. There really wasn't much that got her more excited than a potential sugar high. "Besides, it's free."

"Can't argue with that logic," I said sarcastically, checking my phone for the millionth time and wondering if this was a scam. I'd gotten a text this morning telling me to come in before five o'clock to claim my free half-dozen cupcakes. Normally I would have ignored it, but after mowing the lawn, weeding the garden and front walk, and hanging the garage door back on its hinges, I figured I deserved a cupcake. Or ten. Sometimes I really hated being the man of the family. And I still had to finish that damn TCNJ application tonight.

I squirmed just thinking about what an idiot I'd been yesterday. Walking out of that locker room to find Claudia, sure she was going to take me back so we could start planning next year for real. And then, Traylor. Traylor plastered to my girlfriend.

At least the yard work had been good for working out my aggression. Plus, it had given me time to think. And I had decided that I was 100 percent over her. She could do whatever the hell she wanted with that douche. Really. I was done.

"You never know!" Michelle replied. "Oh! What about the peanut butter and jelly?"

I shook my head, which felt a lot heavier than usual, like it could break off my neck at any moment.

"You get to pick two flavors." I put my hands on her shoulders and steered her toward the line at the counter. "Mom already picked her two and I get two. You should probably get something you know you like."

"Okay," she groused, slouching. "One I know I like and one new one."

"Deal."

The girl behind the counter turned around, and her face lit up. It was True. God. Was she ever not here? At the sight of her I got this horrible twist in my stomach. There was no reason for her to look that happy to see me. Unless she wanted to rub Claudia's new relationship in my face on her behalf.

"Welcome to Goddess Cupcakes!" she announced. "What can I get you?"

"Uh, I got this text about a free half-dozen?" I said, showing her my phone. "Is this legit?"

"Yes! Of course! One hundred percent legit." She looked over her shoulder toward the kitchen. "Tell me what you want and I'll bring it out to you."

"That's okay," I said. "We're going to take them to go."

"Oh. Uh, well, you have to have at least one in the shop."

"Okay! I'll have a triple chocolate!" Michelle said, rising up on her toes.

"Coming right up."

True grabbed a plate and slid open the case.

"What do you mean you have to have one in the shop?" I asked.

"That's how it works!" she replied, looking up at me through the glass. "The promotion. They want you to eat in the shop."

My brow knit. I was so tired I felt like I wasn't processing anything she was saying. "Okay . . . why?"

"God, Peter!" Michelle said, grabbing the plate as True slid it across the counter. "Just shut up and have a cupcake."

True raised her eyebrows like a challenge. I sighed. My stomach *was* grumbling. "Fine. I'll have one of the french toast ones."

"I'll bring it right out to you."

"You can't just hand it to me?" I said.

"Nope," she replied. "Go sit. I'll be two seconds."

We locked eyes in a standoff. There was something shady going on here, but I didn't have a clue what it was or why. Meanwhile, Michelle already had a table and was flagging me down.

"Get me some milk!"

Josie's friends laughed mockingly over their coffees until my look of death silenced them. Yeah, my sister was hyper eighth grader with no boundaries, but she was still my sister.

"Two milks, too, please," I said, fishing out my wallet.

After last night I was down to four dollars. I paid for the two small cartons of milk and sat with my sister, waiting for True to bring over my cupcake. I could tell Josie's friends were whispering about me and I turned my back to them, hoping like hell they wouldn't come over. The last thing I felt like doing was explaining their existence to Michelle.

"Here you go," True said, placing a plate in front of me. Then she sat down.

"Um, what's up?" I said.

"I have a fifteen-minute break, so I thought we could chat."

"About what?" I asked flatly.

She turned to smile at Michelle. "I'm True."

"I'm Michelle, Peter's sister," Michelle said, sucking chocolate off her thumb. "You have awesome hair."

"Thanks," True said, flipping it over her shoulder. "And you have really pretty eyes."

Michelle almost choked. "Really? Thanks!"

"I only speak the truth." True crossed her arms on the table. "So, what's up with you and Claudia?"

Michelle's very pretty eyes widened. She worshipped the ground Claudia walked on and basically freaked when I told her we weren't together anymore. I shifted in my seat. "Nothing. We broke up."

"I know. But what's up? Do you still like her?"

The table of Josie's friends had gone quiet. I didn't think they were close enough to hear our conversation, but I wasn't sure.

"Why? It's not like it matters," I said, pushing myself back in my chair. "She's with that Traylor"—I looked at my sister and chose my words carefully—"guy," I said, thinking *asshole, jerk, dickwad.*

"He's her rebound guy!" True exclaimed, shoving my arm like we were old friends. "Trust me. She doesn't like him."

"She doesn't?" Michelle asked hopefully, her mouth full of cake.

The twist in my gut loosened, and I got this fluttery feeling around my heart. "You think?"

"Of course not," True said loudly. "Look, you broke her heart, but only you can mend it. You simply need to prove to her that you love her."

I snorted an embarrassed laugh even as images of that day on the beach, the day I'd almost told her how I felt, flashed through my mind. Suddenly my throat closed over, just like it had that day too. I cleared it and ripped the wrapper off my cupcake, throwing it down on the plate like some kind of statement.

"No one ever said anything about love," I told her, and took a big, casual bite of my cupcake.

"Well, but you do. Love her, I mean. Right?"

Her smile was stiff. She seemed like she was holding her breath. I cocked my head at her, considering as I chewed. I knew I had loved Claudia then. And if she'd asked me the same question in the locker room yesterday, I probably would have said yes. But that was before. Before I'd seen Claudia trying to touch her tongue to Keegan Traylor's tonsils. Before she'd publicly humiliated me. Before I'd started to feel completely unsure about whether anything we'd ever had was real. Yesterday had made me doubt everything. How could I love Claudia now?

"I mean, I don't know. I do . . . miss her," I said, lowering my voice in case Josie's friends could hear. "But what do I know about love?"

"Oh, don't be a wuss, Peter!" Michelle exclaimed. "You and Claudia were totally in love. You're just terrified to say it because of the divorce."

"What?" True and I asked.

"We're totally learning about it in health class, in our psychology section?" she rambled, then took another bite of her cupcake. "Children of divorce are more likely not to trust their mates and are slower to show their love. I thought it was crap because I'm in love, like, every other week, but obviously for you it's true."

"No, it's not," I said automatically.

"Yes, it is!" she cried, spraying crumbs over the table.

Gross. I handed her a napkin. "Dude. Eat with your mouth closed."

"I *am!*" she replied, sighing with her hand over her lips. She waited until she swallowed before adding. "God! I'm just trying to help."

"So do you think that's it?" True asked me. "Do you think you love her but are just . . . afraid to say it?"

"I don't know." I took another huge bite of cupcake and stared at the bathroom door in the corner. This was a pretty heavy conversation for a Sunday afternoon. Especially a Sunday afternoon following a night of drinking and a day of hard labor.

"Look, people break up sometimes, but it's okay to get back together," True said. "So you wanted to sow your wild oats, see what else was out there, date some sophomore with big—"

"Hey," I said, silencing her. My face burned, but luckily Michelle was too busy licking icing off her fingers to have heard what True was saying. "That's not why I broke up with her."

There was a long silence. True looked baffled. "So, why, then?"

"Because!" I said under my breath. "I couldn't . . . All I could think about was how we were going to have to break up. Eventually. Like, before college. It was like I was obsessed with it. How she was gonna move on without me, find some guy better than me—"

"There's no guy better than you," Michelle said matter-of-factly.

"Thanks, Michelle, but that's what you think. What about what Claudia thinks?"

"Oh!" True sat back hard in her chair, a smile crossing her face. "So it wasn't that you needed space! It was separation anxiety!"

"What are you, some kind of shrink?" I asked.

True ignored the question. "Claudia doesn't want someone better than you! She doesn't want anyone *but* you."

She said it with such conviction that I almost believed her. Then the door to the shop opened with a tinkle of bells, and my heart dropped out of my body. Claudia had just walked in with Keegan Traylor's arm around her. They were so focused on each other, they didn't see anyone else in the room, including me. I watched as they sat down on the bench behind a window table and immediately began to maul each other. Lauren walked in behind them and slouched down across from them. Her arms were crossed over her chest, and she stared in the opposite direction like she was fed up. Like she'd been watching this go on for hours.

Perfect. This was totally perfect.

I turned around, stone-faced, and looked at True. "Yeah, that really looks like I'm the only guy she wants."

True seemed paler than she had a second ago. "I see your point, but I—"

"We'll take the rest of the cupcakes to go. Michelle, tell her what you want," I said gruffly, getting up and keeping my back to Claudia on the way to the door. "I'll wait for you outside."

As far away from the windows of Goddess Cupcakes as I could get.

CHAPTER FORTY-ONE

Claudia

"Can you believe that woman thought that was her space?" Keegan laughed, reaching for his bottle of water.

"I know, right?" I said, smiling as he squeezed my shoulder.

"Well, she did have her blinker on," Lauren stated, pressing her thumb into a leftover crumb on her plate and sucking it off.

"Yeah, but you're supposed to pull up in front of a spot and then back in." Keegan lounged in the booth with his arm spread across the top of the bench. "That's the law."

"Did you notice she had a handicap symbol on her license plate?" Lauren asked.

"Lauren," I said through my teeth.

"So?" Keegan raised his palms.

"So, I don't know, it might have been nice if you'd driven up the block and let her have the space. I mean, it's a beautiful day and we don't mind walking, right, Claudia?" she asked, looking expectantly at me.

"So I'm supposed to let her break the law because she's got a walker?" Keegan asked, snorting. "That's some crap. These people want to be treated like everyone else until they can get the advantage on something. You think that's right?"

"Are you serious?" Lauren asked, her face going blotchy.

I sat up straight, sensing this conversation was about to get out of hand. Lauren's mother had a bad case of multiple sclerosis and had needed a wheelchair to get around since we were ten, so she was particularly in tune with the special-needs community. I would have thought that, being a future physical therapist, Keegan might have been more sensitive to people with disabilities or injuries, but maybe it's one of those things—until you live with it, you can't really know. Anyway, the last thing I wanted was for my best friend and my new boyfriend to hate each other. And to express that hatred in front of everyone in the jam-packed cupcake store.

Plus, Keegan had been totally cool when I'd asked if Lauren could come along today. Did she have to be so ungrateful?

"I think what Keegan is trying to say is, the law is black and white and it's supposed to apply to everyone," I explained.

Lauren stared at me. "So let's say grandma is trying to get up a flight of stairs and she starts to have a heart attack, are you not going to help her because she once told you she was perfectly able to do it herself?"

My cheeks burned. "No—I just—Can we talk about something else?"

"I'm gonna go get another cupcake," Lauren said, standing.

"You sure about that? There were about a thousand calories in the one you just ate," Keegan told her, eyeing her plate.

I pressed my lips together. If Keegan had said that to any of my other friends, he would have been in for a world of hurt. At least Lauren didn't care about her weight and knew how to take a joke. She always appreciated honesty and a good sense of humor. That was why I had figured she'd get along so well with Keegan.

Still, I held my breath when she didn't immediately respond. The quicker the comeback, the more fine she was. A slow burn from Lauren was never pretty. She looked me in the eye, and I tried as hard as I could to get across a silent plea.

"Gee, thanks so much for your input, Keegan," she said finally, with false sweetness. "But I can assure you, I know what I want."

With a flip of her curls, she strode over to the counter, where she grabbed True and practically dragged her into the corner for a chat. True. I needed to talk to her too. To thank her for hooking me up with Keegan in the first place. And to tell her that Peter and I were not going to happen. After everything she'd done for me—heaven knew why—I figured she deserved to know what was going on.

Over in the corner, Lauren was gesturing wildly along with her rant. Maybe I'd talk to True later.

"I don't think she likes me," Keegan said matter-of-factly, sipping his water.

"Lauren? You have to give her some time to get to know you," I suggested, cuddling closer to him. "She's probably still adjusting to me being with someone other than Peter. She was a big fan."

As soon as the words were out of my mouth, I caught my breath. What was I doing mentioning my ex in front of him?

"Oh yeah?" he said, leaning back to look me in the eye. "And what was so great about Peter?"

I shifted, picking up my empty cupcake wrapper just to have something to focus on. I started to tear it into little strips, raining crumbs over the plate. "We don't have to talk about him."

"No, really. I want to know. Is he as perfect as everyone says he is?"

I blinked, but kept tearing. I couldn't have looked Keegan in the eye right then if I'd tried. "People say he's perfect?"

"You hear things," he said, sniffing and looking across the room. "Like how polite he is, how he goes to church every week, volunteers, had a sixty-seven percent completion rating last year. . . ."

I glanced at Keegan's profile as he rattled off Peter's attributes, and suddenly it dawned on me. He was jealous of Peter. It was so ironic I almost wanted to laugh. The only reason I'd gotten together with Keegan in the first place was to make Peter jealous, and now Keegan was the one with the envy problem.

My heart swelled, flattered that he could ever be jealous over me. But did he really think I was going to dump him and go running back to Peter because he had a better QB rating?

He was so sweet it killed me.

I dropped the shredded cupcake wrapper and reached up to touch his face, turning him to look at me.

"Peter Marrott is no Keegan Traylor," I said.

Something caught in my throat as I said it, but I chose to ignore whatever it was as Keegan's wide grin spread across his face.

"Damn straight," he said.

And this time, I kissed him.

CHAPTER FORTY-TWO

True

I'd gotten everything wrong. Everything. As I walked home from work on Sunday afternoon, I couldn't even see straight, because my brain was having a hard time keeping up with the list of mistakes I'd made. Peter hadn't broken up with Claudia because he needed space and wanted to date other girls; he'd done it because he couldn't take the dread of losing her anymore, so he'd gotten it over with. Hooking her up with another guy would have been a perfect strategy if he'd simply gotten distracted by the idea of a hotter girl, but he'd been afraid of her moving on, and I'd talked her into doing just that. My jealousy plan had made the situation worse instead of better. And the kicker? Claudia was now falling for Keegan, who from every account would do nothing but break her heart, stomp on the pieces, and skip merrily away.

I skirted around a family walking happily along with their ice-cream cones and wanted to pound my head into the brick walkway. This was supposed to be my calling. My special talent. Why did I keep screwing it up?

A familiar laugh made my shoulder muscles curl, and I turned to find Darla Shayne traipsing out the door of the boutique where she worked, with Orion right behind her. Yep. I'd gotten that completely wrong too. I turned my back on them as quickly as possible and speed-walked the rest of the way home.

Hephaestus's van was in the driveway. I jogged up the walk, opening the door quietly. If he was talking to someone from the Mount, I wanted to catch as much of the conversation as I could. But when I stepped inside, the house was still. I crept over to Hephaestus's room and found the door ajar. Slowly, carefully, I pushed it wide. His bed was made, his laptop computer shut on his desk, and he was nowhere in sight.

Adrenaline pumping, I closed the door behind me. Part of me realized that what I was doing was, on some level, wrong, but I wasn't about to let this opportunity go to waste. If Hephaestus was using something in this room to communicate with Mount Olympus—whether it was with Harmonia or someone else—I was going to find it.

I started with the dresser, searching carefully through each drawer, making sure not to disturb anything in an obvious way. Everything was perfectly folded, from the socks to the boxer briefs and T-shirts. I moved to the closet, shoved my hand inside pockets, rattled hangers, and overturned shoes and boots. Nothing. Finally I turned to the desk and picked up the computer. It looked like a normal laptop. Nothing out of the ordinary. But Hephaestus was a master mechanic. Could he have figured out a way to make it communicate with our world?

I turned the computer on and a blue screen greeted me, then quickly morphed into a picture of a desert at sunset. I stared, waiting for something to happen, and realized I hadn't a clue how to use the thing. I'd worked on some of the desktop computers at school, but those had mouse contraptions for controlling things. This had nothing but a keyboard and a black pad.

I sighed, frustrated, but something told me the answer wasn't here anyway. The machine wasn't giving off any sort of magical, mystical, or otherworldly vibe. I slapped it closed and walked into Hephaestus's bathroom, giving it a cursory look. It was about the same as I'd last seen it, except the toilet was cleaner.

"Come on, H," I muttered to myself. "What're you hiding?"

And that was when my eyes fell on the mirror. It was a spectacular piece of work, hung over the desk since the day Hephaestus had arrived. It was clearly of his own making. The intricacies of the woven metal frame were impossibly detailed, and the whole thing seemed to glow in the waning sunlight.

I stepped closer to the mirror, narrowing my eyes at my reflection. The glass was flawless, not a nick or a stain or a smudge. It was the only artifact of Hephaestus's own making that he carried with him. The only evidence of the god he used to be.

My skin tingled. This had to be it. Hephaestus's connection to our world. If I could get this thing to work, would I be talking to Harmonia? Or would someone less sympathetic answer the call?

Suddenly I didn't care. I wanted news from home. News I heard with my own ears, not through Hephaestus's possibly disloyal filter. I reached for the mirror tentatively, laying one hand on its frame. Nothing. I clutched the cold metal with both hands. Again, nothing. I waved my hand in front of my reflection. No response. I laid my palm against the glass. Nothing.

But it did leave a nice, obvious handprint.

"Dammit."

I ripped off my T-shirt, straightened the tank top beneath it, and quickly wiped the glass clean. Then I stood back and tapped my fingertip against my chin. Perhaps it had some kind of password.

"Open," I said.

The mirror stared back at me, obstinately ordinary.

"Converse," I tried.

I leaned in closer, now able to see every pore on my nose. I stared as hard as I could, imagining I could see through to Mount Olympus. Willing it to be so.

"Harmonia?" I whispered. "Sister, please. Hear me."

Nothing.

Frustration burbled hot inside my chest. If ever there was a time I needed to use my power, it was now. I clenched my fists, closed my eyes, and concentrated my energy, thoughts, and emotions on the mirror. *Work,* I thought, sending the wish out into the ether. *Work!*

My eyes opened. Nothing.

I groaned loudly and turned away from my reflection, so annoyed with my inadequacy I couldn't look myself in the eye any longer. If I had my earthen window, I could see any place at any time just by willing it. I could have looked into Hephaestus's room whenever I wanted and see what he was doing. I realized, suddenly, how much I had taken for granted my whole existence. If I ever made it back to Mount Olympus, I'd be sure to appreciate everything I had, from my family to my powers to my calling. But especially Harmonia. It wasn't until she'd been torn away from me that I realized how much her counsel meant.

I took a deep breath and slipped my T-shirt back over my head.

There was every possibility that the mirror would work only for Hephaestus, no matter what I did. I had to catch him in the act of using it, but how? He could hear me coming on these creaky floors from a mile away. There was always the chance of spying him through one of the windows, but he usually kept the blinds drawn.

My phone vibrated in my pocket, and I pulled it out. It was a text from Wallace.

DID U GET MIA'S #???

I groaned and texted back. It took me three tries to get the one word typed correctly.

SOON!

I closed the window and saw the tiny square drawing of a camera. Everything inside me froze, then suddenly overheated. A camera. Of course. If I could set up a camera inside this room, it could act as a mini earthen window.

Technology really could be my friend.

For a moment, I considered leaving my phone with the camera turned on somewhere in the room, but it was too bulky. Hephaestus would surely spot it. I needed a tiny camera. Something I could position on the light fixture above the bed and train at the desk and the mirror above it.

And I knew just how to get one. My conjuring power. This constituted an emergency, didn't it? I might have an enemy, a mole, living under my own roof. Someone who could derail my entire mission or, worse yet, lead Artemis and Apollo right to me. I had to know for sure whether I could trust Hephaestus.

Besides, would Zeus really notice one tiny spy camera? One tiny zip of my power? Even as I entertained these thoughts, I knew I was crossing a very serious line, but I couldn't help it. I needed answers.

I closed my eyes, clenched my fists, and imagined a tiny spy camera inside my hand. It appeared instantly. Just like that, I had my very own earthen window on Earth. I took a breath and waited to see if anything else would happen. If Zeus would whirl me back to the Mount for punishment or send one of his guards to flay me.

But there was nothing. No sound save for the sweet chirping of the birds outside the window. I was safe.

Now I had to figure out how it worked. There were two pieces. One, clearly, was the camera because it had an adjustable tube with a tiny lens at the end of it. The other must be something to catch whatever was transmitted through the camera. It looked as if it could plug into a computer, but I had no computer of my own.

That, however, was a conundrum for another time. Right now, I had to get this camera in place before Hephaestus got back from wherever he was.

I climbed up onto his bed and reached for the chandelier. It was a big bowl-like frosted glass thing, and I was able to attach the camera to one of its spindles, hiding most of the mechanism inside the glass. Then I twisted the tubing so that the lens faced roughly in the direction of the mirror. Gods, I hoped I was right about that thing. Otherwise this was going to be one big waste.

At that moment, the front door slammed. I was so startled I jostled the camera, and it fell into the bottom of the chandelier bowl. Cursing under my breath, I grabbed for it, but my hands had started to sweat and it slipped right from my fingers. Clenching my teeth, I latched onto the camera, refastened and repositioned it, my hands shaking the entire time. I was about to drop to the floor again, but it was too late. The door to Hephaestus's room swung open and there he was, staring up at me.

"What the hell are you doing?" he asked.

Yet another emergency.

Lightbulb, I thought desperately.

A small round bulb appeared inside my hand, which was hidden within the frosted glass bowl. I held it up.

"I noticed one of your lights was out the last time I was in here, so I changed it for you," I lied breathlessly, jumping down from the bed.

The mirror rattled when my feet hit the floor and I blinked, hoping I hadn't jostled it into a precarious position when I was manhandling it. If the thing came crashing to the floor, the jig would definitely be up.

"Okay . . . thanks," Hephaestus said slowly, glancing around the room.

"Everything okay?" I asked him, my heart pounding in my ears.

"Yeah. I just went out for some exercise," he said. "Everything okay with you?"

I was edging past him out the door, feeling as though I couldn't get away fast enough. "Yeah! Fine! Just got back from work, so I'm gonna go shower."

"Right. Cool," Hephaestus said.

"See ya."

Pocketing the supposedly dead lightbulb, I ran upstairs and into my room, closing the door behind me. Only then did I let out a breath. That was close. But when I turned around, I stopped breathing again. The sand timer was more than halfway through its cycle. I didn't have much time left to match my next couple, and Claudia and Peter were more estranged than they'd ever been.

With a sigh, I sat down on my bed and pulled out the second half of my spy device, wishing I wasn't so dense with computers. Luckily, however, I had an expert at my disposal. But if I was going to ask Wallace for another favor, I was going to have to return it. I took out my phone and texted Lauren.

CAN YOU SEND ME MIA ROSS'S #?

In two seconds, I had the digits. I was really starting to like these cell phones.

"True!" Hephaestus thundered at the top of his lungs.

My heart vaulted into my mouth. He'd found the camera. He must have. But how? He couldn't stand, and there was no way he could have seen it from his angle.

"What?" I shouted.

"Get down here!"

At that moment the front door slammed, and I heard my mother's voice. "What is it? What's happened?"

I ran out of my room and barreled down the stairs. The two of them were situated near the landing, my mother staring at Hephaestus, him looking up at me.

"It's Artemis and Apollo. They've gotten to Hera," he said, his chest heaving.

My hand grasped the railing. "What? What does that mean? How do you know?"

"Harmonia," he said. "She warns that they've focused their efforts on the queen, doing everything in their power to send Hera over the edge, so much so that Zeus has now banished them to Etna to try to remove them from Hera's presence."

"But they can get back from Etna," my mother said, fiddling with a golden A pendant I hadn't seen before. "There are the tunnels. . . ."

"Of course they can," Hephaestus snapped. He wheeled closer to the staircase and looked up at me, desperate. "If they get back to

CHAPTER FORTY-THREE

Peter

"Saturday night was pretty sick, right?" Josie said, lifting her legs across my lap at the lunch table. She took out a lollipop, unwrapped it, and then brought it to her tongue. "When are we going to do it again?"

"Which part?" I asked, sliding my hand up her thigh. I felt nervous doing it, which was weird. We'd done a lot more than that on Saturday night. But then again, I wasn't exactly sure how far we'd gone. We hadn't had actual sex, though. I was sure I'd remember that. But when I concentrated as hard as I could, my memories were nothing but flashes. Flashes of her closed eyes, her open mouth, and her naked upper body.

After that, nothing.

"Every part," Josie replied. "God, I wished I lived in the city. This stupid town is *so* boring."

Oh. So she was talking about the driving-into-the-city part. Not the being-with-me part.

The double doors to the cafeteria opened, and everyone turned to stare. Ten guys in tuxedos walked inside in a straight line and over to a nearby table. They made a semicircle around a couple of

Hera and she loses her temper, those two will be here in no time."

"Well, what can we do?" my mother asked. "Appeal to Hera ourselves?"

"How? We can't communicate with her," I replied shakily. Then I looked at Hephaestus. "Unless you know of a way."

"To communicate with the queen? How would I know that?" he demanded.

My fingers closed around the second half of the spy cam in my pocket. I had my suspicions, but as of now they were only that—suspicions.

"We can pray to her," my mother said bitterly. "Offer a sacrifice. Perhaps that will get milady's attention. Perhaps she will take pity on my wrongly banished daughter, and that will purchase the time you need." She walked over and laid her hand over mine. "'Tis a dangerous profession, this."

"Indeed," I replied with a small smile.

At least I knew that my mother had finally come around. If she was willing to pray to Hera, her archenemy, then she definitely had my back. But with Apollo and Artemis coming after me, I had the awful feeling her pleas wouldn't be enough.

girls, someone blew into a harmonica or something, and then they started to sing. It was the latest boy band ballad that was played every fifteen seconds on the radio, and when they were done, one of the guys pulled out a rose and asked Ashlynn Simone to homecoming.

"Yes!" she screeched, jumping up to kiss him.

Some people applauded, and then the guys split up and went to their lunch tables. I guess they went here, but I didn't recognize half of them.

"See?" Josie said, sucking on her lollipop. "Boring."

"You're not into homecoming?" Gavin asked from across the table.

She lifted one shoulder, and her feet rubbed together on my leg. "It's not that I'm not into it, if someone wanted to ask me." She looked away casually, but I could see her trying to check my reaction out of the corner of her eye.

My pulse started to race. Did that mean that she wanted me to ask her, or that she didn't want me to ask her? Automatically, I glanced over at Claudia's table. She was eating a yogurt as she talked with her friends. The sunlight streaming through the windows brought out the golden strands in her hair. I started to feel this awful sort of pit open up in my stomach, and I heard True talking inside my head.

Saying that Claudia wasn't over me. That Keegan Traylor was just her rebound.

But then I saw Keegan Traylor with his tongue down her throat, and the pit closed up.

"I just wouldn't want them hiring the frickin' boys' choir to do it," Josie finished finally. "I mean, how unoriginal can you be?"

"So you just want something bigger? Better?" I reached over

and tugged her chair closer to mine, forcing her knees to bend. She screeched and laughed as she careened into my side.

"More creative," she clarified. "Why? You have someone in mind?"

I shrugged. "Maybe. Maybe not. I'm not sure I'm creative enough for you."

Josie's smile slowly curled across her face. "Oh, I think you'll do fine."

I grinned back. So there it was. Like a pre-asking. I was going to homecoming with Josie Morrissey. Not Claudia Catalfo. And knowing that for sure felt like a true ending. Like it was really over and there was no going back.

CHAPTER FORTY-FOUR

True

"Is this something I can get arrested for?" Wallace asked.

The receiving end of my spy camera was in his hand, the connector hovering right next to the side of his laptop. Classes had just ended for the day, and we sat in the back corner of the library, my palms itching like crazy.

It was a fair question. Most likely, if Hephaestus and I were actual members of the human race and documented citizens of this country, then yes, we could probably get arrested for what we were about to do. Suddenly my senses were heightened by an exhilarating sizzle of impending danger.

"Probably?" I ventured.

Wallace, to my surprise, smiled. "Cool." And then he plugged the thing in.

A small camera-shaped icon appeared on his computer screen. Icon was a word Wallace had taught me that morning, when I'd kept referring to the buttons on my phone as illustrations. Wallace clicked it and typed something into a box, and then a spinning wheel appeared.

"This could take a minute. This was my laptop three laptops ago."

"I really appreciate you lending it to me," I told him. "I swear I'll find a way to pay you back."

"You got me Mia's number," he said, blushing slightly. "Now I just have to get the guts to use it."

"I'm sure you will." I smiled. "And if you don't, I'll figure out a way to get you guys in the same room."

"Yeah?" he asked hopefully.

I tilted my head. "It's what I do."

A box opened up on the screen. "Here we go."

Wallace clicked something and a new window opened—a pure color picture of Hephaestus's room, angle on the mirror. My breath caught.

"It works!"

"Yep. You've just started recording," Wallace said, leaning back in his chair. "Why are you spying on your own cousin again?"

I opened my mouth to reply, not knowing what I was going to say, but then two figures walked up behind us, their shadows reflected on the screen. I quickly reached up and slapped down the screen on the laptop.

"True," Lauren said. "We need to talk."

I turned around in my chair. Lauren stood with a handsome hulk of a guy in a varsity jacket. He had a low brow, deep-set eyes, and a broad, open face.

"This is Gavin Dunnellon," Lauren said. "He's Peter's best friend."

I stood up. "Oh. Nice to meet you."

"Yeah. You too," he said. He nodded at Wallace. "What's up, Wall-E?"

"Not much, Gap Denim," Wallace replied.

"We need to talk about Claudia and Peter," Lauren whispered, leaning toward me as the librarian walked by, pausing for a bit longer than necessary to eyeball us. "Everything's going to crap."

"Yeah, you mentioned that yesterday," I said, recalling the vise grip she'd put on my arm at Goddess.

"Well, now it's even deeper in the shitter," Gavin said. "Peter's gonna ask that Josie girl to homecoming unless we do something about it. And Lauren says that for some reason, you're the person to talk to."

At that moment, Orion and Darla walked in, their hands clutched between them as they whispered together. They glanced around furtively, then went directly into the back corner, where I could only imagine they were going to suck face some more. My heart shriveled at the edges, and I could see it in my mind's eye, drying up and turning black inside my body cavity.

I took a deep breath and focused on Lauren and Gavin. I had allies here. I could either retreat inside and feel sorry for myself, or I could work with them to get their friends back together and get one step closer to my goal. Three couples and Orion would wake up and forget about Darla. Three couples and he'd be mine again.

"So you guys are certain—one hundred percent certain—that Peter and Claudia are meant for each other? That these people they're currently with are wrong?"

"Totally," Gavin said with a nod.

"Beyond totally," Lauren added acidly.

I heard Darla giggle and the sound of something hitting the floor. My teeth clenched.

"Fine. Then what we need to do is show them how very wrong these people are for them," I said. "Once we get them broken up with their respective mismatches, we can concentrate on getting them back together."

"Okay," Gavin said. "How do we do that?"

The sound of slurping, clear as day, sent a disgusted shiver down my spine. I pressed my fist into my palm and told myself to concentrate. *Do your job and this will be over. Do your job and everything will be fine.*

"Let's sit."

They both pulled chairs over to surround the small study carrel Wallace still occupied. We looked at him. He stared back.

"Should I go?" he asked.

It was clear from his hopeful expression that he didn't want to. He was obviously intrigued, and for once the kid wasn't playing games on his phone. He was engaging in life. I saw no reason not to let him stay.

"No," I said. "Maybe you'll have some ideas."

Wallace beamed.

"Okay," I said, looking at Gavin and Lauren and doing my best to ignore the sighs of pleasure coming from the far corner. Where the hell was that snooping, suspicious librarian when I needed him? "Tell me everything there is to know about Peter and Claudia. What do they do for fun? What do they want? What do they need? And most importantly, what was it about their relationship that worked, and what didn't?"

Gavin and Lauren looked at each other cagily, as if they didn't want to answer that last question.

"I need you to be completely honest for this to work," I told them. "Can you do that?"

They each sucked in a breath and nodded. "I can," Lauren said.

"Me too," Gavin replied. "But we gotta make this quick. I've got practice in fifteen minutes."

Wallace opened up the laptop again and clicked open an empty document. "What're you doing?" Gavin asked him.

"Taking notes," Wallace said matter-of-factly.

I smiled. "Perfect. Now let's do this."

CHAPTER FORTY-FIVE

Peter

"Nice work out there today, man," I said, and slapped Gavin on his shoulder pad.

He doubled over, hands over knees, and gasped for air. We'd just finished postpractice laps, in full pads, which Gavin hated. He sometimes even threw up afterward. Remembering this, I took a step back. Puke would be tough to get out of cleats.

"Thanks, Pete." He stood up, arching his back. "I felt like cracking some skulls."

"Well, you definitely did that." I glanced over my shoulder as the stragglers came across the finish line and either collapsed on the grass or made a move for the water jug. "I think you might've given Chen a concussion."

Gavin shrugged with a small smile. "Occupational hazard."

We laughed and loped over to the water. Gavin cleared his throat. "So how're things going over at the soup kitchen lately?" he asked. "They made that announcement at church this weekend, about needing more volunteers?"

"Yeah, Marcy roped me into a few shifts this week," I said, shaking my head as I remembered how she'd cornered me after services.

Her frizzy gray hair had been pulled back into sort of a puff ball behind her head, and I was so out of it I'd found myself staring at it the whole time she talked. She wanted me to do four shifts, and considering the guilt I was carrying over my Saturday night activities, I'd immediately said yes. Usually I barely squeezed in one or two. I had no idea how I was going to manage four.

"What if I come with?" Gavin asked, leaning down to pull off his cleats.

My face lit up. "That'd be awesome."

"Cool. And maybe we could ask the girls to come with us," Gavin suggested. He pulled off his sock and stared down at his red, sweaty foot as if he'd never seen one before.

"The girls?" I asked, thinking of my sister Michelle and his sister Mary, who was away at college, so that didn't make sense.

"Yeah." He pulled off his other cleat and sock and tossed them on the grass, then sank onto the bottom bleacher. "Josie and Tara?"

"Oh." I blinked. Somehow I had a hard time putting Josie together with anything church-related. It was as if it didn't add up. When I thought of Josie, I instantly got turned on. Church was exactly the opposite of that. But what would it hurt to ask her? "Um . . . sure. You think Tara would want to?"

Gavin pushed his sweat-soaked hair back from his face. "She volunteers at the animal shelter, and she does a lot of outreach work with her synagogue. I think she'd be into it."

"Okay. Cool," I said, surprised that he knew so much about Tara Schwartz's life. I thought about the conversations Josie and I had had, and I realized I knew practically nothing about hers. Was she religious? Did she go to church? Did her parents? Did she even have parents?

Well, of course she had parents. But did she live with one or the other or both or someone else entirely? I had no clue. And suddenly I felt morbidly ashamed. I'd been inside their house. I'd done things with their daughter. And I'd never even given them a second thought. When it came to Claudia's family, I was an expert. I knew that her dad lied about his golf score, that her mom had a thing for mint ice cream, that her sister recorded every makeover show on TV, and that her brother kept a plastic worm farm in his closet.

I felt a pang, thinking about Claudia's family. Like I missed them. I wondered if they missed me.

"You in there, dude?" Gavin asked.

"Yeah. Sorry."

I had to focus on the now and forget the past. Claudia and I had been together for a year and a half. That was a lot of time to get to know each other. Maybe if Josie and I logged a couple of hours behind the counter at the soup kitchen together doling out the food, I could find out a few more things about her. She couldn't exactly come on to me in that setting.

"I'll ask Josie tonight," I said, feeling slightly more positive about the whole thing.

Gavin looked up at me and smiled. But it was a weird smile. Too wide, too satisfied, for what we were talking about. For a second I wondered if maybe *he'd* gotten a concussion.

"Perfect," he said. "This is gonna be perfect."

CHAPTER FORTY-SIX

Claudia

Ballet shoes shooshed and scraped across the gleaming wood floor of the Studio as the eighth-grade pointe class gathered their things and greeted their parents at the door, their chattering voices filling the airy space. I sat down on the corner chair to lace up my shoes, relishing the slip of the silky ribbon between my fingers. For the next two hours I didn't have to think. All I had to do was dance.

"Hey there." Lance dropped down on the chair next to mine and stretched his arms over his head. "So, I'm driving you to the auditions on Saturday."

It was a statement, not a question.

"Actually, I hadn't thought about it," I told him.

He put his hand on his chest. "You hadn't thought about it? I'm deeply offended."

I laughed. "I guess I've just been more focused on the actual audition. The piece I'm going to perform . . . the terror of the whole thing . . ."

"Understood," he said. "But we are carpooling, yes?"

"Sure," I said, realizing that if I drove down there alone I'd probably psych myself out, and if I drove down there with my parents, *they'd* probably psych me out. Lance and I would just sing and laugh and try not to think about where we were headed. "That'd be fun."

"You know it will be," he said with a smile. Then he got up, executed a mean brisé, and sank to the floor to stretch.

My cell phone beeped, and my heart did a brisé of its own. Somehow, whenever I got a text, I still pictured Peter's face. But I supposed that was only natural. It had been less than a week since we'd uncoupled. I concentrated on shoving the thought of him aside. Once his smile had vanished, I pulled out my phone. The text was from Keegan.

JUST GOT OUT OF THE SHOWER. WHERE ARE U?

If it's possible to blush from head to toe, I did it. Was Keegan *sexting* me? Was I supposed to, like, text back what I was wearing? I couldn't participate in that. Not only was the very idea already making my throat close over, but I wouldn't have a clue where to start. Best to ignore it. Pretend it wasn't happening.

BALLET REHEARSAL ABOUT TO START. GOTTA GO.

I hit send and shut off my phone, but I was shaking so hard I couldn't finish my laces. I sat back and took deep breaths instead. And unintentionally pictured Keegan's naked, wet body.

"What's with you?" Lauren asked, peeling a banana as she took Lance's vacated chair. "You look like you just swallowed your tongue."

"Nothing. I'm fine." I bent down to make another attempt at my right shoe, now shoving Keegan from my mind. It wasn't lost on me that there was a lot of mental boy-shoving going on lately, and I wondered what it said about who I was. Was I a slut? Boy obsessed? Or plain old confused? Whatever the case, now was not the time to figure it out. "What's up with you?"

"Nada mucho." Lauren slumped in her chair, in the way that drove Madame Helene completely insane, and chewed on her banana. "How're things with the magnificent Keegan?"

There was his naked body again. I choked on my own breath. Why was she using the term "magnificent"?

"Fine. Good. Normal. Why?"

She took another bite. "Just curious."

I managed to knot the ribbon behind my calf and sat up, posture perfectly straight. "You don't like him, do you?"

"What?" Her eyes were wide as she swallowed. "No! Of course I like him. If you like him, I like him."

"Really?" I asked, dubious. Lauren had never been one to not form her own opinion before. "I mean, you did try to warn me off him in the beginning."

"Oh, that." She waved a hand. "So he broke Felicity's heart. Doesn't everyone break a heart or two at some point?"

"Um . . . I guess."

"Just because he didn't like her, doesn't mean he can't like you." She slung her arm heavily around my shoulder as Mia and her friend Alicia traipsed in the door, followed quickly by Lance's one male compatriot in our class, Craig Churgin. The room began to fill with conversation as everyone chose stretching spots and got down to work. "In fact, I think you should invite him to the recital."

I felt a shock of nervousness at the mere suggestion of this.

"Isn't that a little . . . soon?" I asked as I rolled one ankle, then the other. "I mean, he's not even my boyfriend. Not technically."

"It's not like you're asking him to marry you," Lauren said, finishing off her banana. She released me, folded up the peel, and shoved it in the side pocket of her bag. "You're asking him to sit on his butt for two hours and watch some pretty spectacular dancing, if I do say so myself."

For some guys, that's actually worse than a marriage proposal, I thought.

"If he's into you, he's going to want to be there," she said, standing. "Ballet is your first love. Any guy you're with should respect that, right?"

I looked up at her, cool trepidation filling my chest. "I guess."

She paused, lifting one heel and then the other, loosening up her feet. "Unless . . . you think he's the kind of guy who wouldn't support you. Do you think he's that kind of guy?"

"No." I stood up and reached back for my right ankle to stretch my quad. "No. He's definitely not. He thinks it's cool that I'm into ballet. He said it the first day we met."

"Then ask him," Lauren said, walking to the center of the floor and dropping down into a split. Her brown eyes were clear when she looked up at me and seemed huge as they reflected the track lighting overhead, pink and yellow and white. "What've you got to lose?"

"Nothing," I said, even as my stomach clenched. "I'll ask him tomorrow."

I sank down next to her and mimicked her pose, reaching for one toe and then the other, trying to figure out why I suddenly felt so uncertain. Was it that I didn't think Keegan wanted to come, or was it that I didn't think I wanted him to come? Part of me felt like dance recitals were for families, friends, boyfriends. People who truly mattered. People who would appreciate my hard work and sweat and tears. Did Keegan fit that bill?

"Good evening, class!" Madame Helene called out, emerging

from her office. She walked over to her iPod and switched it on. The opening strains of her usual warm-up music flowed from the speakers. The class scrambled to its feet. "To the barre, please?"

We scurried noiselessly to the barres along two adjacent sides of the room and began our drills. I breathed in and out as I lowered into plié after plié, but I couldn't stop thinking about Keegan. About how I would ask him. About what he would say. But every once in a while, Peter's face would creep into my thoughts. His voice would sound in my ear, asking . . .

You're really going to ask that tool over me? You really want him there and not me?

I remembered the expression of pride on Peter's face after *The Nutcracker* last year, the one show he'd been able to attend. How he'd kissed me on the forehead and handed me a single red rose. How he'd pulled me close and whispered in my ear, "I told everyone in my row that you were my girl. I couldn't stop smiling."

I felt sick, suddenly. Sick and hot and tearful. How could he have said that to me then, but not want to be with me now? What had changed? What had I done wrong?

What I wouldn't give to hear him say that to me again.

But it didn't matter. Because he was never going to come to another of my recitals. I was with Keegan now. And I liked Keegan. He was laid-back. He was chill. He was so easy to laugh and let everything roll off his shoulders. There was so much about Keegan that I liked. Not the potential sexting, but everything else.

Lauren was right. I should ask him to our recital. I just hoped *he* liked *me* enough to say yes.

CHAPTER FORTY-SEVEN

True

I walked into the house after an insane shift at Goddess Cupcakes that night, tense from spending the entire walk home looking over my shoulder, waiting for Artemis and Apollo to jump out from behind a car or a potted plant or a Dumpster and slay me. I locked both locks behind me and let out a massive breath. The house was quiet. I glanced down the hallway toward Hephaestus's room, and the crack under the door was dark. My mother would just be leaving the mall now, having been on the closing shift at Perfumania. I had plenty of time to do what I needed to do.

Heart pounding from side to side and back to front, I raced upstairs and into my room, closing the door silently behind me. At my desk, I placed Wallace's hand-me-down computer next to the sand timer, which was getting ominously low. So ominously low, I felt as if I could hear every last grain of sand hitting the growing pile at the bottom of the hourglass, sliding down the hill and hitting the thick sides. I pulled my sweater off and tossed it over the thing. Right now, I needed to concentrate.

"Please work, please work, please work."

I opened the computer and turned it on, sitting down and

kicking my shoes off as it booted up. Then I opened the camera program like Wallace had taught me to do back at the library and clicked open the screen marked "Recorded Footage." There was seven hours, thirteen minutes, and forty-two seconds of it.

"Yes," I said under my breath.

Salivating, I moved my finger over the touch pad—I now knew it was called a touch pad—and clicked the triangle that, I'd also learned today, meant "play."

The footage began. Hephaestus's room was empty and still. And it continued to be empty and still for a good fifteen minutes until I finally remembered that he'd worked a shift at the garage right after school today, and I hit the double triangle button, which meant "fast-forward."

I sat back and watched the unchanging screen. The only evidence of the passage of time were the minute movements of the leaves on the trees outside his window, fluttering now and then in the breeze. Finally, once I'd scrolled through three hours plus of the same thing, the door opened, and Hephaestus entered. I sat forward like a shot and hit play again.

Hephaestus hoisted his book bag onto his bed, then wheeled over to the window. He used a metal hook to reach up and lower the shade. My heart skipped in excitement. This was it. This had to be it.

Then he started undressing. I gulped. Hephaestus tugged off his jacket and hung it in the closet, then pulled his T-shirt off over his head. That was when I started to sweat.

Hephaestus had the single most perfect torso I had ever seen on a human being. There were muscles everywhere. Big, defined ones. And his arms were sinewy and strong, bulging whenever he moved. I could see a tattoo on his left pectoral muscle, just above his heart, and I leaned in for a better look, but then he turned and pushed his chair into the bathroom.

Five minutes later, the shower came on, and it was more fast-forwarding until, finally, he emerged in a clean T-shirt and jeans, looking refreshed. He pulled his books from his bag and brought them over to his desk.

Great. Now I was going to watch the guy do his homework? I was just about to hit fast-forward again, when his head popped up and he looked at the mirror. My eyes darted to it as well. The frame was glowing.

I leaned forward in my seat, my fingers itching, my heart in my throat. Hephaestus quickly shoved his computer and books aside. I waited for a face to appear in the glass, wondering if that was even how it worked and wondering if that face would be my sister's or someone else's. Then Hephaestus gripped the handles on his wheelchair with both hands and pushed himself up until his legs hovered inches above the seat. With one mighty grunt of effort, he flung one arm out to touch the mirror.

There was a flash of light, and the screen in front of me went black. Not the entire computer, just the small window opening that had been showing his room.

"No!" I shouted. "No! No! No!"

I clicked the play button a thousand times. Clicked fast-forward. Clicked everything. The timer was still running, which meant the camera still thought it was recording, but there was nothing. Nothing but an infuriating black screen.

The power of the mirror, once activated, must have fried the transmission. It took some serious self-control not to rip the computer in half at its hinge. Instead I got up, tore the pillows from my bed, flung the bedspread to the floor, and pounded on the mattress as hard as I could with both fists. I picked up the biggest pillow and whipped it over and over and over into the wooden footboard, sweat popping out along my brow, tears squeezing from the corners of my eyes. I wanted to see my sister. I wanted to know if it was she who Hephaestus was talking to, or some unknown enemy. I needed to know where Apollo and Artemis were. What they were plotting. I couldn't take the not knowing anymore, having no news from home, no contact with those I loved, no clue as to whether I was going to be suddenly attacked and mortally wounded at any second.

It wasn't fair that I didn't get to know. It wasn't fair.

Finally, after a few minutes of this humiliating fit-having, I ran out of steam. I sank to the floor of my room atop a pile of folded and crushed pillows and breathed. A few tears streamed down my face, but I didn't sob. I was angry and frustrated more than anything. I felt weak. I felt impotent. I felt out of control.

These feelings didn't sit well with me. I was a goddess. I was supreme. I was not this sniveling, desperate wuss.

"I just want Orion back," I said aloud, resting my head down on the nearest pillow and clutching the corner in one hand. "I just want to go home."

CHAPTER FORTY-EIGHT

Claudia

As I walked down the long family-photo-lined hallway of Keegan's second floor on Tuesday afternoon, peeking into rooms with him, I could feel the weight of the recital ticket in my backpack, tugging at the vinyl, pulling down on the straps so heavily my shoulders were tilting backward.

What was he going to say? What would I do if he laughed?

"And this," Keegan said, opening a thick wooden door and flicking on the lights, "is my room."

Suddenly the ticket no longer mattered. I eyed Keegan nervously. It was a weekday afternoon, no one else was home except his little brother, who was glued to the Wii in the basement two floors below, and there we were, standing at the threshold of his bedroom. Did he really expect me to just walk in there like this moment wasn't loaded with a thousand different questions and expectations? But then, maybe it wasn't. Maybe he had no intention of doing anything other than showing me his autographed baseball collection.

Yeah, right, Lauren's voice said inside my head. *Because that's exactly what guys think about when showing the girl they've been Frenching all weekend their room.*

Keegan walked inside and stood back against the door. I could either slip in past him or make an excuse to bail.

"What do you think?" he asked. "I cleaned it up just for you."

"Yeah?"

Now it felt like I had to go inside, so I did. It was perfectly male. Blue-and-gray-plaid bedspread, football posters on the dark-blue walls. Dark wood furniture. A scent that was both flannelly and sweaty at the same time. It reminded me of Peter's room, except that it was bigger and there was more furniture. I had always thought guys were supposed to be messy, but neither one of these guys were. Every book on Keegan's shelves was lined up and pushed back, every shelf dusted, every piece of sports memorabilia set and angled in its place.

He closed the door, and the silence surrounded me.

"It's nice," I said, because I had to say something. "Very clean."

"Glad you like it."

He was right behind me now, his breath tickling the skin of my neck. He nudged my backpack off my shoulders and it hit the floor, the fingers of my right hand curling instinctively around the strap and holding fast. Before I could turn, his lips touched my shoulder, bare thanks to my wide-necked T-shirt, and then he was inching that neckline wider, kissing down toward my arm. When the fabric wouldn't stretch any farther, he made his way back, across my shoulder to my neck and slowly up to my ear.

Was this really happening? No parents, the door closed, alone in the room with a guy I'd known for less than a week? What was I doing? This was so not me. I had to get out of there.

And then his hand slipped around my waist, gripped my shirt at the front, and turned me around. I took one look into his deep-brown eyes and my brain actually said, *Oh, who cares?* Then my body took over.

We kissed. A lot. Standing there in the middle of his bedroom, we kissed and kissed and kissed, his hands traveling up and down my back, into my hair, down my spine, over my butt and back up again. I gripped the back of his striped polo shirt with both hands, feeling childish and grown-up at the same time. Childish because I had no clue what to do with my arms or legs, grown-up because wasn't this the definition of a grown-up moment? Kissing a guy I was just getting to know in the middle of his bedroom alone with a zillion possibilities of what might happen next vibrating around our bodies like thousands of tiny supercharged ions?

After what seemed like forever and also like five seconds, he started to walk me backward, inching his feet one at a time toward his bed.

Suddenly my brain started working again.

I couldn't let him get me to the bed. If I let him get me to the bed, that was like saying I was open to doing things that I wasn't entirely sure I was open to doing. Things I'd never even done with Peter.

Peter. My heart stopped when my brain landed on his name.

I pulled my lips away from Keegan's. At that moment, the sides of my T-shirt were clenched in his fists at either hip, exposing a strip of skin above my waistband. He looked me up and down like I was the single sexiest being on the face of the planet, and for that split second, I wanted to say, *Oh, who cares?* again.

But I didn't.

"Wait," I said instead.

"We don't have to do anything you don't want to do," he rasped, although I could tell in his eyes that he was hoping there wasn't anything I didn't want to do.

"No, it's not that." Even though it was. And now I had to figure out exactly what *it* was. My eyes fell on my bag, which was now behind him. "I wanted to ask you . . . before I forget . . ."

I went to my backpack and bent down self-consciously to pull the ticket out of the back zipper pocket. Putting distance between us, even momentarily, felt good. I felt solid again. Like I could think straight.

"Do you—I mean—would you . . ."

The ticket fluttered in my trembling hand. Apparently my mouth was not keeping up with my brain.

"Would you come to my recital on Friday night?" I asked. And I held my breath.

Keegan glanced at the ticket. His face was blank. It was as if he'd never seen a ticket before in his life and didn't know whether he was supposed to take it from me, swat it to the ground like a bug, or crumple it up and eat it. After a long, breathy pause, he finally plucked it from my fingers.

"Sure," he said. "I'd love to."

The force of my elation hit me so hard I was shocked. I didn't know until that very second how much it meant to me that he say yes. And when he did, I wanted to throw myself into his arms.

So I did.

"Thank you," I said.

"Anytime," he replied, touching his lips to mine. "I bet it's awesome, watching you dance." He moved my hair behind my shoulder, and his expression turned serious. "I bet you're the most beautiful dancer there is."

Everything inside me went liquid, molten and hot. "Really?"

He nodded, as if he was so taken, so emotional, so aroused, I guess, he could no longer speak. So I sat down on the bed and looked him in the eye. And after that, there was no need for either one of us to speak at all.

CHAPTER FORTY-NINE

Peter

"How long do we have to do this for?"

Big Tom, the elderly man across the serving table from us, shot me a look like *Who the hell is this girl?* Honestly, I was right there with him. Ever since the moment we'd walked through the door of my church's basement, where the soup kitchen was located, Josie had been whining. Whining about the smells, whining about the people, whining about having to stand the whole time. Unbelievable.

I carefully ladled mashed potatoes onto Tom's plate.

"Enjoy, Tom."

"Have a good night, kid," he replied. But he looked like he couldn't imagine how I possibly would.

I waited for him to lumber away to the gravy bowl before I turned to Josie. "I told you. Gavin and I signed us up for a two-hour shift."

"Two whole hours?" she moaned, bending slightly at the waist. She was wearing a white tank top with her breasts pushed up inside it, and tiny blue shorts, her long hair tied into two braids. Every male in the room, from the homeless family men to the other youth group volunteers to the ancient security guard in the corner, had checked her out at one point or another. It wasn't like I was going to tell anyone how to dress, but if she thought that was an appropriate outfit for volunteering . . . well, she was wrong.

"Why don't you talk to some people?" I said. "Have some fun."

"Fun?" she griped, staring down at the salad tray. "This place is a crap hole. No one has fun in a crap hole."

Marcy Fiore happened to be walking by with a full tray of chicken at that exact moment. I swear I thought she was going to dump the whole thing over Josie's head. I took Josie's wrist and steered her a few feet away toward the dessert table.

"Tara's having a good time," I pointed out, nodding across the room where Tara Schwartz was hanging out with a whole troop of little kids. It looked like they were playing duck-duck-goose, laughing in a circle on the linoleum floor. Over at the far end of the serving table, Gavin talked with a couple of younger guys in construction gear. His eyes darted to Tara, and he smiled. I hadn't smiled once since we'd picked Josie up.

"Well, Tara's an idiot," Josie said. She wrapped both her arms around one of mine and pulled me toward her chest. "Let's get out of here. We can go get some food, maybe head back to the playground." She tipped her head up, resting her chin near my shoulder and blinking up at me suggestively. For the first time I noticed how fake her huge eyelashes looked. Maybe they *were* fake.

This awful, red-hot anger bubbled up inside me, and I shrugged away from her. "I'm gonna eat here."

I silently counted to ten as I went back to my station.

"You're gonna eat this slop? Seriously?" she said loudly. "Those aren't even real potatoes. They're made from gross boxed powder."

Half the room fell silent. Gavin glanced over nervously. Marcy dropped the chicken tray with a *thwap*. She put one plastic-gloved hand on her hip and stared me down.

"Do you hear yourself?" I asked Josie through my teeth.

"Whatever." She checked her phone. "I've been here over half an hour, which means I can officially put it on my transcript. I'm out."

She walked over to Marcy with her yellow volunteer slip and held it out to her. I thought Marcy might ball it up and shove it down Josie's throat, but instead, her angry face went serene. She took the slip from Josie, leaned into the table to sign it, and handed it back.

"Thank you," Josie said, her nose in the air.

"Anything to facilitate your leaving," Marcy replied.

Gavin snorted a laugh. Josie's jaw dropped. She turned to me, braids flying. "Are you coming?"

"I told you. Two-hour shift," I said coolly. Then I held my breath. "And also, don't expect any big invite to homecoming."

"What?" she snapped. "You're dumping me?"

I sighed. "If that's what you want to call it."

Josie groaned and stormed out, dialing her phone. "Mom! You have to come get me!" she demanded before the door slammed behind her. "I don't care if you have dinner on the stove, come get me!"

I was surprised when a few people clapped their hands. One guy even hooted his approval. I shook my head as I slapped some potatoes onto a young mother's tray.

"You're better off without her," she said.

"Thanks," I mumbled, too annoyed and baffled and embarrassed to come up with anything else.

Gavin approached me slowly. I made a point of moving the

potatoes around the pan, dragging them toward me and pushing them back again. I couldn't look him in the eye.

"You okay, man?" he asked.

"I'm fine."

My fingers gripped the ladle like it was the only lifeline attached to the *Titanic*, and my face was actually pulsating. Thoughts of Claudia filled my mind. The last time she was here, she'd come right from ballet in sweats and sneakers, her face still shining from her workout. She'd let Big Tom twirl her around in the center of the room. She'd laughed with this group of girls who had looked at her like she was a movie star. She'd charmed everyone. That was the word. Charmed.

I felt like Josie had just trashed that memory.

"What the hell was I thinking?" I asked, dropping the ladle. "Why did I break up with Claudia?"

Gavin hesitated, pressing his fingertips into the tabletop. "I don't know. You never told me."

"Yeah, well, I don't know either." I sighed and stared down at the food. "That True chick said something about separation anxiety. Is that even a thing?"

"Hell if I know." Gavin shrugged. Then he quickly blanched and crossed himself, like saying the word "hell" in church was bad. Which was insane, since the priests said it every other Sunday in their sermons. "Look, man, who cares why you did it? It's in the past now. If you want Claudia back, you should do something about it."

"Like what?" I asked, banging the ladle against the side of the tray. Potatoes fell from it in big white globs. "She's hanging out with that Keegan Traylor jackass."

Our eyes locked and we both crossed ourselves.

"Yeah, but they've been together less than a week," he said. "You guys were together for over a year. She can't like him as much as she likes you."

A tiny spark of hope warmed my chest. "You think?"

"Definitely. Call her. See what's up." He looked over at Tara, who was running around a circle of sitting kids, giggling, and he smiled. "You never know."

Could it be that easy? Could Claudia really want me back so much that she'd just forget about the great Keegan Traylor?

I breathed in for what felt like the first time in a week. "You're right. I will."

Marcy finished distributing some of the chicken, then walked past us on her way back to the kitchen.

"Marrott," she said, wiping her brow with the back of her hand, "I'm a big fan of forgive and forget, but do me a favor and don't bring that girl back here. Ever."

"Don't worry," I told her confidently. "You won't be seeing her again."

CHAPTER FIFTY

True

I was just finishing up my inventory of the cupcake display, when someone stepped up to the counter. I felt a chill go down my spine and looked up, half expecting Apollo to be sneering down at me. Instead I was looking directly into Orion's eyes, and he was smiling.

"Has anyone ever told you you look cute in that apron?" he said.

I glanced down, a blush taking over my face. "Thanks." Surreptitiously I looked around, expecting to see Darla finding a table for them, but she wasn't there.

"No Darla?" I asked.

Now it was his turn to blush. "Not tonight. I'm here with my family."

He gestured over his shoulder at a table near the far wall, and I couldn't help staring. His family. His made-up, completely fabricated family. His "mom" had highlighted shoulder-length blond hair and wore a light-blue fitted hoodie over black yoga pants. His "dad" had on a white shirt and a loosened tie and was checking his cell phone, simultaneously running a hand down the blond hair of Orion's sister, Amy, who looked to be about ten.

"Weird," I said under my breath.

"What?"

"Nothing. What can I get you?"

Orion placed his order, and I walked up and down the counter, slowly placing the cupcakes on plates. "So . . . how are things? With you and Darla?"

"Good." He shrugged. "Fine. She's pretty cool. How about you and Wallace?"

I turned around, banged an empty ceramic plate into the side of the display case, and sent the whole thing clattering to the floor, where it shattered into five jagged pieces.

"Oops," Orion said as some of the patrons applauded.

"I don't . . . what do you mean me and Wallace?" I asked.

"Wallace . . . the kid with the bangs." He made this gesture over his forehead like he was combing his hair forward. "He's your boyfriend, no?"

I stared at him, stunned. "Um, no."

"Really?" Orion's eyebrows shot up.

"Really."

"You're sure?"

"One hundred percent sure."

Orion's brow creased. "Oh. Well, that sucks."

"Um, True? You gonna clean that up?" Torin asked me, holding out a dustpan.

I took the pan and practically collapsed to the floor, gasping for air as I swept up the mess. Orion thought Wallace was my *boyfriend*? How? Why? And what the hell did he mean by "That sucks"?

I stood up with the pan in my hand.

"What do you mean, that sucks?" I demanded.

Orion's Adam's apple bobbed. "Just that I—I mean—I thought—" He cleared his throat and glanced over at his family, who were happily chatting. I was so tense with anticipation I was starting to shake. "Every time I saw you, you guys were together . . . with the hugging and the earbud sharing and the lunch-having . . . so I just figured . . . Otherwise . . ."

"Complete a sentence!"

Orion blinked, startled.

"Sorry. I didn't mean to yell." I took a breath, barely daring to hope, barely daring to think. "Otherwise what?"

"Nothing." He suddenly looked like he wanted to be anywhere but here. "Forget it."

Otherwise what? I thought. *Otherwise I would have asked you out? Otherwise I would have let myself fall madly in love with you?*

What, what, what?

"Hey, True. Your shift is over." Torin helpfully took the dirty dustpan out of my hand. "Why don't you go clock out? I'll finish up here."

I couldn't move. They both looked at me like they were afraid I might explode. Which at that moment was a distinct possibility. What I really wanted to do was grab Orion and shake him, make him tell me what he was feeling. But I couldn't. Not without him thinking I was even more insane than he already thought. So instead, I turned on shaky knees and somehow walked myself into the break room without fainting.

Otherwise what? Otherwise what?

For the rest of my existence I was going to hate the word "otherwise."

Inside the office-slash-storage room, I leaned over the computer and carefully typed my employee code into the box next to my name, feeling half-catatonic. It was as if nothing around me was real. Nothing made sense. And I was moving in some sort of vacuum.

Otherwise what? Otherwise what?

At least my shift was over. I needed to go home. I needed to take a bath. I needed some time to think. As I slipped my arms into my denim jacket, I suddenly felt as if someone was watching me from the back of the room. Instantly the catatonia fell away and the tiny hairs on my neck stood on end, then started to dance. I felt a dread deep within my heart that could not be mistaken.

Apollo and Artemis. They'd found me.

I whipped around, my arms raised for a fight.

"Whoa! Hey! It's just me!"

It was my manager, Dominic Cerlone. He must have come in from tossing the garbage in the Dumpster outside.

"Sorry!" I dropped my arms. "Sorry. I thought—" I paused. It wasn't as if I could tell him what I thought. "Sorry."

"It's okay," he said, running his palm over his dark, thinning hair. "I just wanted to talk to you for a second."

"What's up?" I asked, glancing toward the door to the restaurant. How I wanted to walk out there and make him finish that sentence.

Otherwise . . . what?

"It's come to my attention that you've been giving away some free cupcakes lately," Dominic said, sitting down on the edge of his beaten and battered desk chair. He folded his hands together in front of his mouth. "I need you to know this is unacceptable."

My heart sank like a god falling to Earth. "Am I fired?"

"What? No." Dominic laughed. "No. Every teenager I hire does this in the first couple of weeks, handing out food to their friends, eating dinner here as if chocolate and sugar are two of the essential food groups. If I fired every one of them, I'd be working the counter on my own."

I leaned one hand into the shelf of cupcake wrappers and napkins behind me. "Thank you."

"But it can't keep happening," he said seriously. "Consider this your warning. As of now, you're on probation. A cupcake doesn't leave that case unless some money goes into my register. Got it?"

Probation. I felt like I was on probation with everyone. Zeus, Hephaestus, Ares, Orion, even Claudia, in a way, since the jury was out on whether she was still down with my plan. Probation had become my natural state of being.

Otherwise what?

"Got it," I replied. "It won't happen again."

"Good." He nodded and turned to his computer. "Good night, True."

"G'night," I replied.

I was just about out the door when my cell phone rang. The screen read GAVIN DUNNELLON. I quickly hit the talk button as I stepped outside.

"Hello?"

"True? It's Gavin."

"Hey," I said, taking a deep breath and leaning back against the cool outer brick wall of the building. "What's up?"

"I just wanted to tell you, it worked," Gavin said. "I went with Peter and Josie to the soup kitchen tonight, and she made this huge scene and bailed. Peter is *pissed*. And he's talking about getting back together with Claudia."

"Really? That's incredible!" I said.

At least something had gone right tonight.

"Totally. What's up with Claudia and Keegan?" he asked.

"I don't know. I'll call Lauren and get an update. We'll talk at school tomorrow, okay?"

"Cool. This is fun." Gavin sounded giddy. "I feel like we should have some kind of code name."

"I'll leave that to you," I said. "I've gotta go. But thanks for calling."

"See you tomorrow."

As I cut across the parking lot, my feet crunching on the asphalt, I tried to focus on the positive. This thing with Peter and Claudia was going to work out. I could feel it. Before the end of the week, I'd have them falling in love for real, and I'd be two-thirds done with my mission.

And if not, then maybe I'd just have to move on to Wallace and Mia. Or find someone new. Maybe it was about time I kicked things up a notch.

"You didn't really think you were going to get away with this, did you?"

I froze at the sound of Hephaestus's voice, then slowly turned. He sat in the middle of the parking lot, vibrating with fury. In the palm of his right hand was my tiny, now useless, spy camera.

"How did you—"

"Get up to my light fixture?" he asked, wheeling toward me. "I had a hunch, so I got a friend from work to come over and he found it. Does Aphrodite know you were spying on me?"

His skin was waxy, and he spit when he talked.

"No," I said. "She doesn't know anything about it."

"What did you see?" he demanded with a glare.

"Nothing." I lifted my chin. "The camera died as soon as you fired up your magic mirror."

He blinked and withdrew, as if he'd just been slapped. "How could you do this?" he asked. "Why can't you just trust me?"

"Don't you get it, Hephaestus?" I demanded. "I can't trust any-one. How do I know you're not working with Hera to sabotage me and keep me and Aphrodite stuck here forever? How do I know you don't still hold a grudge against my parents? If you had only been honest with me—"

"I have *always* been honest with you!" he snapped. "I kept the secret because your parents requested it of me. And the only thing I've done since arriving here is help you. If you can't look to those facts and see me as a friend, then I don't know what else to say to you."

"So you have no ulterior motive?" I said, holding my jacket tighter around me. "You have nothing to gain from being here, other than feeling good for helping a friend?"

Something shifted behind his eyes. It was minuscule, but unmistakable. He *was* hiding something. I was sure of it.

"I can't do this anymore," he said, turning his chair around. He dropped the camera on the ground, then swiftly, ceremoniously, crushed it beneath his right wheel. "Until you come to your senses, don't bother talking to me."

"Fine," I bit out. "I won't."

I waited for him to make his way around the corner of the building before I turned in the opposite direction and stormed off.

CHAPTER FIFTY-ONE

Claudia

Peter. I was meeting Peter. I sat at my usual table in the library after school, not studying, because any second Peter was going to walk through that door and we were going to "talk."

I looked down at my phone. The text he'd sent after fifth period was open on the screen. I'd looked at it fifteen thousand times in the last three hours.

MEET IN LIBRARY AFTER SCHOOL? I NEED TO TALK TO YOU.

Of course he did. Because he was jealous. Because he realized that I was in a relationship and, just like True had predicted in the beginning, wanted what he couldn't have.

But that was what was really different now. He couldn't have me. I was with Keegan. Keegan cared about me. He was coming to my recital on Friday, even though it meant coming straight from practice to be there on time. Keegan and I were a couple now. After what we'd done together yesterday afternoon, I was more sure of that than ever.

I just had to stay strong. If that's what this was about. If Peter really did want to get back together. Maybe he just wanted help with his math homework or something and—

There he was. He practically filled the doorway. And he was wearing that maroon-and-white-striped rugby shirt that I'd gotten him for Christmas last year. The one I loved so much I'd briefly thought about breaking into his room and stealing it during my darker moments last week.

He saw me right away and walked over. "Hey."

Annoyingly, his voice still sent pleasant shock waves through me. "Hey."

After a second, he pulled out the chair at the end of the table, diagonal from me, and sat. And then he took my hand, drawing it out of my lap and into his.

Holy crap. This was happening. And I couldn't breathe. But I was with Keegan now. Keegan, Keegan, Keegan.

"I'm sorry," Peter began, his voice thick with emotion. "I'm so sorry for breaking up with you. I was so stressed that day and I didn't know what I was doing. I'm so sorry, Claudia."

I cleared my throat. I thought of Keegan, who was supposed to call me later and maybe pick me up from dance class. Keegan, who gave me chills every time he touched me.

"Will you . . . take me back?" Peter asked. "Will you . . . be my girlfriend?"

His forehead was wrinkled, his eyes hopeful. My heart flipped and sputtered, bucking and tripping like a desperate, confused, newly born fawn.

And then I said, "No."

Peter sat up. "What?"

"I'm sorry, but no," I said, feeling a bit like I was about to jump off a building. "I've moved on."

Peter dropped my hand. "With Traylor?"

I looked at him, annoyed by the accusatory tone in his voice, like he thought he might get to choose who I moved on with. "Yeah. With Keegan Traylor," I said, my voice wavering annoyingly.

"You've got to be kidding me. We were together for a year and half!" he protested. "I thought that you—I thought that we—"

I held my breath, dying for him to finish his sentence. Instead he huffed a sigh.

"What's so great about Keegan Traylor?" he demanded.

My jaw dropped. "Well, first off, he's funny. And he's laid-back. He's never once snapped at me for no reason."

Peter hung his head.

"He's coming to my recital on Friday, even though it's not exactly convenient for him. He makes me feel like he actually wants to be with me, like he cares about the things I care about, which is more than I can say for you."

Peter stared at me. He looked deflated. "I made you feel like I didn't want to be with you?"

"Sometimes," I said, faltering a bit at his naive tone. "For the last few months you just . . . I felt like you were pulling away. Every time I tried to talk to you about college, you bit my head off. . . . You walked out on me the day I got my audition. . . . It was like you were angry all the time."

I swallowed hard, impressed by my own bravery. I'd told him what I really thought, how I really felt.

"Separation anxiety," he said under his breath.

"What?"

"It's a real thing!" he said loudly, like a protest. "I looked it up. You're so afraid of someone leaving you that you push them away. It's the subconscious exerting control or some crap."

"Oh." I felt this odd sort of pang in my chest. He'd broken up with me because he was scared of losing me? Was that possible?

He leaned forward, elbows on his thighs, hands forming a tee-pee over his nose and mouth, and sighed. "I thought . . . I thought that you, like, couldn't wait for us to graduate. I felt like you were trying to get rid of me. That there was no way for me to be part of your future."

He hung his head. My body felt like it weighed fourteen thousand pounds.

"Oh, Peter."

It was the only thing I could say without bursting into tears. Why hadn't he just told me this instead of breaking up with me? If we could have talked about it last week, before the pain and anger and confusion and plotting and planning and Keegan. Maybe then, things would have been different.

Suddenly he pushed himself up and started out of the room. My heart caught in my throat. "Peter."

He turned to me hopefully, which made me feel like a jerk when I reached into my backpack and pulled out his class ring.

"I should give this back to you."

"This isn't happening," he said breathlessly. His face was like stone. He didn't move a muscle. I placed the ring on the table and got up.

"I'm sorry, Peter," I said clearly, almost unable to believe I was actually saying the words. "It's too late."

CHAPTER FIFTY-TWO

Peter

"Where are we going? I just wanna go home," I muttered to Gavin, sounding like a big fat baby as we trudged across the football field. Practice had sucked. Of course it had sucked. Claudia had picked Keegan over me. Everything sucked.

Of course, if I did go home right now, it wasn't like there was anything awesome waiting for me there. My mother had finally laid down the law and said that if I didn't finish at least three applications by the end of the night, I was grounded for two weeks.

Did I mention how everything sucked? Somewhere in the distance, the marching band was practicing. The trumpet was louder than the other instruments and playing a mournful tune. The perfect soundtrack for my life.

"There's someone you need to talk to."

Something about the way Gavin was talking was off. He swiveled his head from side to side, wearing these mirrored sunglasses like he was some kind of FBI agent. Or the Terminator.

"Why are you being so weird?" I readjusted my bag on my shoulder as we got closer to the Snack Shack on the home side of the field. The sun beat down on my back like an assault. I turned my baseball cap around so the bill covered my neck. "You do know this is only open on game days."

He just looked at me. At least I think he did. It was hard to tell with those glasses.

"You're really starting to freak me out," I said.

Then we came around this hedge line, and I stopped walking. Lauren was sitting at one of the white plastic picnic tables with True. Great. The girl who'd given me false hope about getting Claudia back, and my ex's best friend. What was this, some kind of bizarro intervention?

"You again?" I grumbled.

"She's here to help," Gavin told me. He looked at True and removed his sunglasses, folding them carefully. "Operation Love Sack has hit a snag."

"Is that what we're calling it?" True asked.

"That doesn't even make any sense," Lauren said, screwing her face up.

"Yes, it does!" Gavin countered. He might even have whined.

"How? How does that make any sense?" Lauren asked with her arms crossed over her chest.

"Because! He's, like, the linebacker trying to get to the quarterback, and Claudia's the quarterback trying to, you know, evade the sack." He stopped and blew out a breath, hands on his hips. "Can we just do this?"

"Will someone tell me what the hell is going on?" I demanded.

"We're gonna help you get Claudia back," Lauren said matter-of-factly.

My shoulders tensed, and I shot Gavin a death glare. He was going to pay for dragging me up here for this. "It's too late. She already rejected me."

"We know," Lauren and True said at once.

So she'd told them. Already. Told them about how pathetic Peter tried and failed to win her back. Probably laughed about it with them, wondering how I could be such an idiot. I deflated at the thought, sitting down on the bench next to Lauren and slumping against the table.

"What do I do?" I asked.

"Well, you can't just ask her out again, clearly," Lauren said, shaking her dark curls back over her shoulders.

"Clearly," I said through my teeth. I'd always liked Lauren, but right then, she was completely getting under my skin.

"You have to do something to make it up to her—the breakup, I mean," True said, leaning into the edge of the table while Gavin stood over us, like our very own Secret Service agent.

"What makes you such an expert?" I asked True.

True narrowed her eyes. "Trust me. I have a lot of experience with this stuff."

I sighed. So everyone felt like being cryptic today. Cool.

"You have to show her that you never stopped caring about her," True said. "That you care about the things that matter to her. Her future . . . your future. Together."

"I tried to tell her," I said, turning my palms up.

"It's not enough. You need to do something," True said firmly.

"Like what? What can I do? After today I'm not sure she's ever going to talk to me again."

"You could come to our recital, for starters," Lauren said.

"When's that?" True asked.

"Friday night," Lauren said.

The girls looked at me hopefully. "I could do that. I mean, I'd have to break my pregame ritual, but—"

"So break it," Lauren interjected.

"I don't know," True said, biting her lip. "I don't think it's big enough, just showing up."

I groaned and crossed my arms on the table, dropping my head onto them. The conversation I'd had with Claudia earlier rang in my mind. Everything she'd accused me of was true. How I'd been snapping at her, how I'd been angry so much, how I'd bailed on her when she'd found out she got the audition—letting my own insecure crap ruin her big moment.

Suddenly my head popped up. For the first time in my life I understood why cartoonists are always drawing lightbulbs over their characters' heads, because that was what it felt like. My whole brain shone with an idea.

"The audition," I said quietly.

"What?"

I pushed myself up, practically bursting with excitement. "I've got it, you guys. I know how I'm going to get Claudia back."

CHAPTER FIFTY-THREE

True

Peter was a genius. Once I'd heard his plan, I knew for sure that he was in love with Claudia. What I needed now was for her to remember how much she loved him. If only I'd never brought Keegan into this equation. Then there would be nothing standing in Peter's way.

I sat near the wall of the Studio that evening and watched Claudia's friend Lance lift her into the air with seemingly no effort, then place her gently on her toes so she could continue her gorgeous, elegant movement across the floor. As soon as they were done rehearsing, I was going to corner Lance and talk him into helping us. Then I'd have done my part. I just wished Keegan would help me out and do his part—start acting like the jerk everyone knew he was deep down.

"Beautiful, aren't they?" Lauren asked.

"Absolutely," I replied.

Dozens of dancers lined the walls around us, sitting with their legs outstretched or curled under them, every one of their pretty faces rapt with attention. The music swelled, a piece by Mozart that I knew very well, and Claudia executed her last set of pirouettes, finishing up in Lance's arms. The room went wild.

I stood up, hoping to grab Lance on his way to the bathroom or the locker room or wherever he'd go next. Instead the dance teacher, Madame Helene, intercepted him to go over a particular move. She waved Claudia off, and she jogged over to join us, tugging a bottle of water out of her canvas ballet bag.

"How was it?" she asked.

"Amazing as always," Lauren replied, slapping hands with Claudia.

She took a swig of water, then pulled out her phone. Something on the screen made her freeze. "Oh."

"What?" Lauren asked.

"Nothing. Just . . . I was texting Keegan between classes about picking me up tonight and he wasn't getting back to me. . . . But he texted me fifteen minutes ago."

She showed us the screen.

CAN'T PICK UP 2NITE. SRY.

My lips pursed. No explanation, no promise to call her later. He was blowing her off. Which was, of course, a good thing. In the grand scheme.

"Can I get a ride home?" she asked Lauren.

"Of course."

Claudia quickly typed in a text, her pale fingers trembling. I leaned right ever so slightly to read over her shoulder.

NO PROB. GOT A RIDE. WHERE WERE U TODAY?

She sat back as she hit send, her posture straight as she leaned her thick bun against the wall behind us.

"So what did you think, True?" she asked, glancing down at her phone.

Nothing. She tapped it against her light-pink tights.

"It was lovely. This is really a great dance school," I told her. "And you're a beautiful dancer. I'm sure you're going to ace that audition on Saturday."

She gave me a small smile. "Thanks. I'm so nervous about it."

Her eyes darted to her phone again. Still no response. The silence began to feel awkward, even as the other dancers on the floor started to stretch out and mess around, laughing and making up silly dance moves. Lauren turned her phone over and over and over atop her thigh.

"Do you want to get some food after this?" Lauren asked.

"Um, sure," Claudia said.

She turned her phone's screen up and then checked it. Nothing.

"Why isn't he responding to any of my texts?"

I decided to play devil's advocate. "He did respond to one. . . ."

"Yeah, but when he knew I was in class. When he knew I wouldn't be able to text back," Claudia said.

"Well, maybe he has his phone off," Lauren suggested.

"Keegan? Never. He needs to be connected twenty-four-seven."

She looked her phone over like something might be wrong with it, toggling the switch on the side, checking some setting or other.

"Just give him a few minutes," I said. "He might be in the middle of something."

"You're right," Claudia said. "Sometimes I don't hear my phone go off when it's in my bag."

So we sat there. And waited. And watched the phone. And Madame Helene going through some movements with Lance. And the other dancers. Until eight full minutes had passed and Madame

Helene finally clapped her hands for attention and there was still no reply from Keegan Traylor.

"Let's give Claudia and Lance a break!" Madame announced. "Places for the finale, everyone."

The other dancers scurried into place along the sides of the room.

"I'm going to go make a call," Claudia said, already moving toward the door.

Lance walked past me and over to his black vinyl bag in the corner. He pulled out an energy bar and started to eat, perched on the edge of a chair.

"Okay. I'll be here," I said to Claudia. But I'm not even sure she heard me. She was already pushing through the door and onto the sidewalk.

"You gonna talk to him?" Lauren asked under her breath.

"Now or never."

She gave me a conspiratorial smile, then joined her friends on the dance floor. I stood in front of Lance, and his brow knit.

"Remember me?" I asked.

"True, right? How could I forget?"

"Good, because I have a favor to ask you."

He sat up straight, intrigued. "I'm listening."

"I need some information about your audition this weekend," I told him, sitting in the empty chair next to his. "We're planning a little surprise. . . ."

CHAPTER FIFTY-FOUR

Claudia

Twenty-one hours, thirteen minutes. That was how long it had been since I'd received a text from Keegan. The guy who I'd let take my shirt off and a lot more on Tuesday afternoon. The guy who I'd thought was now, basically, if not officially, my boyfriend. Meanwhile, I'd texted him at least a couple dozen times and called. Had he lost his phone? Had he been in some kind of coma? Had he been kidnapped by aliens? What? As I pulled my Prius into a spot in front of St. Joseph's Preparatory on Thursday afternoon, I hoped against hope that he had a legitimate excuse. Because otherwise . . .

I looked at my eyes in the rearview mirror and wasn't exactly impressed by what I saw. I saw uncertainty, nervousness, and fear.

Because, well, otherwise, I didn't know what I was going to do.

The front doors of the school opened, and a horde of boys spilled out onto the steps with Keegan at the lead. I cut the engine, opened the door, and got out, straightening my skirt and flipping my hair over my shoulder. Somehow, flipping my hair always made me feel a tad more self-assured. I wasn't sure why, but whatever worked.

Keegan was laughing as he hit the bottom step, but he stopped laughing when he saw me approach. His face, in fact, fell. He knew he was in trouble. Which meant he *had* gotten my messages. Now I was pissed.

"Claudia!" he crowed, his expression suddenly brightening again.

He said good-bye to a couple of friends, slapped a hand or two, and then turned his full attention on me. I stopped about three feet away from him, clinging to my ballet-shoe key ring with both hands, so he had to step forward to envelop me in a warm, leather-scented hug. I, however, remained as stiff as a board.

"What's up? What're you doing here?" he said.

"Did you get my texts?" I asked. "My voice mail?"

A cloud moved in front of the sun as Keegan thought it over. He pushed his hands into the pockets of his jeans. "Which ones?"

I shifted from foot to foot. I couldn't tell if he was serious or messing with me, but either way, I felt hot and uncomfortable. "Keegan, come on. I texted you a dozen times yesterday, at least."

"Oh, right! Sorry. Yesterday was crazy." He pulled his phone out and looked at it, hitting a few buttons as if that was doing anything. "And then last night, my phone was off. My parents are doing this lockdown thing, making me study for my final SAT attempt. I didn't really check it until I got to school this morning."

Lies. That was the first word to pop into my head. Keegan always had his phone on. Even if his parents had taken it away from him for a few hours so he would study, he would have turned it on the second he got it back. Anyone would have. But he looked so contrite and innocent, standing there with that big, lovely smile on his face. I couldn't muster up the confidence to call him on it.

"So what's up?" he asked finally. "Is everything okay?"

His hands were in his pockets again.

"What do you mean?" I asked.

"Well, there must be something wrong if you felt like you had to drive all the way over here just to talk to me."

I looked away, confused and defeated, insecure and awkward. He was the one who'd done something wrong, right? So why did I suddenly feel out of line?

"No. Not really," I said. "I was just . . . confused."

Keegan blinked. The bells in the tower on the campus church began to toll, ringing long and clear from very nearby. The sound vibrated my bones and seemed to shake the ground beneath my feet.

"Confused?" he said eventually. "Because I didn't call you back for one day?"

I swallowed. "Well when you put it like that—"

Keegan turned toward the parking lot, shaking his head. I could see his blue car gleaming in the sunlight a few rows behind mine. He started to walk, giving me no other option other than to fall into step with him.

"What is it with you people? Just when I think we're starting to have fun, you get crazy and clingy."

I almost tripped. Luckily, we were passing the driver's-side door of my car at the time. I stopped moving, stopped breathing, stopped thinking. It was as if the reverb of that bell had filled my brain, shuddering the insides of my skull, drowning out everything else.

There were no words for what I was feeling. No words for what he had just done to me. But I had to say something.

"Us people?" I blurted. "What the hell does that mean?"

"You people. Girls. It's like pathetic is your default setting. I'm sorry I can't be there for you every second of every hour of every day. I have a life."

My eyes filled so suddenly I almost gasped. No one had ever

called me pathetic before, and it did not feel good. Suddenly I remembered the way Peter's face had crumbled when I'd used the same word on him last week, and I wanted to go back in time and slap my hand over my own mouth.

Instead I stared at Keegan. He looked so different to me. So different from when he'd smiled at me over the Dave & Buster's table. So different from when he'd pulled me to him outside the gym or acted vulnerable at Goddess that day. He had this cocky, defiant look on his face I'd never seen before. The look of a player. A jerk. A user.

Lauren had been right from the beginning. And I had been so, so stupid.

I felt as if someone had just punched me square in the chest. This whole thing had started when I set out to use him. Apparently, when I wasn't looking, he'd turned it around on me. He'd gotten what he wanted out of me on Tuesday afternoon, and now he was showing his true colors.

"Don't worry," I said, mustering my pride. "I have a life too. And it's about time I get back to it."

Hands shaking, I somehow yanked open the car door, got in behind the wheel, and put Keegan Traylor in my rearview mirror as fast as I possibly could.

CHAPTER FIFTY-FIVE

Peter

I went to Claudia's recital on Friday night. I didn't have to—she
wouldn't know I was there unless someone told her—but I wanted
to. I watched her and Lance execute their duet. Watched the crowd
go wild. Gave them a standing ovation. And when the old lady in
the next seat smiled up at me, my throat welled with pride.

"That's my girlfriend," I said.

Then I spent the rest of the night praying to God that tomorrow,
I'd be able to make those words true.

CHAPTER FIFTY-SIX

Claudia

"I'm going to throw up," I said to Lance, pacing in my three feet of space in the lobby of the Lafayette School of Dance. There were dancers everywhere. Tall ones, short ones, skinny ones, skinnier ones. They stretched out against walls, practiced pirouettes in the corners, compared résumés over coffee. There were too many dancers vying for too few spots. How could I have ever thought I was good enough?

"You're not going to throw up," Lance said firmly, holding onto my shoulders. "You're probably just carsick from the drive. That with the nervousness is not a good combo. Why don't you go to the bathroom? Take a minute. You'll feel better once you've had time to breathe."

"Okay. Yes. Good." I said, looking around for a sign to the ladies' room. Instead I was accosted by a series of pretty, perky faces topped by perfect buns and chignons. Lance pointed me in the right direction and gave the small of my back a shove. The door was right in front of me.

"I'll be right here," he said, rather loudly.

"Okay."

I shoved the door open and slipped into one of the three white-walled stalls. The place spotlessly clean. Still, I tugged out one of the paper toilet seat covers, laid it on the seat, and then dropped down, putting my head between my hands.

"Focus," I whispered. "You've done this routine ten million times before. You can do this. You can do it, you can do it, you can do it."

I bit down on my tongue and looked up, wishing my parents and Casey and Lauren were here. Agreeing to carpool with Lance had felt like a good idea at the time, and when he'd picked me up that morning, I'd felt so independent. Like making it through this life-altering event on my own would prove that I was ready for the real world.

But now I just wanted my mommy.

Or Peter.

Dammit. Why had I thought of Peter? I'd been doing so well. I hadn't thought of him once on the ride down here. Well, not in the last fifteen minutes of the ride. Okay, at least not since we'd parked the car.

But now that I was alone and thinking about him, I couldn't stop. I remembered the plea in his eyes when he'd asked me to take him back. His confession about being so afraid of losing me. He'd been so heartfelt, so vulnerable, and I'd just flat-out rejected him. For Keegan. The biggest jerk ever to walk the earth.

What would he do if I called him and told him I'd take him up on his offer? Did he still want me, or had I ruined everything?

Someone pounded on the stall door.

"Are you ever coming out of there?" a nasal voice asked.

"Sorry."

I jumped up and flushed, then yanked open the door. The

girl waiting for the stall wore a black thin-strapped leotard and a leopard-print gauze skirt. She looked me up and down like I was trash. I averted my eyes, washed my hands, and checked my reflection.

"Well," I whispered, "you can definitely beat out that girl."

Then I smirked, rounded my shoulders, and vowed not to think about Peter Marrott for the rest of the day. Except that when I yanked open the door, he was standing right in front of me, holding a dozen red roses.

"Surprise!"

My hands fluttered up to cover my mouth. Behind Peter were True and Lauren, Mia and Wallace, Lance and Madame Helene, Gavin and his new girlfriend Tara. And behind them were my parents, alongside Casey and Corey. My friends and family. They were here. And they were holding embarrassing painted signs. Messages like GO CLAUDIA! and TWIRL TO VICTORY!

"What are you guys doing here?" I gasped, as my mom stepped forward to hug me.

"Peter called us," she said, beaming over at him. "He said he was organizing a caravan to come down and cheer you on."

"We couldn't miss that," my dad said.

"You did this?" I said to Peter, releasing my mom. "But you have a game tonight. . . ."

"We'll make it back in time," he said with a shrug. He was wearing a black polo shirt that made him look older somehow, more sophisticated, but still my Peter. "We wanted to be here for you." He cleared his throat and lowered his voice. "I wanted to be here for you."

My heart was so full I thought it might pop. We both looked around at our audience, and they quickly turned away, pretending to be enthralled by the black-and-white framed dance posters decorating every wall.

"Claudia, whatever happens next year, I want you to know, I'm going to be there for you from now on."

"Peter," I whispered. "I'm so sorry about the things I said to you. I can't even—"

"It doesn't matter," he said. "I'm over it. As long as I can be with you."

Before I could answer, the door to the audition room opened with a squeal. A hush fell over the gathered crowd.

"Claudia Catalfo!" a woman with a clipboard called out.

My heart hit the ground. My mouth went dry. This was it. This was the first moment of the rest of my life.

"Oh my God," I gasped.

Peter smiled. He tossed his head back, flinging his bangs off his forehead. As always, they fell right back where they'd been. "Kick some ass," he said.

"I will," I told him confidently, grinning from ear to ear. And somehow I knew that I would. Knowing that these people were here to support me, how could I not?

"I love you, Claudia," Peter said.

Somehow the grin on my face widened. "I love you, too."

He leaned in and gave me a gentle but firm kiss. "And just so you know," he whispered. "When you come out of there, I'm going to ask you to homecoming."

I squeezed his hand, giddy beyond belief. "Just so you know, I'm going to say yes."

CHAPTER FIFTY-SEVEN

True

The job was done. The timer had turned. And if the kiss a victorious Peter was now planting on a blushing Claudia at the center of the field postgame was any indication, my latest match was one that was going to last.

As an added bonus, Wallace and Mia were now sitting in the almost empty bleachers cuddled together over his iPad. I had talked Lauren into driving me, Wallace, and Mia down to Princeton yesterday, forcing the two of them to share one small backseat for over an hour, during which they'd discovered a mutual love of spinach pizza, a shared obsession with Angry Birds, and some kind of ancient Boy Scout/Girl Scout connection I couldn't quite understand. Whatever it was, it was working for them. Perhaps I'd already sent my third couple out on their journey to true love.

I looked around at the torn-up football field, the smiling faces of the retreating fans, the yellow school buses, the GO RAMS! banners, the packs of students milling around the Snack Shack, and felt at peace. I was a human now and for better or for worse, I was starting to feel more human. This place was becoming my home. It was scary, but at the same time, exhilarating, to feel a part of something—to feel real. I took a deep breath and relished the moment.

Almost as if to mock me, Orion's laugh sounded nearby and I turned. He was standing at the top of the bleachers along with a group of football players, cheerleaders, and other random students, with his arm around Darla's waist. I wished like anything I could be next to him, hearing his voice, holding his hand.

I turned away, sparing myself the torture. Claudia and Peter were now moving across the field toward the school, her head resting comfortably against his shoulder. That was what I wanted for myself. That simple intimacy. Was it so wrong that I wanted it with the guy I loved?

Otherwise what? Otherwise what?

No, I decided. It wasn't so wrong. And I was going to do something about it. I'd spent so much time meddling in other people's lives over the past few weeks, I could spend five seconds meddling in my own.

I started up the steps toward Orion and his friends, wondering what it was going to take to extricate him from Darla's grip, when I realized he was no longer there. Darla, Veronica, Josh, Charlie, Katrina, Gavin, and a few other jocks were still hanging out, but Orion had disappeared. Of course. Right when I'd decided to swan-dive off the high wire.

"Where in the world did he—"

The most awful peal of electronic noise split the air so suddenly and so loudly, it made everyone in a half-mile radius cringe. Then someone cleared his throat, and the sound blasted through the speakers set into the booth behind the bleachers.

"Sorry about that."

It was Orion's voice.

"I just wanted to say that Darla Shayne, I think you're the most beautiful girl at Lake Carmody High, and I would be honored if you'd go to the homecoming dance with me."

Every girl in hearing distance let out a sickening "awwwww" of delight.

"Oh, this is Orion, by the way."

Darla ran up to the open window in the booth, and suddenly Orion's face appeared.

"Yes, yes, yes!" she shouted.

And then they kissed. They kissed a lot. They kissed and kissed and kissed, and hot fireballs of fury roared to life inside my chest. My bones began to shake. My every cell vibrated from the heat of my rage. I closed my eyes and tried to contain it. I could see only destruction. I saw the bleachers collapse beneath Darla's feet. Saw the ceiling cave in upon the Orion who was not my Orion. I felt the entire Earth begin to quake beneath my feet.

Someone screamed. My eyes flew open and my heart stopped beating. The walls of the announcer's booth were, in fact, trembling. Startled birds took flight from trees as somewhere nearby a car alarm began to blare. People gripped guardrails, lay prostrate on the ground, clung to one another in terror. That was when I realized that the ground was, in fact, shaking. That I had made it shake. My anger had caused an earthquake.

This was very not good. I had to make it stop. I took a deep breath. With every fiber of my being, I concentrated on my center. I closed my eyes and calmed my heart. And then, finally, the world grew still.

So. Maybe not so human after all.

"What the hell was that?" Josh Moskowitz shouted.

"An earthquake. That was an earthquake," Charlie told him.

Everyone started chattering and making calls, checking to see if loved ones were okay. I had a feeling they were going to find out that this particular earthquake was very localized, that no one else they knew had felt a thing. Fear coursed through my veins. What I had just done was unacceptable. It was too big, too dangerous, too noticeable. Zeus must have seen it, and if he had, I was soon to be in a huge amount of trouble.

Orion raced out of the booth and grabbed Darla, who sobbed and clung to him like she would never let him go. I turned my back on them and got out of there as quickly as possible, before I could cause any more damage. Before I could unwittingly bring them even closer together.

CHAPTER FIFTY-EIGHT

True

I walked into my house on shaky legs, surprised that I had not yet been summoned back to Mount Olympus. That I had not yet been punished, or at the very least, chastised, by Zeus or Hera or Ares. Perhaps no one had noticed after all. Perhaps I was still safe. I took a deep breath of the oak-and-dust-scented air, trying not to think of the very public display of affection that had caused my momentary lapse of reason.

I couldn't believe I had let something so petty almost ruin everything. I should have been celebrating. My mission was more than halfway complete. Tomorrow I would start searching for another set of soul mates, just in case Wallace and Mia proved to be too easy to be true, and before long Orion wouldn't even recall having uttered the name "Darla Shayne," let alone kissing her.

"Everything's going to be fine," I whispered to myself. "If you can just hold on to your head, everything is going to be fine."

I closed the door behind me and froze. Hephaestus was waiting at the bottom of the stairs. The little hairs on my arms and along the back of my neck stood on end. I readied myself for a confrontation.

"Waiting for me?" I asked him.

He looked me in the eye. I'd never seen him appear so vulnerable. My defenses instantly died away. "I've decided to tell you the truth," he said. "I do have an ulterior motive for being here."

"You do," I said resignedly. I so hated it when my father was right. "Is it because of my parents? Are you using me to get back at them somehow?"

"No. It's not that," he said, raising one palm. "And I wouldn't say I'm using you. My being here is mutually beneficial."

"So how does it benefit you, exactly?" I asked.

He blew out a sigh. "I want to get back to Harmonia."

That brought me up short. I stepped into the doorway between the foyer and the parlor, leaning back against the cool, carved wood that framed it. "Explain."

Hephaestus rubbed his brow for a moment. He adjusted his wheels and edged over until we were directly facing each other. Out on the street, a car whizzed by, its horn honking, a pack of girls screaming happily out the windows, celebrating Lake Carmody's latest win.

"Do you have any idea what it's like to be torn away from your true love?" Hephaestus asked passionately.

"Yes, actually, I do," I replied, trying not to think about my own personal earthquake.

He blinked. "Right. Of course. Sorry. Well, try living that way for over two thousand years."

"So the two of you really were in love," I said quietly, mournfully. I shook my head, staring down at the frayed fringe along the edge of the parlor's largest rug. "How could she have kept this from me?"

"You know how private she is," Hephaestus said. "How cautious. She didn't want to tell anyone until she was absolutely certain my love for her was pure. But before I had a chance to find a way to prove it to her, I was flung from Mount Olympus for the last time. I thought I would never see her again—that I would never be able to show her how much I cared for her."

"But you found a way," I said, looking into his aching eyes.

"I did." He nodded and touched the back of his hand to his nose. "One morning many years ago I awoke to find a twisted ball of metal next to my bed. I could tell in an instant that this material held divine properties. To this day I have no idea which god or goddess gifted me with it, but I somehow knew exactly what I had to do. I forged that mirror, and Harmonia's face appeared in the glass. When I saw her that day I thought I would truly die from longing, but instead it gave me a newfound hope. Now my only hope is that I live long enough to hold her again."

"How long have the two of you been communicating?"

He lifted his shoulders. "A few centuries now."

Centuries. She had kept this secret for so long.

"And she truly loves you? You're certain of this?"

"She does." His eyes shone, and I knew he was telling the truth. "It may seem silly, but we both thought that if I helped you, then you and Aphrodite . . . maybe even Ares . . . might plead my case with the king—help me get an audience with him. If it came from your parents especially, considering our history, he might be willing to listen, and maybe he'd let me come home."

His lament was so sincere, his hope so pure, that it opened up something deep inside me. I knew that I could trust him again, felt guilty for having ever doubted him. It was time for me to share my truth with him as well.

"I have something to tell you, too," I said, standing up straight.

"What is it?" he asked.

"Well, perhaps I should show you."

With a flick of my hand, I released the lock on his chair and pushed him backward six inches. His hands flew instinctively to his wheels, and his eyes widened.

"Your power?" he hissed, wheeling back to his position.

I nodded. "And that's not the only one."

I knelt in front of him and placed my hand, palm up, in his lap. I envisioned a yellow sunflower, and suddenly it appeared there.

"Oh my gods," Hephaestus said. "How?"

"I don't know," I replied in a whisper, tossing the bloom on the couch. I stopped short of telling him about the earthquake, not ready to receive the tongue-lashing he was sure to unleash. "My father thinks they're returning of their own accord. That I'm so powerful in my own right that they can't be kept from me."

Hephaestus whistled, long and low. "That won't make Zeus happy."

"That's what Ares said."

"You must be careful," Hephaestus said, reaching for my hand. "Promise me you won't use them for fun. Only in emergencies."

He sounded just like my father. Maybe the two of them weren't as different as they believed. Not that I'd ever share that opinion with either of them.

I looked down at his fingers locked around mine, and my palms began to sweat. What I had done earlier had not been on a lark. I had lost control—a fact that frightened me to my core. But if I could focus on my mission, it wouldn't happen again. I simply needed to be more careful from here on out.

Whatever the future held, I felt heartened by this conversation with Hephaestus. I wasn't alone in this. Thanks to Harmonia, I wasn't alone.

"I promise," I said. "And I also promise that whatever happens, when this is over, I will do everything in my power to get you home."

Hephaestus smiled and kissed the back of my hand like a true gentleman. "Thank you," he said. "You have no idea what that means to me. And to Harmonia."

I lifted my shoulders and looked up at the ceiling, knowing in my heart that Harmonia was watching. "That's what sisters are for."

We held each other's gaze for a long, peaceful moment, and in that moment I somehow knew that we were going to get through this. Everything was going to be okay. Orion and I were going to return home to Mount Olympus, and we were going to bring Hephaestus with us.

Then, suddenly, Hephaestus's head snapped to the side. His whole body went rigid.

"What is it?" I asked.

"Harmonia. She's calling."

He turned his chair and raced down the hallway to his room. The mirror's frame glowed so brightly it was near blinding. Breathless with excitement, anticipation, and fear, I stepped into the room behind Hephaestus. He raced to his desk, shoved himself up, and touched the mirror.

Harmonia's beautiful face filled the screen. Her red hair floated around her like she was lying in the calm waters of a lake. My heart swelled with joy. I'd never been so happy to see anyone in my long, long existence.

"Harmonia, what is it?" Hephaestus's voice was filled with concern.

I blinked, and for the first time noticed that Harmonia's face was creased in worry. I had been so blinded by my excitement over seeing her again that I hadn't noted it.

"Harmonia?" I said, approaching the mirror.

"Eros!" Her eyes widened at the sight of me. "Sister, it is so good to see you. I wish it were under merrier circumstances."

"What is it?" Hephaestus repeated. "What's wrong?"

Harmonia glanced over her shoulder, frightened by something in the background we couldn't see. She was so startled that I automatically reached for the mirror, as if I could somehow press through it and protect her. Then she turned to face us once more.

"You shouldn't have done it, Eros," she said gravely. "You should have kept your temper."

A sizzle of fear went through me.

"Done what?" Hephaestus demanded.

"The earthquake. Everyone knows about it. Everyone saw."

Hephaestus craned his neck to glare at me. "You caused an earthquake? Have you lost your mind?"

"What does this mean?" I asked Harmonia. "Is Zeus angered? Is he bringing me back?"

"No, but Hera has used your carelessness as an excuse," Harmonia said.

I sank like a stone onto the edge of Hephaestus's bed. "An excuse to do what?"

"She's sending Artemis and Apollo to Lake Carmody to retrieve Orion."

"What?" I breathed.

"It gets worse, my sister. It seems Apollo has been spying on me, knowing that if you tried to contact anyone here, it would be me. He heard me speaking with our father and . . . they know. They know it was you who brought him down from the heavens. They know you are in love."

The whole world went gray. I closed my eyes, the air around me seeming to blister with fear.

"I'm so very sorry, Eros," Harmonia added, desperate. "I should have been more careful."

"They'll kill me," I whispered. "The queen must know they'll kill me."

"She's making a sport of it," Hephaestus said, his tone dire. "She wants to see a battle."

My stomach twisted into knots. "How long do I have?"

"No time at all," Harmonia said. "Artemis and Apollo are already there."